✧ **W9-CAP-438**

PRAISE FOR THE NOVELS OF v, 9

#1 NEW YORK TIMES BESTSELLING AUTHOR
BARBARA FREETHY

"I love *The Callaways*! Heartwarming romance, intriguing suspense and sexy alpha heroes. What more could you want?"
-- *NYT Bestselling Author* **Bella Andre**

"I adore *The Callaways*, a family we'd all love to have. Each new book is a deft combination of emotion, suspense and family dynamics. A remarkable, compelling series!"
-- *USA Today Bestselling Author* **Barbara O'Neal**

"Once I start reading a Callaway novel, I can't put it down. Fast-paced action, a poignant love story and a tantalizing mystery in every book!"
-- *USA Today Bestselling Author* **Christie Ridgway**

"In the tradition of LaVyrle Spencer, gifted author Barbara Freethy creates an irresistible tale of family secrets, riveting adventure and heart-touching romance."
-- *NYT Bestselling Author* **Susan Wiggs**
on Summer Secrets

"This book has it all: heart, community, and characters who will remain with you long after the book has ended. A wonderful story."
-- *NYT Bestselling Author* **Debbie Macomber**
on Suddenly One Summer

"Freethy has a gift for creating complex characters."
-- ***Library Journal***

Also By Barbara Freethy

The Callaway Series
On A Night Like This (#1)
So This Is Love (#2)
Falling For A Stranger (#3)
Between Now and Forever (#4)
Nobody But You (Callaway Wedding Novella)
All A Heart Needs (#5)
That Summer Night (#6)
When Shadows Fall (#7)
Somewhere Only We Know (#8)
If I Didn't Know Better (#9)
Tender is the Night (#10) *Coming soon!*

Lightning Strikes Trilogy
Beautiful Storm (#1)
Lightning Lingers (#2) *Coming soon!*
Summer Rain (#3) *Coming soon!*

The Wish Series
A Secret Wish
Just A Wish Away
When Wishes Collide

Standalone Novels
Almost Home
All She Ever Wanted
Ask Mariah
Daniel's Gift
Don't Say A Word
Golden Lies
Just The Way You Are
Love Will Find A Way
One True Love
Ryan's Return
Some Kind of Wonderful
Summer Secrets
The Sweetest Thing

The Sanders Brothers Series
Silent Run
Silent Fall

The Deception Series
Taken
Played

To Lisa for all her wonderful help and support!

IF I DIDN'T KNOW BETTER

BETTER

The Callaways #9

BARBARA FREETHY

HYDE
STREET
—PRESS—

HYDE STREET PRESS
Published by Hyde Street Press
1325 Howard Avenue, #321, Burlingame, California 94010

Printed in the United States of America

Cover design by Damonza.com

ISBN: 978-0-9961154-3-8

One

―→ ➺➤ ⥸⥷ ⥷ ―

"I'm not running away," Mia Callaway said forcefully as she looked into her older sister Annie's disbelieving eyes. "I'm helping Mom. She can't clean out Aunt Carly's house with a broken foot, and I have some time on my hands, so I said I would do it."

"You're going to drive five hours down the coast tomorrow to Angel's Bay and spend the summer clearing out Aunt Carly's house, which could probably be on one of those shows about hoarders?" Annie Callaway asked doubtfully.

"It can't be that bad."

"Aunt Carly has been collecting junk for forty years."

"I doubt she would call souvenirs from her travels— junk," she said defensively.

"What happened to your job?" Annie asked. "You worked so hard to get that position at the museum. It was perfect for you. And what about Grayson? I thought he was the perfect guy."

Mia sighed. "He definitely turned out to be less than perfect. It's too long of a story to get into now."

They were standing on the sidewalk in front of her cousin Nicole's house, where a huge combined bridal/baby shower was about to begin. At least two dozen Callaway females were waiting inside, and she did not need that kind of attention on her now somewhat dismal life.

She opened the passenger door of her car and grabbed her two presents, then tipped her head toward the house where balloons adorned the porch railing. "The party is starting. We should go inside."

"We have a minute," Annie said, tucking a strand of her long, dark red hair behind her ear. Unlike Mia, who had blonde hair and blue eyes, Annie had inherited her mother's red hair and green eyes. Those eyes were now staring at her with stubborn determination.

Mia had thought she'd get the most pointed questions from her mother or her twin sister Kate, but her mom's fractured ankle and Kate's FBI training, had apparently kept their focus elsewhere. Annie, who, at twenty-nine, was three years older than Mia, rarely kept that up-to-date with her life. Nor did her three brothers who probably had no idea she'd lost her job or her boyfriend. But that was a good thing.

Being the baby in the family, she'd grown up under the protective eye of two parents and five siblings, and she was more than a little tired of being under their microscope, which was another good reason for going away.

"I'm not going inside until you tell me what is going on with you," Annie said, determination in her eyes. "I'm worried about you, Mia. Kate is the one I expect to go off on a whim or some crazy adventure, not you. You've always had your act together, a solid plan, a list of goals. So what is the deal?"

"There's nothing to worry about, Annie. Things didn't work out with Grayson, and I decided to leave the museum." She'd actually been asked to leave, but she didn't need to get into that. "I'll find another job, but I could use a break. I've been working nonstop for the last four years." Actually, she'd been working nonstop her entire life: buried in books, chasing goals, trying to be the smartest person on the planet, or at least her family, only to find out she'd been about as dumb as anyone could be.

"What did Grayson do?" Annie asked, a sharp, speculative gleam in her eyes. "And don't say it was nothing."

"I don't want to talk about Grayson. This day is about Nicole and Maddie. Let's focus on making their party special."

Since her cousin Nicole was about to give birth in three weeks, and Maddie Heller was set to marry Mia's cousin Burke in a month, the family had decided to throw a combined bridal/baby shower. With so many Callaways celebrating so many happy events these days, it had become necessary to put some of them together.

"Fine, I won't press you anymore right now," Annie said. "But I'm still not sure going to Angel's Bay is a good idea. It's so far away. And what is there to do?"

"Clean out Aunt Carly's house."

"That doesn't sound too exciting. I still feel like you're running away from something, and I hope you know you can talk to me. I realize I haven't been the most attentive big sister, spending all my time at work, but I am here for you."

"I know that. Stop worrying. I loved visiting Aunt Carly in Angel's Bay. I can't wait to get back there. The beach is wild and beautiful. I love the shipwreck legend and the angel stories. Plus, I want to take care of Aunt Carly's house. She's the one who gave me my first set of paints. She told me stories that made me love art and history. I'm really going to miss her. We had a special bond."

"I'm going to miss her, too, not that she and I were as close as the two of you were, but she was always fun when she came to visit."

"Usually on her way back from a trip somewhere."

"Crazy Aunt Carly," Annie said with a smile. "She and Mom might have been sisters, but they were as different as night and day."

Mia nodded. Her mother was a hard-working nurse who'd married a firefighter and raised six kids. Her Aunt Carly had never married, although she'd had numerous *lovers,* as she liked to call them, and she'd traveled all around the world.

Carly had died a few weeks earlier when she was on a boat that capsized in the Indian Ocean. It was difficult to believe she would not come home with yet another great story to tell. But at least she had died having the time of her life. What more could anyone ask?

"We should go inside," Mia said.

Before they could move, Sara, Chloe, and Emma came down the sidewalk with bags of presents in their hands.

Emma, a petite blonde with bright blue eyes, was a fire investigator and another one of her cousins.

Sara, a dark-eyed brunette, was married to Emma's brother Aiden. With Sara was her adorable, almost two-year-old toddler Chloe, who had a mass of brown curls to match her mother and a rebellious personality that was all Aiden. Even now, Chloe was tugging at her mother's hand, eager to get to the party.

"One minute, Chloe," Sara said firmly, as she and Emma exchanged hugs with Mia and Annie. "How are you doing, Mia? I heard you might be looking for a new job."

"News travels fast in this family."

"I have a friend who works at the Palace of Fine Arts. Let me know if you want me to make a call," Sara said.

"Thanks. I'm going to take a few weeks off before I decide my next move."

"Lucky you," Emma said. "I can't remember the last time I had weeks off in the summer."

"That's because you adore your job and never want to leave it," Sara teased Emma.

Emma grinned. "Actually, my adoration is now more focused on my husband, but between him and my job, I get even less time to myself."

Mia knew that Emma wasn't really complaining, not with the glowing smile on her face.

"Go now," Chloe demanded with another tug on Sara's hand.

"She saw the balloons and got excited," Sara said with an apologetic smile.

"I'm excited, too," Mia said. "Let's go to the party."

When they stepped onto the porch, Nicole threw open the door to greet them.

Like her sister Emma, Nicole had blonde hair and blue eyes, but she was also enormously pregnant, carrying all her baby weight in the front of her slender frame.

"Welcome," Nicole said, giving them each a hug.

"How are you, Nic?" Mia asked, lingering behind as the others made their way into the house.

"As big as a house and happy as can be, but I must admit that I am a little tired." Nicole rubbed her baby bump with an affectionate hand. "My miracle child has been kicking a lot lately. I think she's eager to meet everyone."

"We're eager to meet her, too. Where's her older

brother Brandon?"

"Ryan and Sean took Brandon and Kyle to the park," Nicole explained, referring to her husband Ryan and her brother Sean, and the twin boys who were now eight years old.

"How is Brandon handling the idea of a new sibling?" she asked. Brandon had been diagnosed with autism when he was two, but he had recently improved in some areas of language and communication, which was not only due to intensive therapy, but also the reunion with his twin brother—another miracle that had been bestowed on Nicole.

"I don't think Brandon gets it yet, but Kyle is over the moon. And whenever Kyle is happy, Brandon is happy. That's the way with twins, I guess. You would know that better than me."

"Kate and I were never quite as tightly linked as Kyle and Brandon, but we do sense when one of us is in trouble and needs a call, a hug, or a kick in the ass."

"I have a feeling Kate would usually be the one to deliver that kick," Nicole said with a laugh. "Anyway, come in. I'm sorry your mom couldn't come. I heard she fell down some stairs."

"Yes. She was carrying some boxes down from the attic, and she tripped. She's all right, but she fractured a bone in her foot, sprained her ankle, and has to stay off her feet for a while. She's not happy about it. Where's your mom?"

"In the living room." Nicole waved her hand toward the crowded room off to the right of the entry. "Make yourself at home. There's food in the dining room, drinks in the kitchen, and plenty of people everywhere."

Mia was used to large gatherings. Growing up in the Callaway family meant every party involved at least twenty to thirty immediate family members, and this joint shower was no exception.

She'd always liked being a Callaway, having a solid family around her, although being a Callaway also came with responsibility. Her father had been a firefighter like her Uncle Jack and several other relatives. And while not every Callaway saved lives, a lot of them did something to better the community or the world, setting the bar quite high. She'd fallen quite a ways under that bar in recent weeks, but she wasn't going to think about that today.

As she moved toward the living room, she ran into the bride-to-be coming down the hall. Maddie Heller was another beautiful blonde with a happy glow, obviously looking forward to her upcoming wedding. Maddie reminded her of her Aunt Carly. Like Carly, Maddie had been a free spirit, traveling the world before falling for Burke and choosing to marry and settle down.

Maybe it was about time Mia joined the free-spirit crowd. Certainly trying to do everything exactly right and meet everyone's expectations had not worked out well.

"So glad you could come," Maddie said, giving her a hug.

"Are you getting nervous about the wedding?"

"Not even a little bit. Burke is not perfect, but he's the perfect man for me."

"I'm so glad you found each other. I can't wait to see you two walk down the aisle."

"You're still coming, right?" Maddie asked. "Did I hear something about you going to Angel's Bay for a while?"

"Yes, but Angel's Bay is only an hour or so from Santa Barbara, so I'll be able to make the wedding."

"Good. I'm counting on you being there."

As Maddie left to say hello to someone else, Mia

walked into the living room.

Her Aunt Lynda waved her toward the couch. "Come sit next to me, Mia."

Lynda Callaway, a blue-eyed blonde in her late fifties, was married to Mia's Uncle Jack and was both mother and stepmother to eight of her cousins. She was also one of the nicest people Mia had ever known.

"I'm sorry about your mother's fall," Lynda said, as Mia sat down next to her. "And I'm also sorry about your Aunt Carly. She was such a lovely, energetic woman. I got a postcard from her on my birthday a few months ago. I couldn't believe she remembered. The postcard was from Paris. She told me she'd rented a loft for a month and was spending her days painting by the Seine, drinking wine at dusk and talking to handsome men in the moonlight." Lynda laughed. "What a life."

"I'll say." The restlessness she'd been feeling for weeks grew stronger as she thought about her aunt's words. Maybe her aunt had died too young, but she'd certainly lived well.

"Your mom said you're going down to Angel's Bay to clear out Carly's house," Lynda continued.

She nodded. "Yes, it might take a few weeks. Aunt Carly had a lot of stuff."

"Well, there are worse things than spending August at the beach."

"I know. It's a tough job, but someone has to do it," she said lightly.

"Can I give you one little piece of advice, Mia, if you don't mind?"

"Of course not," she said, tensing at the question. She didn't know how much the rest of the family knew about her problems, but she was hoping very little.

"Don't be in a rush to throw things away. Sometimes

what people leave behind is more important than you think. And there's a healing to touching and holding items that meant something to the person you loved."

Lynda's words brought unexpected moisture to her eyes. "I agree."

"Oh, I'm sorry. I didn't mean to make you cry." Lynda gave her an apologetic smile.

"I'm fine. I'm just a little emotional."

"As you should be. Loss is always difficult. But you're the perfect person for the job, because you love history and art. I think you're going to find both in your Aunt Carly's house."

"I am curious to see what's there. The last few years she rented out the cottage at the back of her house to artists passing through town or local painters needing a place to create their art. Aunt Carly never asked for rent money, but she did request that each artist leave behind one piece of original art when they moved on. I can't help thinking I might make a real discovery in that cottage."

"That does sound like a possibility."

"It looks like the party is starting," Mia said, as Emma took center stage.

"Just a few games. I promise they'll be fun," Emma said with a laugh, as her news was received with groans of displeasure.

Emma's determined gaze told the group that they were going to play whether they wanted to or not. "We're going to mix it up between baby and bridal, so our two favorite girls, Nicole and Maddie, will each feel special," she added. "Let's start with you, Nicole. You have to guess what's in the diaper bag that Ria is holding." She motioned toward the dark blonde holding an overstuffed tote bag in her hands.

Nicole shook her head. "I can't."

"Come on, you have to play," Emma said with a frown. "I know you think games are silly, but they're fun, too."

"I can't." Nicole stood up, a pained expression on her face as she held her stomach with both hands. "My water just broke. I'm in labor. Oh, my God, I'm in labor. It's too early. It's too soon."

"You'll be okay, Nicole," Lynda said, jumping to her feet as she rushed toward her daughter. "We're going to get you to the hospital."

"I'm going with you," Emma said.

"I'll call Ryan," Sara put in.

"I'm sorry, Maddie," Nicole said. "I'm wrecking your party."

Maddie waved a hand in the air. "Don't be silly. We'll celebrate after you deliver your beautiful daughter."

"It's too early. I wish Shayla were here," Nicole added, referring to her younger sister, who was also a doctor.

"She'll be at the hospital," Emma reassured Nicole as they left the living room.

"Never a dull moment at a Callaway party," Annie said, coming over to her.

"You can say that again. I hope everything goes well."

"It will," Annie said confidently.

"Okay, the party will now go on," Sara declared, taking charge. "We'll just focus on Maddie and celebrate Nicole's baby when she brings her home."

As Sara started the next game, Mia thought about how many of her cousins were making big moves in their lives with babies and weddings. She'd been stuck in a rut, but she was going to get out of it, starting tomorrow with a very long drive down the coast.

Two

As Jeremy Holt drove through the streets of Angel's Bay on Monday afternoon, he wondered why he'd ever made the decision to come home. On the other hand, had he really had a choice?

Two months ago his life had been completely different. He'd just finished his twelfth year in the Army, and his fourth year as a member of the Army's elite Delta Force. Then an IED blast had sent him to an operating room in a military hospital in Germany. It had taken four hours to stop the internal bleeding and repair shoulder muscles decimated by shrapnel. When he'd woken up, his future had looked a lot different.

Rehabilitating his shoulder was possible, but it would be a long and painful process, and he might never recover full range of motion or the physical strength he needed to do a very challenging and dangerous job. His future with Delta was in jeopardy, and he'd be in denial if he thought otherwise.

He'd never shied away from hard truths, but this was one truth he wished he could look past. He loved the Army. He'd enlisted after high school graduation, and in the military he'd found his family, his skill set. He was good at his job. What the hell else he was good at, he didn't know. But he was going to have to find out.

It wasn't just the potential loss of his career that had sent him reeling, it was also the letter that had arrived two weeks after his surgery. The letter had come from the children's services department in San Francisco. It had been following him around the globe for almost a month before finally reaching his possession.

The news had been shocking.

He had a daughter—an eight-year-old kid named Ashlyn Price. His child was the result of a one-night stand nine years ago with a woman named Justine Price.

Justine had been killed a month earlier in a robbery. Ashlyn had no other living relatives, so she'd been put into foster care until her father could be located—and he was her father.

He'd flown to San Francisco and met a shy, dark-haired, dark-eyed, skinny little girl who mumbled a few words when she absolutely had to, but beyond that she seemed to have no interest in speaking to him. He'd been expecting anger, surprise, or joy at his arrival, but she'd given him no reaction whatsoever.

He'd tried to explain to her that he hadn't known about her until now, but it was difficult to know if anything he'd said had sunk in. Ashlyn had shut down emotionally after her mother's death, and the social worker he'd spoken to in San Francisco had told him to be patient, that Ashlyn needed time to heal and a relationship could take a very long time.

Ashlyn needed to learn to trust him. She also needed to feel safe, and that would require structure, predictability, consistency, and lots of therapy.

He'd accepted his parental responsibility without a second thought. He might not have loved her mother—or even barely remembered her—but he would never walk away from his child. He just had no idea how to be a father.

They'd spent the first two weeks together in a vacation rental in San Francisco. He'd thought about staying in the city and getting an apartment so Ashlyn could go to school with her friends, but the city streets terrified her. The convenience store robbery that had left her mother dead had traumatized her. She visibly shrank when he took her in the car or tried to get her to walk down the street with him. It had become clear to him that he had to make a change.

Since his most recent address had been an Army barracks on the other side of the world, he'd needed somewhere else to go. His good friend Kent Palmer had told him it was time to come home.

At first, Jeremy had resisted the idea. It wasn't like he had a family waiting with open arms to welcome him back or who were dying to get to know his daughter, maybe help take care of her.

No, the only relative he had left in town was a gruff, cold father who still spent most of his days at sea and his nights with a bottle. It had been that way since Jeremy was eleven years old. There was no reason to expect things to be different now.

But he didn't need his father to make things work. What he needed was a safe place for Ashlyn, and the charming coastal town of Angel's Bay couldn't be any safer.

Kent had helped him find a rental house and a good therapist for Ashlyn. Unfortunately, the first visit with the therapist had not gone well. He hoped today would be different.

He parked his car in front of the Redwood Medical

Clinic and checked his watch. He had ten minutes until Ashlyn's appointment ended. He got out of the car to get some air. As his feet hit the pavement, he saw Kent pull up in his patrol car, then get out and walk toward him.

At six foot four, Kent was long and lanky with short, dark blond hair and brown eyes. He was dressed in uniform and obviously on duty, but he didn't look particularly stressed out. Jeremy doubted being a cop in Angel's Bay put too much pressure on a man who'd been a soldier for ten years of his life.

"How's it going?" Kent asked with a friendly boyish grin that took Jeremy back to the old days when they'd been two kids getting into trouble.

"Not bad. What are you doing here?"

"Taking a break. I thought I'd see how Ashlyn's session went today."

"We'll see. The first one didn't do anything."

"Did she put up a fight to go back?"

"She doesn't put up a fight to do anything. I wish she would. Anger would be easier to deal with than...nothingness. It's like she wants to be invisible. I talk to her and try to play with her, but I get no response. I've bribed her with toys and candy. Her bedroom looks like the inside of a toy store, but nothing interests her. She spends most of her days lying on her bed, staring at the ceiling. I was actually thinking of painting a picture up there, just to give her something to look at."

"That's not a bad idea, but I have confidence that Eva will help Ashlyn. She knows how to deal with trauma. I saw her a few times when I first got back, and talking to her really helped put things into perspective."

"I hope so." His first impression of Dr. Eva Westcott had been a positive one. The thirty-year-old psychologist had a pleasant, soothing manner and a quiet confidence that commanded attention. His brows drew together as he thought about the rest of Kent's statement. "I didn't know you'd seen a shrink when you got back here or that you were having any issues. You never told me that."

Kent shrugged. "It wasn't that big of a deal. I couldn't sleep for the first few weeks. I was feeling like a zombie. I ran into Jamie Adams one day. He told me that Eva Westcott had helped him when he got out of the Army and that she was great with soldiers. I thought it couldn't hurt. Plus, she's not bad to look at," he added with a sparkle in his eyes.

Jeremy smiled. "I can see how that factored into your decision. How's Jamie doing these days?" The younger man had left the Army three years ago.

"He's working in construction. He got his contractor's license, and he's been busy building the new homes going up at the north end of town. He hires a lot of ex-soldiers, if you feel like swinging a hammer."

"Not at the moment."

"You were lousy with tools anyway."

"I wasn't that bad."

"You weren't that good. You hammered your shirt to the fence, remember?"

"I remember that I was twelve at the time," he said dryly. "I've picked up some skills since then."

"Well, I have a better idea for a career change if you're looking to make one. We're going to be hiring one or two more officers in the fall; I think you'd be perfect."

"I'm not a cop."

"You could be. It's a good job. I know you're not ready to give up on Delta, but just keep it in the back of your mind."

"Fine. I'll think about it. Speaking of Jamie Adams, isn't that his sister?" Jeremy asked, as an attractive blonde walked out of the clinic. She had on a slim-fitting blue dress under a white physician's coat. As she paused to check something on her phone, he couldn't help thinking that Charlie, as they used to call her, had grown up quite nicely.

"That's her. Charlotte—over here," Kent said with a wave.

She lifted her head and smiled, then walked over to join them. "Hi Kent." She paused, her eyes widening with recognition when she saw him. "Jeremy Holt? Is it really you? I don't think I've seen you since high school."

"I'm back."

"I can see that. How are you? Jamie tells me you're quite the hero, that the Army is going to run out of medals to give to you."

"He exaggerates."

"Really? I don't remember you being modest, Jeremy."

He laughed and tipped his head in acknowledgement. "Life experiences have a way of humbling you. So you're a doctor here at the clinic?"

"Yes. I'm an OB/GYN. I just delivered a happy, healthy boy to his very excited first-time parents. It never gets old." She paused. "And I'm not Charlotte Adams anymore. I got married last year to Joe Silveira, the chief of police. I don't know if you've met him…"

"Not yet," he said.

"Well, I'm sure you will. He's wonderful. Kent can attest to that."

"Best boss I've ever had," Kent said.

"I better go," Charlotte said. "I expect I'll be seeing you again soon. Angel's Bay has tripled in population since you left, but it's still a small town."

"You don't have to tell me that."

She laughed. "I left for a long time, too, Jeremy, but when I came back, I found it very difficult to leave. Be warned, Angel's Bay will put its spell on you."

"She's right," Kent said, as Charlotte walked away. "I'm not in any danger of falling under the Angel's Bay spell, not while my father lives here."

"Have you seen your dad yet?"

"I saw him for about five minutes last week. I called first and told him I wanted to come by his apartment and talk to him about something important. I thought that might make him skip his afternoon cocktail, but I was wrong. His love affair with Jack Daniels is as strong as ever. I told him I had a daughter. That sent him on a rant of how irresponsible I'd always been. So I left. I don't need any further contact with him. Frankly, the last thing I want to do is expose Ashlyn to him."

"You need to talk to him when he's not drinking."

"And when would that be? He leaves before dawn to fish, and by afternoon he's back in the bar."

"I've had some sober conversations with him. In fact, I thought he'd been sober for several years. I have a feeling you coming home set him back."

"It doesn't matter. I've spent too many years of my life worrying about him; it's about Ashlyn now."

"Has she told you anything about her mother, their life, the robbery?"

"Absolutely nothing. I get only yes, no, and nonverbal answers. It's making me nuts, I have to admit."

"Well, you're used to getting quick results when you put your mind to something, but this is different."

"Very different. I have no idea how to talk to a little girl. And I don't know what her mother told her about me. I also don't know why Justine never tried to find me to let me know she was pregnant or had a child. I would have done the right thing. I would have supported her."

"She didn't know you. You didn't know her."

"We made a kid."

"Yeah, but who knows if she could have even found you after that night. She might not have known your last name."

He would have thought that was possible if Justine hadn't put his name down on the birth certificate, because he hadn't remembered Justine's name until the social worker had shown him a photograph and given him the date of Ashlyn's birth. He'd counted backward and realized that he'd hooked up with Justine while he was on leave in Miami. He'd been celebrating his twenty-first birthday, and she'd been on spring break.

They hadn't done a lot of talking that night. It had been sex and drinking and more sex and more drinking. He'd left the next day for an eleven-month deployment, and he'd never seen or heard from her again.

"She put me down as the father; she just didn't tell me," he said.

"Maybe it's better that she didn't. You might not have had the career you've had if she'd told you she was having a baby. It would have changed your life."

He knew that and there was a selfish part of him that was a little happy that he hadn't had to figure out how to be a father at twenty-one. But there was also another part of him that felt angry with her silence and the distance she'd put between him and his child.

If Justine hadn't died unexpectedly, would he have ever known he had a daughter? Somehow he didn't think so.

The door to the clinic opened, and Dr. Eva Westcott walked out with Ashlyn.

His daughter had no expression on her face, and her

hands were in the pockets of her shorts, making it clear she had no interest in holding Dr. Westcott's hand.

Eva was an attractive, cool blonde who wore a straight black skirt and a cream-colored blouse.

Jeremy couldn't help noticing that Kent stood up taller when Dr. Westcott approached.

"Hello," Eva said calmly, as she walked Ashlyn over to the car. "Ashlyn and I had a good talk today."

"Really?" he asked, unable to keep the doubt out of his voice.

She gave him a pointed look that told him that wasn't the right thing to say.

Ashlyn walked past him and got into the car without saying a word.

"Sorry," he muttered. "Did she really talk to you?"

"She responded to some pictures that we looked at together, a few words here and there. This is going to take time, Mr. Holt."

"Please call me Jeremy. I do understand that it will take time. I just want to know how I can help her get better faster."

She gave him a compassionate smile. "Just be there for her. Ashlyn needs to learn how to trust you. Only then will she be able to share her emotions and her thoughts."

"How do I get her to trust me?"

"Be her father."

"I don't really know how to do that."

"Well, she doesn't know what she expects you to do, either. She lived alone with her mother. Having a father is as foreign to her as having a daughter is to you. You'll find your way together."

"I hope so." He paused. "Why do you think she won't talk?"

"Her voice is the one thing she can control when

every other part of her life is in chaos. But she can speak, and she will."

"When?"

"When she has something she needs to say."

"Great," he said, feeling even more frustrated by that vague answer.

She gave him a sympathetic smile. "I'll see you on Friday. Please feel free to call if you have questions before then."

"Thanks."

"Do you have a minute, Eva?" Kent asked.

She checked her watch. "I have a patient in ten minutes."

"It won't take that long. I'll walk you to your office."

As Eva and Kent went into the clinic, Jeremy got behind the wheel of his SUV. He'd always driven a truck, but he'd needed a more family-friendly car since he got Ashlyn, so he'd joined the SUV crowd.

Ashlyn stared straight ahead, her hands clasped together in her lap.

"Are you hungry?" he asked. "I was thinking we might pick up a pizza on our way home." He was getting used to answering his own questions. He took her silence for a yes. "Great, we'll do that then. Dr. Westcott said you had a good talk today," he added, as he pulled out of the parking space. "One of these days you and I are going to have a good talk, too. I want to get to know you, Ashlyn, hear about your life. I have a lot of questions. You probably do, too. We don't know much about each other, but we're family. And we're going to be together." He gave her a sideways glance and realized her expression hadn't changed a bit. She looked frozen. Had she even heard him?

Maybe there was more wrong with her than even Dr.

Westcott knew.

On the other hand, there was something about the set of her profile that reminded him a little of himself. He'd withdrawn from the world after his mom passed away from cancer. It was the only way he knew how to deal with the well-wishers who really just pissed him off with words that made no sense to him.

"You know," he said, thinking he'd just found a way to connect to her. "I lost my mom when I was eleven, just a few years older than you. I didn't like it when people tried to make me feel better. I really hated when they said things like *she's in a better place*, or *she's watching down on you from heaven*. I didn't think any place without me could be better, and I didn't want her watching me; I wanted her to be there with me." He realized that he'd never expressed those thoughts out loud until now.

"You're never going to forget your mother, and you'll always miss her," he continued. "But I do know that your mom would want you to be happy again, and I'm certain that she'd want me to make sure you had a good life."

Actually, he didn't know that at all.

If Justine had wanted him to be part of Ashlyn's life, wouldn't she have included him in it while she was alive? Maybe he was the last person she would want raising her daughter.

He looked over at Ashlyn again. She'd turned her head, but not in his direction. Now, she was looking out the side window. Was the fact that she'd moved at all a good sign or a bad one? Or was he just going to drive himself crazy by analyzing every tiny movement?

Probably the latter, he decided.

With a sigh, he turned on the radio and hoped the music would take some of the tension away.

Thirty minutes later, after a stop at Rocco's to pick up pizza, salad and garlic chips, Jeremy drove home, thinking that he had another silent, uneventful Friday night in front of him.

His life had certainly turned completely upside down, he thought, wondering if it would ever go back to right-side up.

As he parked in front of his house, he was surprised to see a car in the driveway next door. The house had been empty since he'd moved in, and the neighbor on the other side had told him that the owner had passed away a few months earlier.

He was even more surprised when he realized that a woman was standing on the roof of that house, outside a second-story window, and was waving her arms to get his attention.

He quickly got out of the car.

"I need help," she yelled.

He could see that. The trellis next to the house was in pieces in the yard. She'd obviously climbed up to the second floor before the fragile frame of wood had given way.

"I thought the window would open all the way, but it's stuck," she explained, motioning her hand to the window behind her that was open about three inches. "Can you help me? I can't get in, and I can't get down. Do you have a ladder?"

He glanced back at Ashlyn, who had gotten out of the car and was watching their interaction. She actually seemed somewhat interested in the blonde woman trapped on the roof next door.

He looked back at the woman. "I might. Who are

you?" He moved closer to her house, noting that the woman was prettier than he'd first realized. She had wavy blonde hair that fell past her shoulders and a really great body displayed in a pair of shorts and a knit shirt that clung to her breasts.

"I'm Mia Callaway. This is my Aunt Carly's house. She died last month, and I've come to clean out her house."

"Why don't you have a key?"

"I do have a key, but it didn't work."

"So you decided to climb onto the roof?"

She made a face. "It wasn't the best idea I've ever had. I saw the window ajar and thought I could pop it open and save myself a trip to the locksmith. It was a long drive down here, and I was tired."

"Where did you come from?"

"San Francisco. Look, we can chat, but I'd rather do it down there or in the house. So what do you say, can you help me out?"

"I'll see if there's a ladder in my garage."

"You don't know?"

"I rented the house two weeks ago. I haven't looked all that closely at the garage." He turned back to Ashlyn, who'd also moved closer but was still about ten feet away from him. "I need to help Mia get off the roof. I'm going to get a ladder out of the garage. Do you want to wait in the house? I'll let you in and then come back."

He was expecting her to nod and run toward their house, because so far she hadn't shown much interest in anyone, which had made him feel marginally better, since her dislike didn't seem to be only focused on him.

Instead, she shook her head and sat down on the grass right where she was standing.

"Okay, I'll grab the ladder. You stay right there," he

said.

"I'll keep an eye on her," Mia offered. "What's your name, sweetie?"

He saw Ashlyn look in Mia's direction, but she didn't answer.

"Her name is Ashlyn," he said, then walked down the short driveway to the garage.

"You have a very pretty name," Mia said. "I like your long dark hair, too."

He appreciated Mia's effort to engage Ashlyn, even though she was getting absolutely nothing back.

As he pulled the ladder off the wall, he winced, his left shoulder protesting the movement and the weight, a reminder of how far he was from his normal state of health. He shifted the ladder to his right side and walked next door. He managed to get the ladder up against the house with a minimal amount of effort and pain.

"All right, there you go," he said.

"Thanks." She moved forward and then paused, as she peered over the side. "It looks a lot higher when you get closer to the edge."

"Seriously? You're nervous to come down?" he asked in amazement. "You climbed up what was probably a fifty-year-old trellis without a second thought."

"Well, I've had time to have second thoughts," she retorted. "But I can do this. I just have to take the first step. It's going to be fine. I won't fall. It's not like I've never been on a ladder before."

"Hey, I've got a pizza that's getting cold. Are you done with the pep talk?" He wondered how he'd gotten stuck with a woman who wouldn't shut up and a kid who wouldn't say a word—talk about extremes.

"I'm just being careful. I won't fall, will I?" Her worried gaze sought his.

"I just heard you say you won't, and I believe you." He put both of his hands on the ladder. "First step is the hardest."

"Right."

Despite her answer, she didn't move.

He hesitated and then climbed up the ladder until he was close to the roof. "Take my hand." He held out his right hand, happy again that it was his left shoulder that had been ripped apart.

"I might knock us both off the ladder," she said doubtfully.

"You won't."

"Are you sure?"

"You're going to have to trust me."

She took a breath and then put her hand into his. Her fingers were warm and soft, and he felt the strangest sensation in the pit of his stomach as his gaze met hers. He was startled by the blue of her eyes; the kind of blue that mirrored the deepest part of the sea. A man could drown in those eyes, but that man was not going to be him, he told himself firmly. He had enough problems in his life without adding a woman into the mix, especially a woman who seemed a little too impulsive for her own good.

He held onto her hand while she awkwardly climbed onto the ladder, and then he let go so he could get down. When he hit the ground, he kept a careful eye on her as she made her way safely down.

She took the last step with a relieved sigh and a triumphant smile. "Made it."

She acted like she'd just breached the summit of Mount Everest.

"Yes, that was quite the feat," he drawled. "Maybe next time come up with a better plan for coming down before you go up."

"My plan was to open the window, get in the house, and then come downstairs and open the front door. I usually do plan out everything, but I decided when I came to Angel's Bay that I was going to shake things up, be more spontaneous."

"Well, you did that."

"Thanks for your help, Mr…"

"Holt—Jeremy Holt. So what's next? You're still not in the house."

"Right. I'll call a locksmith and see if I can get someone out here before it gets dark."

The sun was falling fast. She had about ten minutes of light left, and he doubted she would find a locksmith to come out quickly at six thirty on a Friday night, but he'd let her deal with that.

While she called the locksmith, he gave Ashlyn a smile. "I'll put the ladder away and then we can go inside and eat. Do you want to get the food out of the car?"

His question brought her to her feet, and she ran toward the car while he moved down the driveway.

When he closed the garage door, he was surprised to see Ashlyn walking toward Mia's house instead of their front door. She paused right in front of Mia, waiting for her to get off the phone, then she lifted up the pizza box with the salad bag on top like an offering to the gods.

"That smells good," Mia said, glancing past Ashlyn to Jeremy. "You should go and have your dinner."

That was his thought exactly, but Ashlyn seemed to be entranced by Mia. He didn't know what was happening with his daughter, but he thought he should go with it.

"Why don't you come next door and have some pizza with us while you wait for the locksmith?" he suggested.

Surprise flashed across her face. "Really? I wouldn't

want to impose."

"All evidence to the contrary," he said dryly. "Feeding you will take less effort than getting you off the roof. I think Ashlyn would like you to join us."

Mia looked at Ashlyn. "Do you want to share your pizza with me?"

The little girl nodded.

"Then I'm going to say thank-you," Mia said. "I'm starving. I didn't want to stop on my way down. I got kind of a late start, and I wanted to get here before dark."

He led the way to his house, with Mia and Ashlyn following close behind.

Once inside, he said, "Why don't you wash your hands, Ash? We'll be in the kitchen."

Ashlyn handed the food to him, then ran up the stairs. It was the fastest he'd ever seen her move.

"The locksmith said it would be about an hour," Mia told him, as they walked down the hall and entered the kitchen.

"That should give you enough time to eat."

"Are you sure there's enough?"

"We have plenty. Ashlyn won't eat more than one piece, and even I can't finish off an extra-large pizza by myself." He pulled out the salad and garlic chips and put them on the table along with the pizza. "What do you want to drink?"

"Anything is fine."

"Water, milk, orange juice and apple juice is about all I have."

"Water is good."

She looked around the room while he grabbed a water out of the refrigerator.

"Have you lived here long?" she asked.

"Just two weeks. It's a rental."

"Oh, that makes sense. I thought an older couple lived here."

"Apparently, they moved out a few months back and decided to keep it as a rental."

She nodded and sat down at the table. He could see the questions gathering in her eyes, and it didn't take long for the first one to reach her lips.

"So I don't want to pry," she began.

"Ashlyn lost her mother two months ago. She's dealing with grief and trauma. Those emotions seem to have stolen her voice."

"I'm so sorry," she said, compassion entering her pretty blue eyes. "That's terrible. You both must be devastated."

"Ashlyn's mother and I weren't together," he said, realizing she'd jumped to the wrong conclusion. "I actually didn't even know I had a child until last month."

"Really? She didn't tell you?"

"No. Ashlyn and I have been together for three weeks, one week in San Francisco and two weeks here. She didn't have any other relatives to take her."

"Well, I'm sure she's lucky to have you."

"So far, she doesn't act like she feels lucky, but that doesn't matter. I just want her to get better, talk again, smile, laugh, and be a normal little kid."

"You'll get there," she said, as he sat down across from her.

He wished he felt as confident.

"So her mother never told you she was pregnant?" Mia continued. "Was your relationship over before she found out?"

"It wasn't a relationship. It was a hook-up: my twenty-first birthday, her spring break, a lot of tequila."

Mia nodded in understanding. "Got it. I'm surprised

that she didn't tell you, though. It must have been difficult for her to be a single mother at twenty-one. What about her parents?"

"All I know is that they've been deceased for some time." He paused. "Justine put my name on the birth certificate, but she never tried to find me, and I doubt I'll ever know why."

"Would you have been difficult to find?"

"I was in the Army, so difficult, yes, but not impossible. I asked Ashlyn if her mom had told her about me, and she just stared back at me with those big brown eyes of hers that should be full of life but aren't. Anyway, she might not like me, but she seems quite drawn to you."

"I was always good with kids. As a teenager, with a not-so-great social life, I made a lot of money babysitting."

He had a difficult time believing she'd had any lack of a social life. She was pretty, friendly, and had a killer body that he appreciated even more now that she was sitting in his lighted kitchen. He tried to shake that thought out of his head. "So you said you're here to clean out your aunt's house?"

"Yes. Aunt Carly died unexpectedly in an accident. She was a world traveler and quite a collector. I haven't been in her house in years, but I remember it being filled to the brim with all kinds of things: statues, carvings, paintings, old books, and scarves. She loved scarves—she wore them every day. She loved jewelry, too—the older the better. I bet she has some pieces that are a hundred years old."

"Sounds like you're about to open a treasure chest," he said, seeing the light of anticipation in her eyes.

She smiled. "It feels a little like that. But I don't want you to get the wrong idea. I loved my aunt. She and I were soul mates. We had a special connection. She introduced me to art; she taught me how to paint. She inspired me so much. I am really going to miss her. The only thing that gives me peace is that she died having an adventure. She was always about living life to the fullest. She used to give me a hard time, asking me what I was waiting for, when I was going to start living..."

Her voice trailed away as a shadow entered her eyes. She looked at him with pain now in her gaze. "I don't know what I was waiting for, what I'm *still* waiting for. How do you decide when it's time to stay on the path of certainty or jump into the unknown?"

"Interesting question for a woman who had trouble coming down a ladder," he said. "For you, I think the path of certainty might be the only choice."

She made a little face at him. "I was speaking metaphorically."

"I find it's better to live in reality, not metaphoric possibilities."

"That's probably a good idea. I climbed up to the roof, because I was trying to be more bold, take more chances, not just wait for someone to rescue me."

"And yet—"

"I know you had to rescue me," she said, cutting him off. "But that wasn't supposed to happen."

"That's the thing with taking chances; you don't know what will happen. Most people would say that's what makes taking a chance exciting."

"I know my aunt would say that." She sighed. "I don't know why I just told you all that about myself. I guess five hours on the road with only myself to talk to has loosened my tongue."

"I don't know why I told you anything, either, but I guess living with a kid who acts like I'm invisible has made me appreciate conversation more than I used to."

"Be careful what you wish for. Once Ashlyn starts talking, she might never shut up."

"I look forward to that day. How long do you think you'll be in Angel's Bay?"

"A few weeks. I have some time and there's no better place than Angel's Bay in the summer. It looks like you and I are going to be neighbors for a while, Jeremy."

She gave him a smile that literally stopped his breath. "Great," he muttered.

She laughed. "Don't worry. I'm not going to be a problem. I'm usually quite responsible—all evidence to the contrary."

He couldn't help smiling as she threw his words back in his face. He realized that it was probably the first time he'd felt amused by anything in over six weeks, and as he found himself unable to look away from her sparkling eyes, he realized that Mia Callaway was going to be a problem, a beautiful and quite possibly irresistible problem. But he had enough on his plate without throwing a woman into the mix, didn't he?

Three

❧

It was the strangest dinner she'd ever had, Mia thought, as she finished up her second slice of pizza and looked across the table at her companions. Ashlyn had eaten one slice quite slowly and spent the rest of the time staring at Mia. It was a very intense stare, too, questioning in some way that Mia couldn't begin to understand.

She wondered if she reminded Ashlyn of her mother, if that was why the little girl seemed so fascinated by her. Or maybe it was just that she was female, and Ashlyn felt more comfortable with her than with the strange man who'd shown up at her door saying he was her father.

Mia couldn't imagine how that would have felt. She'd been lucky to grow up with solid parents, wonderful siblings, and an amazing extended family. But this little girl had apparently been raised by a single mom, suffered a terrible loss, and had been handed off to a man she never met. No wonder she didn't want to talk. She probably had no idea what to say to her father.

Mia's gaze drifted across the table to Jeremy Holt. He was more than a little attractive in a rough-edged kind of way. He had dark brown hair and brown eyes, much like his daughter, but there was no waifish softness about him.

His short-sleeved T-shirt revealed muscular arms and a broad chest, and his jeans clung to a frame that didn't appear to have an ounce of fat on it. He was tan, too, his skin darkened by the sun. She got the feeling that he spent a lot of time outside, and she couldn't help wondering what he actually did for a living. Maybe it was time to find out.

"So, Jeremy, what do you do for work?" she asked.

"I'm in the Army."

That explained the solid, ripped physique. "Are you on leave?"

"Yes."

"Because you're a dad now," she ventured, when he didn't continue speaking.

"And because I was injured six weeks ago. I need to rehab my shoulder," he said, rolling his left shoulder back with a wince. "It's going to take time to get back to one hundred percent."

"Do you want to go back?"

"Yes," he said without a hint of doubt. "The Army has been my life for the past twelve years, but it may not be my choice as to whether or not I go back. The physical requirements for my unit are extremely high." He paused. "Do you want the last slice of pizza?"

She realized he'd deliberately changed the subject, but she didn't want to pry into his personal life, so she followed his lead. "No, I'm full, but it was excellent. Where did you get it?"

"Rocco's."

"I've never heard of that place."

"It's down by the harbor. I think it's new. Have you spent a lot of time in Angel's Bay?"

"I spent several summers here when I was a teenager, but I haven't been here since then. I kept meaning to come down for a visit, but life got in the way. I feel badly about that now." She let out a little sigh, then said, "What about you? What brought you to Angel's Bay?"

"Ashlyn. I grew up here, but I left at eighteen, and I had no intention of coming back until everything changed."

"Why wouldn't you want to come back to Angel's Bay? It's so charming."

"And small and boring."

"Well, that's part of the charm."

"Not when you grow up here."

"Did you know my Aunt Carly?"

"No, I didn't. Aside from a few weekend visits, I haven't spent much time here in the last decade."

"You probably wouldn't have run in the same circles anyway."

"Probably not." Jeremy looked at his daughter. "If you're done eating, Ashlyn, why don't you take your plate to the counter? You can watch TV for a while if you want to."

Ashlyn hesitated, and then she slowly got up from the table. After putting her plate in the sink, she walked back to the table and sat down, her arms crossed in front of her small chest.

"I guess we're more interesting than TV," Mia said lightly.

"Or *you* are," he said dryly. "What do you do for a living?"

"I was working at the Kelleher Art Museum in San Francisco until recently."

"What happened?"

"It's a long story, but I'm now unemployed, and I'm free to clear out my aunt's house. My mom was going to do it, but she broke her foot, and it would have been difficult for her to get down here any time soon. I'm actually looking forward to going through the house, and I think I'm the perfect person for the job. If any of my other siblings had come down here, they'd probably just start throwing things away without even looking at them. They don't share my appreciation for history or sentiment. Plus, what could be better than summer in Angel's Bay?"

"I can think of a few things. How many siblings do you have?"

"Five."

"Big family."

She nodded. "I'm the youngest and I have a twin sister. Kate just finished training to be an FBI agent, so she's pretty busy."

"FBI? That's impressive. What's her focus?"

"I have no idea. Everything seems to be classified. Kate has always been more adventurous than me. She would have had no hesitation climbing down a ladder," she added with a self-deprecating smile.

He smiled as he said, "What do the rest of your siblings do?"

"They're all pretty much over-achievers. Dylan and Hunter are firefighters. Firefighting is a tradition in the Callaway family. My father is a retired firefighter, and my uncle is second-in-charge of the San Francisco Fire Department. I also have a bunch of cousins in the department."

"You didn't want to fight fires?"

She laughed at that suggestion. "Not in a million years. I try not to even think about how much danger my family could be in any time they get a call."

"What about the other siblings?"

"Ian is a scientist. Don't ask me what he does, because it's also classified for me to know about. My sister Annie is a graphic designer, and she has been building websites and brands for companies the past few years. She's starting to get in with a celebrity crowd, which is fun." She paused. "What about you? Do you come from generations of soldiers?"

"No, I'm the first, and I'm an only child."

"What about parents? Do they live here in Angel's Bay?"

"My father does."

At his words, Ashlyn's head swung in her father's direction for the first time.

Jeremy jolted, as if surprised by the sudden eye contact.

"Has Ashlyn met her grandfather?" Mia asked.

"No, not yet." His lips tightened as his daughter gave him a long stare. "He's away right now."

Ashlyn didn't react, but after a moment her gaze swung back to Mia.

Mia wanted to say something to the little girl, but she wasn't sure what.

Then a text popped up on her phone.

"It's the locksmith," she said, getting up from her chair. "He's next door. Thanks for the pizza and getting me off the roof."

"No problem," Jeremy said, as he stood up.

She gave Ashlyn a smile. "I hope to see you again soon. Maybe when I get my aunt's house organized, we can make some cookies. I'm a really good baker."

Ashlyn didn't speak but gave her a shy nod.

"Take that as a yes," Jeremy advised.

"I will. Thanks again, Jeremy. I owe you one."

"You don't owe me anything." He paused, his gaze turning to his daughter. "Ash, I'm going to walk Mia to her house. I'll be back in a few minutes, okay?"

"You don't have to walk me out," she protested, but Jeremy was already ushering her down the hallway, and Ashlyn was right behind him.

"I just want to make sure you get in all right. I don't want to have to rescue you again," he said.

"I think I'll be fine."

"And I think we're *all* going to make sure of that," Jeremy said, as he and Ashlyn walked her across the lawn.

The locksmith, Richard Cummings, was waiting on the porch. He was a bearded, middle-aged man with a friendly smile.

"You're Carly's niece." He shook her hand with a warm smile. "It's nice to meet you, even though it's under terrible circumstances. I can't believe Carly is gone. It still seems like a bad nightmare."

She felt the same way. "Yes, it does. You knew my aunt?"

"Oh, sure. She was a delight—always smiling and friendly. She could tell a smutty joke, too, like a real broad. She's going to be missed."

His words sent a wave of pain through her body. "She will be missed," she echoed, feeling the depth of the loss once again.

"Ah, now, I've made you sad. I'm sorry," he added quickly. "My wife always says I don't pay enough attention to what I'm saying."

"It's fine. You didn't say anything wrong. I get emotional about my aunt every time I think about her. I'm hoping that taking care of her things will be healing."

"I hope so, too. Is this your husband and child?" Richard asked.

"No," she said immediately, reminded that in Angel's Bay, people liked to get into other people's business.

"This is my neighbor Jeremy Holt and his daughter Ashlyn. They were keeping me company until you came."

"Sure, I heard about you from Kent," Richard said with an approving nod. "You're the war hero."

Jeremy gave an awkward shrug at Richard's words.

"What did you do?" she asked Jeremy, a little more curious about him now.

"My job," Jeremy replied.

"He rescued a lot of people," Richard said. "Kent said Jeremy here saved his life."

"We saved each other many times. So, can you get Mia into her house?" Jeremy asked. He was obviously eager to change the subject away from himself.

"Absolutely." Richard turned his attention back to the lock. Within minutes, he had the door open. "There you go."

"Thank you so much," she said. "I don't know why my mom's key didn't work."

"The lock was warped. This will work for tonight, but why don't I change all the locks for you tomorrow and give you a new set of keys?"

"That would be great."

"I'll come by in the morning, unless you're going to be out tonight and will need to get back in?"

"No, tomorrow is good for me. Thank you for coming out after hours."

"No problem. I'll see you soon. You all have a good night."

As the locksmith left, she stepped into the house. She turned on the lights, happy that her mom had made to sure to keep the utilities paid until they could get the house cleaned out.

She took a deep breath as she walked through the entry and into the living room. It was more cluttered than she remembered. She could barely take it all in.

There wasn't an inch of wall space that wasn't covered by a painting or a decorative piece of artwork, and the tables were filled with vases, bowls, small statues, and framed photographs as well as numerous books and magazines on art and interior design. One armchair was filled with fabric swatches that made Mia wonder if her aunt had been planning to redecorate.

"You weren't kidding when you said your aunt had a lot of stuff," Jeremy commented.

She hadn't realized that he and Ashlyn had followed her inside. "I didn't think it would be this much," she confessed. "I remember the house being neater, although my aunt traveled a lot in recent years, and she always had some new project she was working on. I guess organizing and cleaning fell to the bottom of the list."

Ashlyn wandered over to an antique chair that held a beautiful doll with a porcelain face and a flowing white dress that had yellowed with age. But the doll's face was exquisitely pretty, with what appeared to be almost real lashes over the bright blue eyes. Ashlyn reached out to touch the doll, and then abruptly put her hand back into her pocket, flashing Mia a guilty look.

"It's okay," she said quickly, wondering if Ashlyn felt guilty for almost touching the doll or for forgetting that she wasn't supposed to be interested in anything. "My aunt used to tell me that dolls were meant to be played with." She walked across the room and picked up the doll. "And this doll needs a friend. She'll be lonely now that my aunt isn't here anymore. Could you keep her company?"

Ashlyn stared back at her with indecision in her eyes. Then she slowly took her hands out of her pockets and accepted the doll. She sat down in the chair and held it awkwardly in her lap, as if she wasn't sure what to do now that she had it.

Mia looked away, sensing Ashlyn was more uncomfortable with the attention she was getting from her and Jeremy than she was with the doll.

Jeremy mouthed, "Thank you."

She nodded and drew in a breath as she turned her gaze back to the room. "This is going to be a big job."

"I'll say," he agreed. "This one room alone will take you a dozen boxes and at least a few hours."

"I'm almost afraid to look at the rest of the house."

"Well, just remember what you said…"

"What's that?"

"What could be better than summer in Angel's Bay?"

She smiled. "Good point. I just have to take it one step at a time."

"Or one weird statue at a time." He picked up what appeared to be a goat with a hat on its head. "What on earth is this?"

"I'm not sure, but I'll find out. Aunt Carly knew the difference between valuable pieces and junk." At least, she hoped her aunt had known the difference.

"We should go and leave you to it."

"Okay." She was almost sorry to see them leave, but she'd come to Angel's Bay to sort out not only her aunt's house but also her life. She needed to focus on that and not the sexy man next door and his adorable and wounded daughter. She needed to fix her own life, not theirs. She walked them out the door, grabbed her suitcase out of her car and took it back into the house.

Bypassing the living room, she headed upstairs. Her aunt's bedroom was the first door on the left. She glanced inside but didn't feel ready to go in there yet. There would be a lot of emotions in that room, and she wasn't ready for those. She continued down the hall to the guest room she'd used as a teenager.

It was also crammed with stuff. She swept piles of clothes off the bed, changed the linens, and then put on her PJs and climbed under the covers with the odd feeling that she'd come home.

—➤➤◄◄◄—

It was almost midnight when Jeremy turned off the television in the living room and got up with a yawn and a stretch of his stiff limbs. He'd felt both tired and restless since he'd left Mia's house. After Ashlyn had gone to bed, he'd tried to distract himself with a baseball game and surfing the Internet. Neither had really worked. His mind kept returning to the pretty blonde with the most amazing blue eyes and a smile that made him feel like he'd just come in from the cold.

Mia had blown into his life like a gust of refreshing wind. She talked a lot, but she was friendly, kind, and candid about her personal flaws, and he liked her down-to-earth, unpretentious attitude a little too much.

He was supposed to be focused on his daughter, on rehabbing his shoulder, on getting his life together. He couldn't allow himself to be derailed by a woman, no matter how attractive she was.

As he walked across the room to turn off the lights, he couldn't help thinking how empty and bare this house was in comparison to the one next door. While he'd tried to make Ashlyn's room cheerful and bright, he hadn't bothered to change anything in the rest of the house, and most of the furniture was beige or black, with no personality. The house had been furnished to be a serviceable rental, and it was comfortable enough, but it didn't feel like a home.

Then again, did he even know what home felt like? It had been a long time since he'd lived in any house that felt like a home.

He walked up the stairs and opened the door to Ashlyn's bedroom. Taking a quiet step into the room, he saw that she was asleep. She was a tiny figure in the middle of the double bed, but tonight she had a friend with her—the old doll Mia had given to her.

The sight of that doll with its tattered yellowed dress and cracked porcelain face brought mixed emotions. He was happy that Ashlyn had found something she liked, but he didn't understand why she'd chosen this doll over the brand new ones he'd given her, the ones that had been tossed in a heap in the bedroom closet.

For some reason, this doll felt like a rejection of him and an acceptance of Mia, a woman Ashlyn had met hours earlier. What was that about?

He had to admit he felt a little jealous at the connection Ashlyn had made with Mia. He'd been working his ass off trying to get his daughter to look at him, to talk to him, with no results, and then Mia showed up, and his kid suddenly was interested in life again.

Whatever works, he told himself; the important thing was that Ashlyn had found something to care about. It was a step in the right direction.

He was about to leave the room when Ashlyn began to mutter and kick at the covers. Hesitating, he wasn't sure what to do. He didn't want to wake her and scare her. But he also wanted to comfort her.

He was halfway to the bed when she sat up straight and let out a piercing scream, her eyes flying open.

His heart jumped into his throat. Since he'd picked her up from foster care, he'd barely heard her voice above a whisper, so the shrill sound shook him to the core. And it wasn't just the volume; it was also the raw fear in the scream that made him rush to her side.

He tried to put his arms around her, but she pushed him away and scooted back against the head of the bed, staring at him as if he were a monster, but there was a glaze over her eyes that made him wonder if she was seeing him at all.

"It's okay, Ashlyn. You're just having a bad dream," he said in a quiet, firm voice.

She didn't even blink.

"You're safe. I'm here. I'm taking care of you. No one will hurt you, baby."

He didn't know if he was getting through at all, but as the seconds ticked by, her breath started to come more evenly. Her eyes focused on his face as she came fully awake.

He let out a breath, feeling as if he'd just dodged a bullet.

Then she shocked him when she said, "I want Mommy."

His heart broke at the anguish in her eyes, the plea for him to give her the only thing she really wanted—her mother.

"I know you want your mom. I wish she could be here, too." He spoke slowly, trying to choose his words carefully. He didn't know how to explain death to a child, and he didn't want to make things worse. But she was looking to him for answers, and he had to give her something. "We're going to be okay—you and me," he continued. "I know it doesn't seem like that right now, but we'll get to know each other. I think you might like me if you give me a chance."

He swallowed hard, her stare challenging and

unnerving. He'd never wanted to meet someone's expectations more than he did now.

"I'm going to take care of you," he said. "You'll be safe with me, because I will never ever let anyone hurt you. That's a promise, Ashlyn. When I make a promise, I keep it."

She blinked twice, and then slowly got back under the covers. She reached for her doll and hugged it tightly against her chest. The doll was almost as big as she was.

He tucked the covers around her body and said, "Every day will get easier, Ash. We've spent a lot of time getting set up here, but we'll start having fun. We'll go to the beach and surf the waves. Have you ever gone bodysurfing? It's fun. And there are some great bike trails that go along the beach. We can explore them together. It's going to be good. This is going to work."

As he said the words, he felt a bit desperate to convince not only Ashlyn but also himself. He was sailing in uncharted territory, but he was not going to go under. Failure wasn't an option. Not with this relationship. It was the most important relationship of his life.

He wanted to kiss Ashlyn's cheek, smooth her hair, but he was afraid if he touched her, he'd unsettle her again. So he just kept talking in a soothing voice about what they could do in town. As he spoke about the charms of Angel's Bay, he realized that he'd chosen a good place to start over. The town had bored him as a teenager, but as a child he'd loved exploring the beach, the hidden caves, taking bike rides, flying kites, and participating in any number of somewhat cheesy festivals and events that the town liked to put on.

"We're going to be all right," he said again as Ashlyn's eyes closed.

He watched her for another ten minutes, and then he

got up and walked out of the room.

He left the door of her room ajar to make sure he could hear her if she needed him again. He couldn't believe she'd actually spoken three words in a row. It was just heartbreaking that those words had been *"I want Mommy"*.

He wished he could give her mother back to her. He wished he could go back to doing what he knew how to do, but it wasn't only Ashlyn's appearance that made that impossible, he thought, rolling his shoulder back with a painful wince. He still had to get his shoulder back into the shape it had once been in.

As he walked into his own room, he hoped that tomorrow would be better, but he didn't know if he believed that any more than Ashlyn did.

Four

⟶⇒⟫⟪⇐⟵

Mia woke up Tuesday morning, feeling refreshed and eager to take on the day. The locksmith rang her bell just after eight and within the hour had changed the locks on every door and given her a new set of keys to use.

After making coffee and grabbing a granola bar, one of the few snacks she'd brought with her, she walked through the sliding glass doors that led from the family room into the backyard. A horseshoe-shaped brick patio held a large, round glass table with a bright umbrella overhead and six chairs.

Beyond the patio were a grassy area and a rocky path that led to a two-story cottage, whose walls were covered with ivy. The cottage sat at the edge of a bluff that looked over the Pacific Ocean. The view was spectacular and always took her breath away.

She wandered across the patio and grass to the waist-high back fence and looked out at the sparkling turquoise sea. The waves were wild on this part of the coast and the white water splashing against the huge boulders below was intense and somewhat mesmerizing. It was nature in all its glory, and she felt a wave of intense emotion at the churning waves, the constant pull of the tide that came in and went out, reflecting the turbulent feelings within herself.

She'd been churning inside for weeks, and she'd let herself get pushed around in dizzying circles. But she wasn't helpless. She didn't have to go with the tide. She could fight back. She could find her own path. She just had to do it.

Looking at the horizon, she felt more inspired than she had in a long time. This was the same view that had called her aunt to explore the world, and while she wasn't itching to get in a boat or on a plane, she was yearning to start something new, to find a way to be herself and be successful, too.

She would figure it out, she thought, but first things first. Looking away from the view, she wandered around the yard. The rose garden was dying with the drought of summer, the hot sun, and no loving hands to tend the earth.

Someone must have come by and mowed the lawn, as it didn't look particularly overgrown. Maybe her aunt had a gardener come by to do the basics. She'd have to look into that.

Setting down her coffee mug on the table, she took the keys out of her pocket that the locksmith had given her and walked down the path to the studio. Unlocking the door, she stepped inside the cottage and stopped abruptly. While the house had been cluttered, the studio was filled to the brim with artist supplies, paints, easels, canvases, pictures, frames, a table covered with open containers of jewelry beads and hot glue guns, another table displaying a sewing machine and hundreds of scraps of fabrics that seem to be making up part of a quilt. There were clay structures on a shelf next to spools of yarn and colorful knitting needles.

It felt as if a dozen artists had suddenly gotten up in mid task and walked out of the building. Not one thing seemed to be finished or put away.

It was more than a little overwhelming.

She took a deep breath, reminding herself that nothing had to be done in a day. She could take her time. And she was excited about the possibilities. There could be some incredible art in this room. She moved over to the stairs, where stacks of paintings lined the steps that led up to the loft.

She climbed the steps and found a double bed, a small dresser, and a bathroom. The windows showed off another amazing view of the ocean. And an easel with a blank canvas stood by that window, just waiting to be brought to life with paint.

"Later," she muttered to herself, fighting the desire to stop taking inventory and play with the paints.

As an art historian, she didn't just love art; she also loved the stories about the people who made the art, and there were probably many stories that had been started in this very studio. Maybe she would discover a piece of art that hadn't yet been seen by the world. It could happen. And it could be amazing.

"I'm going to do it right," she said out loud. "I'll make you proud, Aunt Carly. I'll make sure everything in here is treated with respect. I know that's the way you'd want it." Smiling at her promise, she went down the stairs. She'd just reached the bottom when the door swung open, and a small figure appeared in the sunlit doorway. It was Ashlyn. She held the doll she'd gotten the night before, and she was looking at Mia with her heart in her eyes. It was so clear that she wanted to connect; she just didn't know how.

"Hi, Ashlyn," she said with a warm smile. "What do

you think of my aunt's studio? She used to let artists stay here while they worked on their paintings or their sculptures or their quilts. Now I just have to figure out what to do with all this stuff."

Ashlyn didn't even blink, and Mia had to admit her wide-eyed stare was somewhat unnerving. No wonder Jeremy had been so happy to have someone to talk to the night before. The silence was probably making him crazy.

"I'm glad you like your doll," Mia added. "I was thinking we should probably wash the dress and see if we can tidy her up a bit."

Ashlyn's arms tightened around the doll. It didn't look like she was interested in letting go of her doll for any reason.

"Or we can wait until she's ready for a bath," Mia continued. "Maybe you could help me clean up in here. I probably need to start taking things outside and see what I have. I could use a helper—if you're not doing anything."

Mia had no sooner finished speaking when Jeremy's voice rang through the air.

"Ashlyn! Ashlyn—where are you?"

She heard the fear and panic in his tone. "Your dad doesn't know you're here, does he?"

Ashlyn just stared back at her.

"Let's go tell him. He sounds worried."

She waved Ashlyn back through the open door and into the yard and yelled, "Jeremy, Ashlyn is over here."

A minute later, Jeremy came through the side gate. He wore a T-shirt and track pants and a shadow of a beard darkened his jaw.

"There you are," he said with relief as his gaze fell on his daughter. "Ashlyn, you can't leave the house without telling me. You can't come over here without asking me if it's all right." He walked over to the little girl and squatted down in front of her. "Do you understand? I was worried about you. Don't do it again, okay?"

Ashlyn didn't answer.

"I need to know that you hear me, that you understand," he said firmly. "This is important, Ash."

Ashlyn finally nodded, her long, tangled hair tumbling around her face and shoulders.

"Good," he said, getting to his feet. He looked at Mia. "I should have figured she'd be over here. But when she wasn't in her room, and the side door was open, I didn't know what to think."

"She's all right."

"I shouldn't have been that worried. This is Angel's Bay, after all." He turned his attention back to his daughter. "We need to go home, Ash. Mrs. Danbury is coming over to watch you while I work out."

Ashlyn immediately shook her head and sat down right where she was standing, as if daring him to drag her back to the house.

Jeremy frowned. "Ashlyn, I have to go. I have to meet the therapist to work on my shoulder. I told you that I hurt it, and I need to get it better."

She gave another defiant shake of her head.

"I could watch her," Mia offered, impulsively stepping into their silent battle. "If it's okay with you, Jeremy."

He hesitated. "I don't know."

"I promise I won't let her climb up onto the roof," she said lightly. "And I told you I was the best babysitter in my neighborhood."

"You have your own things to take care of."

"Ashlyn can help me. I don't want to put your babysitter out of a job, but it looks like you have a sit-in on your hands."

He sighed. "I'll only be two hours. I need to stick to my therapy schedule."

"Of course you do," she said, wondering more about his injury, but that was a story for another day. "We'll be fine."

"Do you want to stay with Mia?" he asked Ashlyn.

She gave him an emphatic nod.

"Okay," he said. "I'll tell Mrs. Danbury she's off the hook. I'll be back in a few hours. Let me give you my number in case you have any problems."

She pulled her phone out of her pocket and they exchanged numbers. "Take your time," she said. "I'm going to start cleaning out the studio. It's a mess, but it seems easier to deal with than to tackle the whole house." She paused, seeing a lingering hesitation in his eyes. "Go. And don't worry about a thing. I will take good care of Ashlyn. You can trust me. Everything will be all right. "

He gave her an odd look. "People have been saying that to me for a while, but I think this morning is the first time I've actually believed it."

The look in his eyes brought a wave of heat to her cheeks. She was obviously reading into his words, but she couldn't help thinking that for the first time in a month, she actually thought everything might turn out all right for her, too.

After Jeremy left, she turned to Ashlyn. "Let's get to work."

Ashlyn got to her feet and followed her back into the studio.

An hour later, Mia had taken a dozen paintings out to the patio and had filled one large plastic trash bag with yarn and knitting supplies and another with fabric swatches and sewing machine accessories. She hadn't been aware that her aunt was into textile art, but apparently at least one or more of her artists had been interested in quilting.

The other items that had drawn her interest were the black-and-white graphic sketches she'd found in a folder labeled *"Carly's Coloring Book Ideas For Grown-Ups"*. She took them over to the patio table and sat down. With Ashlyn at her side, she flipped through the sketches.

These were not the usual kids' coloring book pages. They were detailed pictures of hidden gardens and staircases, jeweled birds and circular mazes. A few of the sketches had been colored in with markers, showing what they could be like when finished.

She hadn't thought about coloring in years, but as she stared at the pictures, she felt an urge to pick up one of the hundreds of brightly colored markers she'd found and do some coloring.

The sound of a female voice lifted her head from the patterned sketches.

Ashlyn bolted across the yard and into the studio as a woman came through the side gate.

"Hello? Anyone home?"

As Mia got to her feet, an attractive redhead in her early thirties walked into the yard. She wore cropped white pants, a bright yellow shirt, and a large floppy hat to protect her pale, freckled skin.

"Hi there," she said with a friendly smile. "I'm Kara Lynch. I rang the bell, but no one answered. Carly was very good friends with my mother and grandmother. They sent me over with this." She held up the rectangular plastic food container in her hand. "Lemon squares and raspberry dot cookies to welcome you to Angel's Bay."

"It's nice to meet you," she said, wiping her dusty hands on her shorts as she moved around the table.

"Oh, my, you've really dug in, haven't you," Kara

said, her gaze sweeping the crowded table.

"I've just barely started." She moved the basket of colored pens out of the way so she could put the dessert on the table. "I'm Mia Callaway."

Kara nodded. "My mother said you were coming in your mom's place. Did you know what you were getting into?"

"Not exactly. I used to spend summers here when I was a teenager, but this house was not nearly as cluttered or messy back then. It almost makes me wonder if something was going on with my aunt. Or maybe she was just having too good of a time to waste a second cleaning."

"I think that was probably the case," Kara said. "Your aunt was a real character. Besides hosting all the visiting artists, she used to teach salsa dancing at the recreation center."

Mia raised an eyebrow. "My blonde-haired, blue-eyed aunt taught salsa dancing?"

Kara laughed. "She was good. She also taught yoga for a while. I took one of the yoga classes. She talked a lot about her time in India, studying yoga with the masters. She was very flexible."

Yoga, salsa dancing, art—was there nothing her aunt couldn't do?

"I didn't realize she had so many talents," Mia murmured.

"Even if she hadn't perfected something, she still wanted to show it off to the world. I always liked your aunt's confidence. She didn't care what anyone thought as long as she was having a good time. I'd like to be more like that."

"Me, too," she agreed, thinking she'd spent far too much time worrying about what other people thought.

"What are you going to do with all the paintings?" Kara asked, waving her hand around the patio.

"I'm not sure yet. I hate to just throw them away, and some of the paintings are really good. They should be on display somewhere." As she finished speaking, she got an idea...probably a bad idea, but she couldn't stop it from taking shape in her head. "Maybe I should put them up somewhere."

"The museum in town might be interested, or one of the art galleries. Angel's Bay has quite an art scene these days. We get a lot of tourists driving up from Los Angeles and Santa Barbara on the weekends and in the summer. Do you think the paintings are good enough? I'm no expert on art, but that one looks like my three-year-old drew it." She pointed to a smudged, messy painting that looked like a ball of colored yarn.

"That one is pretty bad," she agreed. "But what about this one?" She picked up the painting of a solitary sailboat bobbing by a dock. "I like the colors and the brushstrokes. It's technically good, and I think it evokes a mood."

"It feels a little sad and lonely," Kara said.

"Art that makes you feel anything is usually good."

"You should talk to the galleries and the museum. You might start with the Eckhart Gallery on Main Street. Didi Eckhart just took it over after her husband's death, and she was friends with your aunt. She might be the most interested in talking to you about a showing of some kind."

"I'll start with her."

"Do you think you have enough good pieces?"

"There are more in the studio, and I haven't even gone through the storage area on the second floor. The only thing I worry about is whether any of the artists would object to my taking the paintings they left for Aunt

Carly and doing something with them."

"If they gave their art to Carly, then it was hers to do with as she liked, and now it's yours."

"Technically everything here belongs to my mother, but I think she'd like the idea of setting up an exhibition in Aunt Carly's honor. And it would give the artists some recognition, too. She was always about finding undiscovered talent."

Kara smiled at her with a knowing gleam in her eyes. "You remind me a little of myself, Mia. I love to take on big projects and make plans even when I have a ton of other things to do."

Mia laughed. "I have to admit putting on an exhibition sounds like more fun than filling trash bags. But it will all get done."

Kara picked up the sketch of a peacock from the table. "What is this?"

"That is part of a coloring book for grown-ups that my aunt was putting together."

"I've heard of those. They're all the rage now. A friend of mine in Los Angeles just went to a coloring book party. She was telling me how much fun it was. She liked that she could drink a lot of wine and color at the same time, and it wasn't as complicated as quilting or knitting."

"Good point. My aunt was always on trend."

A light came into Kara's eyes as she flipped through the sketches in the folder. "These are all fantastic. Carly drew them all?"

"I think so. The folder had her name on it."

"You know what we should do? We should have our own coloring book party. I can introduce you to my friends and some of your aunt's friends, who would probably love to come. We could have it at my grandmother's quilt store in town. We have a big meeting room upstairs."

"Isn't that for quilting?"

"Oh, we do tons of other stuff up there, too. This will be so much fun."

"I would love to meet some of my aunt's friends, but do you think they'll want to color?"

"I'd say yes, especially if it's in Carly's honor. I'll get my friend Charlotte to help. She's always up for a party. We can make copies of the sketches and preserve the originals."

"I could take care of that," she offered.

"Great. Let's exchange numbers and we'll set a date, probably the sooner the better. How long will you be in town?"

"I don't have a set plan, but I'm thinking at this point at least a few weeks."

"Perfect." Kara gave her another smile. "I do have to warn you that if you stay in Angel's Bay too long, you might never leave. This town has a way of spinning a web around you."

"My aunt told me that once. She said she came here for a summer vacation and never left. Although she traveled a lot, Angel's Bay was home base. Were you born here, Kara?"

"I was, and my family, the Murrays, was one of the founding families of the town. I have ancestors dating back to the original shipwreck."

"Aunt Carly told me the story once, but I don't really remember it."

"The short version is that people were fleeing San Francisco after the Gold Rush ended. One of the ships got caught in a big storm off the coast and split apart. The survivors started the town and called it Angel's Bay in memory of their lost loved ones. Legend has it that angels still watch over the town and miracles can happen."

"Have you seen any of those miracles?"

Kara's face sobered. "Actually, I have."

"Really?" she asked with surprise.

"My husband Colin is a police officer. He was shot a few years ago. I was pregnant at the time. He was in a coma for months. I wasn't sure if he would ever wake up and see our daughter, but he did. And he's perfect now. We added another child last year, so life is pretty crazy and more than a little wonderful."

"I'm sure the last thing you need to add to your list is a coloring book party."

"Well, as I said, I like to take on projects even if I don't have time for them, and this sounds fun and easy enough to throw together. Shall we go for it?"

"Yes," she said. "But tell me what I can do to help. I don't want you to have to work too hard."

"If you can make copies of the sketches, that would be great. We have plenty of markers and colored pencils in the craft part of the quilt store. I was actually thinking that we should stock coloring books after talking to my friend. This will be a good test of how much interest there might be in town for this kind of creative project." She glanced at her watch. "I better run, but let me get your number."

After they exchanged phone numbers, Kara said, "So is that cute little girl spying on us from the cottage your daughter?"

Mia glanced toward the studio and saw a quick movement in the shadows of the doorway. "No, that's Ashlyn. She lives next door. She's rather shy."

"I wish one of my daughters was shy, but they both seem to have their father's outgoing personality."

"And yours," Mia said with a laugh, sensing that Kara rarely met anyone who stayed a stranger for long.

"I suppose that's true. So you don't have a daughter; what about a husband?"

"I don't have one of those, either."

"Interesting. We have some good-looking single men in town."

She laughed at that pointed suggestion. "Thanks, but I'm off men for the moment."

"Bad breakup?"

"You could say that. Anyway, thanks for the dessert and for being so welcoming. I'm really touched by your generosity."

"You're more than welcome. Carly was a really wonderful person—warm, kind, generous, and free-spirited. We all miss her. And we're all really happy to meet you, because she talked about you quite a bit. She said she had a bunch of nieces and nephews but only one who shared her love of art, and that was you."

"Yes, that would be me."

"I'll be in touch. Enjoy the lemon bars; they're my favorite."

"I'm sure I will."

As Kara left, Mia took the lid off the container, her stomach rumbling at the sight of the lemon bars sprinkled with powdered sugar. "It's time for a snack, Ashlyn," she said, thinking she'd go to the cottage and bribe the girl out with a lemon bar. It turned out that she didn't have to bribe her at all.

Ashlyn was practically behind her when she turned around.

She put a hand to her heart. "You are the quietest little girl. Are you hungry?"

Ashlyn nodded.

"Lemon bar or raspberry cookie?"

Ashlyn pointed to the lemon bar.

"That's my favorite, too." She hesitated. "You're not allergic to lemon or anything, are you?"

Ashlyn shook her head.

"Would your dad care if you had this before a healthy lunch?"

Ashlyn repeated the negative shake of her head.

Mia laughed. "Ask a silly question, right?" She handed the bar to Ashlyn, and they both sat down at the table.

"That woman who came by was named Kara," Mia said conversationally. "She was really friendly. She wants to have a party to introduce me to some of my aunt's friends. I think it's a good idea. And she thinks we should color at the party." She reached across the table and picked up one of the patterns. "This does look fun to color. What do you think?"

Ashlyn nodded. Despite her unwillingness to give a verbal answer, she was paying attention.

"Maybe we should try one of the pictures out, see if it is fun," she added, reaching for the top piece of paper. While she did want to make copies before using all the originals, she didn't think one large peacock picture would be missed. She put it between her and Ashlyn and then grabbed some markers. "Let's do it together."

Ashlyn hesitated for a minute, and then picked up one of the markers. It was navy blue, so dark it was almost black. She colored in one of the peacock feathers. Mia chose a bright red and started working on the opposite side of the bird.

She found the coloring surprisingly stress-reducing. It was a nice break from cleaning, and Ashlyn seemed to like it, too. Although, as their efforts got closer together, she was struck by how dark Ashlyn's side of the page was: nothing bright or hopeful, just blacks and browns and heavy blues.

The sadness the little girl was mired in showed in every stroke of the marker. Maybe the coloring would help ease her pain, too.

She wondered what exactly had happened to Ashlyn's mother. Jeremy had said that she'd been killed, but he hadn't said how. Her heart went out to the little girl, and she wished she could do more for her than offer her lemon bars and the opportunity to color.

Ashlyn finished coloring in the last feather with black and then pointed to the lemon bars.

"Uh, I think we should wait on another one of those until after lunch." It was almost noon. Jeremy would probably be back soon.

"Now," Ashlyn said.

The demanding word didn't surprise her, but the voice did. She looked Ashlyn in the eye, and for the first time the girl did not break eye contact with her. In fact, there was defiance in her dark gaze.

"No," Mia said, even though it took every ounce of strength she had not to say yes.

Ashlyn looked shocked by her answer.

"You need to eat a healthy lunch first. I'd make you something now, but I have no food in the house. Your dad will be back soon."

Ashlyn threw her marker in Mia's face and then slid off her chair and ran toward the gate. She'd slipped through the gate before Mia could open her mouth. She jumped up and ran after her, yelling, "Ashlyn, come back."

Five

—➤➤◄◄◄—

As Mia got to the front of her house, Jeremy pulled into the driveway.

He jumped out of the car, concern in his eyes. "What's going on?"

"Ashlyn got mad at me and ran home."

He hurried down the driveway. "She must have gone in the back door. Didn't you tell me everything was going to be fine, that I should feel free to leave her with you?"

She knew his angry words came from concern, but they still stung. "She slipped away from me really fast."

They walked into the backyard and up the steps. The sliding glass door was open.

"Ashlyn," Jeremy called, moving quickly through the hallway toward the stairs.

Mia stayed on his heels all the way up to Ashlyn's room.

Ashlyn was lying on her bed, staring at the ceiling.

"Ash, are you all right?" Jeremy asked, sitting on the bed next to her.

Ashlyn didn't respond.

Jeremy looked to Mia for an explanation. "What happened?"

"She wanted a second lemon bar. I told her she had to wait until after lunch. I would have fed her lunch, but I didn't have any food. I haven't gone to the store yet." She looked past Jeremy to Ashlyn. "I thought we were having fun coloring together, Ashlyn."

"Why didn't you just give her another lemon bar?" he asked, running a hand through his hair.

"Because I thought it would be too much sugar." She paused. "When I said no, she said *now*."

His gaze swung back to her. "She spoke to you?"

Mia nodded. "She seemed pretty upset about my answer."

"Damn," he muttered. "A little extra sugar wouldn't have killed her. She doesn't want anything, Mia. It's the first thing she's asked for in weeks."

"Well, I didn't know that." She looked at Ashlyn. "Ashlyn, I said no, because I care about your health. It's not good for little girls to have too much sugar at one time. But we can have lunch, and then if it's okay with your father, you can have another dessert. What do you think about that?"

Ashlyn finally turned her head to look at her.

Mia's heart tore at the streaks of tears on her cheeks. Why hadn't she just said yes to the damn lemon bar? This little girl was suffering. But it was too late to change the past.

Ashlyn sat up and slid off the bed.

"Okay, good," Mia said with relief. She looked at Jeremy. "So what's for lunch?"

"Whatever we want to order off the menu at…" Jeremy paused, looking at Ashlyn. "Dina's Café?"

Ashlyn nodded.

"Good," he said, getting to his feet. "Why don't you wash your hands before we go?"

Ashlyn walked down the hall to the bathroom.

"Sorry," he said to Mia. "I shouldn't have snapped at you. Connecting with her is so difficult and frustrating that I probably would have given her anything she asked for if she'd said the word out loud."

"Maybe it's good that I didn't give her the second lemon bar. Kids need boundaries, even kids with a lot of issues."

"I suppose."

"What happened to her mom, Jeremy?"

He cast a quick look at the door and then dropped his voice. "She was killed in a robbery at a convenience store. Ashlyn was with her when it happened."

"Oh, my God," she said, horrified by his answer. "No wonder she's so troubled."

"She's seeing a therapist. The doctor told me that it's going to take time and that I shouldn't ask questions about what happened, which means you know as much as I know."

"But surely you spoke to the police."

"I did, and I know the basics. I know who killed Justine. There were a dozen witnesses to the incident. He's going to jail for a long time, and, thankfully, Ashlyn does not have to testify at the trial. I don't want her to ever have to see that man again."

"No, she shouldn't have to do that."

"But what I don't know is exactly what happened that night, other than that they were in the convenience store. I don't know if Ashlyn's mother was killed instantly or if she said anything to her daughter..." His voice trailed away. "I don't know what Ashlyn saw or heard or thought. It's all locked up in her head."

"Maybe one day she'll let it out."

"I hope so. Besides that horrific incident, I know

nothing else about Ashlyn's life, which is also disturbing. The social worker I spoke to had no records on her. She lived with her mother; that's all they knew. She had no other living relatives. Apparently, Justine and Ashlyn had been in San Francisco for a year and before that they'd been in Los Angeles. As for friends, no one came forward to try to take care of Ashlyn after her mom died."

"There must have been someone who knew Ashlyn and her mom. She must have gone to school. They had neighbors."

"The apartment they'd been living in was already rented out to someone else by the time I was informed of Ashlyn's existence. Their meager belongings were put into storage, and I didn't take anything. It's still there waiting to be gone through. I thought it would be more painful for Ashlyn to see her things all boxed up, so I left it alone. I did ask her if she had a favorite doll or stuffed animal, but she just shook her head."

"Where was she living?"

"With a foster family. They had three other kids they were taking care of. They said she was no trouble, but that she didn't speak to them, either. I can't imagine what was going on in her head. She loses her mother. She's placed with strangers."

Her heart went out to Ashlyn. "It sounds awful. No child should have to go through that."

"I thought she'd be happier to see me or that at least she would have questions, but she doesn't."

"I'm sure she does," Mia said, seeing the discouragement in his eyes. "How could she not?"

"Then why won't she talk to me?"

"I'm sure the doctor could give you a better answer than me, but maybe she just needs time to feel safe with you and then she'll open up."

"I hope so."

"You could always try holding a lemon bar hostage," she said lightly, trying to defuse the heavy mood.

He tipped his head. "Good idea. Ash did say something to me last night."

"What was that?"

"I want Mommy."

Mia sighed at the poignant words. "That's rough."

"Tell me about it. The one thing she wants, I can't give her."

"I'm sorry. I guess I understand now why you would have given in on dessert. I was trying to be a responsible babysitter."

"It's not your fault. At least she spoke to you."

"Because she was mad."

"Anger is better than the nothingness I get."

"Don't worry. I'm sure you'll piss her off at some point."

A reluctant smile crossed his lips. "You think so?"

"I think it's pretty much a guarantee. I adored my father, but he still annoyed the crap out of me at times."

"Good to know. So is Dina's Café all right with you?"

"You and Ashlyn can go to lunch on your own. I need to go to the market this afternoon."

"You can shop later. I'm buying you lunch. No arguments."

"Well, I am hungry," she admitted. "I could have eaten a second lemon bar, too."

"How did you bake if you didn't have any food in the house?"

"Kara Lynch brought me a welcome dessert tray. Do you know her?"

"I went to school with Kara. I haven't seen her in years."

"She was really nice. She wants to introduce me to everyone in town."

"That sounds like Kara. Her family has always been at the center of town activities."

"That's what she said. I liked her, especially because she didn't laugh at my new idea."

"What idea is that?"

"I'll tell you over lunch," she said as Ashlyn gave them an impatient look from the hallway. "Someone is hungry."

"I can see that. Let's go."

—➤➤◄◄—

Dina's Café was crowded with both locals and tourists, but they were able to snag a corner booth after just a short wait.

"I came here once with my aunt," Mia commented, glancing around the restaurant. The décor in the café was warm and friendly: seascapes decorated the walls, along with a display case of all the local kids' sports teams sponsored by the café. "It hasn't changed a bit."

"No, it hasn't," he muttered, his lips tightening as his gazed settled on two older men seated at a table by the window.

"Do you know them?"

"Yes. The tall guy with the glasses is Hal Conroy. The white bearded man is Bill Hooper. They're friends with my father. Hal works at Buddy's Bait and Tackle, and Bill runs a bar on Shellview."

"What does your father do?"

"He's a fisherman."

"And you said he's on vacation?"

"I did say that," he replied. "Do you know what you

want to eat, Ash?"

She pointed to an item on the menu.

"Cheeseburgers are my favorite, too," he said. "How about some fruit to go with that?"

She shrugged and then sat back in her chair, her gaze turning to Mia.

Mia was happy to see the anger gone from Ashlyn's eyes. "Are we friends again?" she asked. She heard Jeremy's quick intake of breath and thought he probably didn't like her blunt question, but she had a bit more experience with pissed-off eight-year-old girls than he did.

Ashlyn slowly nodded.

"Good, because we have lots of work to do this afternoon, if you still want to help me. And I hope you do. You did so well on the coloring, I thought we might try some paint."

A light entered Ashlyn's eyes, with a more vigorous nod of agreement.

Mia smiled and turned her attention back to Jeremy, who looked a little confused by their exchange. "As I mentioned, I have a lot of siblings. We fought all the time, often about nothing, but we got over it faster if we just put it out in the open. My father hated drama. He always told me not to go to bed mad at anyone. If we were having problems with each other, he tried to get us to talk things out, not let them fester."

"And that worked?"

"Most of the time. There was still some sulking, and forgiveness didn't always come quickly, but at the end of the day, we always remembered that we were family."

"It sounds like you had a good family."

His tone told her that he had not had that same experience. She wanted to ask for more information, but he'd made it clear he did not want to discuss his father.

The waitress delivered their drinks and took their order, then headed back to the kitchen.

As Jeremy settled in his seat, he rolled his left shoulder and winced with the motion.

"How was your physical therapy?" she asked.

"Painful, but necessary."

"Can I ask you how you got hurt?"

"I fell," he said shortly.

She couldn't imagine that was true. Jeremy was physically fit and athletically gifted from what she could see. If he'd fallen, someone had pushed him. But apparently his injury was also off-limits. She frowned, not liking the boundaries he was setting up. Grayson had done the same thing, deciding what she could and couldn't talk about. "You know, conversation is a two-way street."

"Tell that to Ashlyn," he said dryly.

"I'm not talking to her; I'm speaking to you."

"If you want conversation, tell me about the big idea you mentioned earlier."

It was a good dodge, she thought, but since she suspected that some of his reticence had to do with Ashlyn's presence, she decided to go with the change in subject.

"After taking quite a few paintings out of the studio, I was impressed with the quality of the art. I think it would be a shame to give the paintings away or recycle them as if they were disposable when in reality they represent someone's artistic vision. So I'm thinking that I should display them somewhere, put on a show to pay homage to Aunt Carly and all the talented artists who stayed in her studio to pursue their dreams. Kara suggested I contact the museum or one of the galleries in town. What do you think?"

"I don't know much about art, but since you mentioned you worked in a museum, I'm guessing you do. Although, you skipped the part about why you're unemployed."

"Well, it wasn't because I wasn't good at my job."

"Now who's decided our conversation is a one-way street?" he challenged.

"It's not an interesting story. Right now I'm more interested in discussing my idea. I was thinking I could call the show *Freedom* in honor of the artists who found freedom from their emotional problems through art."

"Are you sure they all ended up free?"

She frowned. "Well, no, I don't actually know anything about the artists. But Aunt Carly did tell me once that she thought art therapy was an under-used method for freeing the soul. She got very spiritual and philosophical after her trips to India and Tibet. I think she even got to speak to the Dalai Lama."

"I wonder what that conversation was about," he mused.

"Knowing Aunt Carly, it was about living well, loving deeply, and peace in the world."

"Peace in the world—what a concept," he said, a cynical note in his voice reminding her that he'd seen a far different world than she had.

"Where did you fight, Jeremy?"

"All over the place. There are a lot of battles going on in the world right now, but let's get back to art. Did you like working in a museum? The few I've been to seem too quiet and too pretentious. I guess I'm just not a museum kind of guy. I know I should appreciate art, but I can't understand why swirls of paint command hushed reverence when they look like nothing but a mess to me."

"You must have been looking at abstract art. The

swirls of paint represent the artist's vision of the world."

"Twisted and colorful?"

"You're being too literal. The Russian artist Wassily Kandisky believed that colors provoke emotions. Red is confidence, green is peaceful, blue is deep and sometimes supernatural, yellow is warm and white is silence. He even assigned instruments to go with the colors. Red is a trumpet and light blue is a flute."

"I think I'm just too practical for art. I deal with what's real in front of me, not what someone wants me to imagine."

"I understand, but I like to be open to possibilities, to be transported through art to another time or place or level of realization." She laughed at his bemused expression. "It's fine. You don't have to like art. A lot of people don't get it."

"But you do."

"Well, I don't love everything. I have certain periods and styles that I enjoy more than others, but I have an appreciation for the artist, for their ability to create something out of nothing. I respect their dedication and the way they put their heart and soul on the line when they put their art up for public consumption. It's a brave moment, and I like bravery, even when it's very, very small." She paused. "I feel kind of silly talking about bravery to you. What I'm discussing is nothing like the kind of courage required to go into war. I don't want you to think—"

"I don't," he said, cutting her off. "I know the difference. One of the reasons I fight is to protect the freedom of people to create art, speak their mind, and live their lives the way they want to."

She stared back at him, feeling herself moved by his words, by the passion in his voice, by the perfect male beauty of his strong face and clear eyes and extraordinary mouth. Her body tingled with feminine appreciation and suddenly she couldn't remember what they were talking about. She just knew that she wanted to keep on looking at him, keep on talking to him. He was quite simply the most fascinating man she'd met in a very long time. He was very different from the men in her usual circle and she liked that even more. She had a feeling he liked her, too, and that was a little scary. She'd come to Angel's Bay to get over a mistake with a man. She didn't need to make another one.

Clearing her throat, she took the conversation back to a lighter level. "So if you aren't a museum kind of guy, what kind of guy are you?"

"I like to play sports: baseball, football, basketball, soccer, golf, occasionally tennis."

"That's a lot of sports."

"I like to compete, challenge myself. I don't know what I'll be up to playing in the future though, maybe miniature golf."

"I have a feeling you'll conquer your weakness."

"We'll see. What about you, Mia? What do you do besides art?"

"Well, I don't do sports. At least, not if I can help it."

"Never? Not even when you were a kid?"

"I couldn't when I was really young. My sister and I were born premature. And while she didn't have any health issues, I had respiratory problems for a long time. I got pneumonia when I was seven, and I almost died. After that, my mom tried to put me in a bubble. It took years for her to realize that I had fully recovered and my health had improved."

"I'm glad to hear you're okay now."

"I'm perfect. But during all those years in the bubble,

I did a lot of reading and painting and schoolwork. It was much easier to excel in art history than to throw a basketball into a hoop."

"You're a little short for basketball anyway."

"True." She didn't know why she'd told him about her health issues. It wasn't something she'd spoken about in a long time, but there was something about Jeremy that made her want to lower her protective barriers. "So now you know about my weakness."

"I've seen no evidence of weakness in you, Mia. Impulsiveness, maybe."

"You're not going to let me forget about climbing up to the roof, are you?"

"Not any time soon." His smile made her stomach do a somersault. The connection between them was ridiculously strong, but their relationship was so undefined. They weren't dating. They were sort of friends, but not really. But there was an honesty between them that she hadn't had with any other man.

Unfortunately, Jeremy's mood abruptly changed when the café door opened and a man walked in.

He was older, fifties she thought, with gray hair, a weathered, lined face and a scruffy beard. He had a solid, broad build and wore jeans and a long-sleeved shirt that displayed the logo for Buddy's Bait and Tackle.

He paused inside the door, his gaze sweeping the restaurant. He saw his friends and started forward, and then froze when he saw Jeremy.

His face paled as his dark eyes moved on to Ashlyn.

Jeremy drew in a sharp breath.

"Who's that?" Mia asked.

Before Jeremy could reply, the man walked over to their table.

"Jeremy," he said, a harsh, rough note in his voice.

"Dad."

She stiffened at the word. "This is your father?"

"Yes," the man said stiffly, answering for his son. "Cameron Holt."

"Mia Callaway."

"And this is my daughter," Jeremy said. "Ashlyn Price."

"Price?" Cameron echoed. "Why doesn't she have your name?"

"I told you why, but you probably don't remember."

A tense silence followed his words.

Mia decided to break it. "I heard you were on vacation, Mr. Holt. Was it somewhere lovely?"

"Vacation?" he queried with a grumble. "Is that what he told you?"

"I might have misunderstood," she said quickly, realizing now it had been a lie.

"Why did you come back here?" Cameron asked Jeremy. "You said you'd never live in Angel's Bay."

"That's a question I keep asking myself," Jeremy replied. "You should join your friends."

"You never did want me around."

"You never wanted to be around," Jeremy returned.

A long, hard look passed between the two men. There was so much anger that the air practically sizzled between them. Ashlyn must have picked up on the tension, because she scooted her chair closer to Mia.

Both men saw the little girl's move. Anger flared in Jeremy's eyes at the action. But the look that Cameron gave his granddaughter was filled with pain. Then Cameron turned and walked over to his friends.

"Are you okay?" she asked Jeremy, seeing the tension in every hard line of his face.

"Fine."

"You don't look fine."

"Just leave it alone."

"Jeremy—"

"I need to take a walk," he interrupted. "Could you stay with Ashlyn?"

"Of course, but I think the food will be here soon."

"I just need a minute. I'll be right back."

When Jeremy left the café, Mia saw his father's gaze follow him out the door. There might be a lot of anger between the two men, but there was something else, too; she just wasn't sure what it was.

Six

—➤➤◄◄◄—

Jeremy walked a half-mile before his pulse went back to normal and he wasn't seeing the world through the colors of rage. He didn't know why he let his father get to him. He didn't know why he ever expected the man to act any differently. Cameron Holt had been pissed off at Jeremy for his entire life, or at least every day since his mother had died.

His father's sister had tried to tell him that Cameron was destroyed by his mother's death, but that had never explained why his father had turned away from him. Not that they'd ever been close.

His father was a wanderer. In his youth, he had traveled the world, crewing for whatever ship needed another hand. And as an adult, he had spent lots of time at sea, sometimes fishing the oceans on the other side of the globe. He was probably not a man who should have ever gotten married or had a child, but apparently when he'd met Tracy Warner, he'd decided she was worth staying home for. So he'd settled in Angel's Bay, saying he was content to fish the Pacific Ocean for the rest of his life as long as he had her.

And his mother was everything his father was not.

She was warm, friendly, interested in people, someone who liked to have friends, to be social, who participated in community events. Sometimes his dad would come along, probably just to humor his wife, but Cameron had always been more content in his own company or with the few men who were just like him. If he had nothing in common with someone, he wasn't going to waste a minute trying to find something to talk about; he'd just move on.

He'd moved on from Jeremy right after Tracy died. He'd gotten his sister to stay with Jeremy the first few weeks. Then it was a series of housekeepers/babysitters until Jeremy was in high school. Then it was just the two of them.

Actually, it had mostly just been him.

Drawing in a breath, he stopped to look at the ocean. The large, rough waves crashing against the seawall in the distance fit his mood quite nicely. That was the thing about Angel's Bay. The calm waters in the bay turned into turbulent waves that could take down a ship, wreck everything in its wake, and make you wonder if you would ever get back to shore.

His life had felt very much like that ocean in recent weeks. But he would get back to shore. He would beat the storm, because he didn't just have himself to save; he had his daughter.

It wasn't about him and his father anymore; that wasn't the family he was interested in. It was about him and Ashlyn. They would be the new Holt family, the one his mother had tried so hard to build while she was alive.

Sadness ran through him as he thought about his mother. She would have loved to have a grandchild, to know Ashlyn. She would have known how to reach his daughter. As a teacher, she'd loved kids—all kids, even the ones who were a little broken.

But Ashlyn would recover. He would make sure of that.

Turning, he walked back to the café, feeling guilty and pissed off that he'd let his emotions get the best of him.

He shouldn't have left Ashlyn with Mia. He shouldn't have walked out on either of them. That had been a mistake. He didn't think Cameron would try to speak to Ashlyn on his own, but Jeremy certainly didn't want that to happen when he wasn't there.

When he entered the restaurant, he was relieved to see that his dad and his friends had left, and Mia and Ashlyn were finishing up their lunch.

"I asked the waitress to keep your lunch warm," Mia told him with a sympathetic smile.

"Thanks."

She motioned to the cheerful middle-aged woman named Connie who had taken their order, and a moment later he had a burger and fries in front of him.

"This place has great food," Mia continued. "Ashlyn enjoyed her meal."

He was surprised to see that Ashlyn had actually eaten almost her entire burger. Maybe her appetite was starting to come back.

"Your dad left right after you did," Mia added. "He didn't speak to us again, in case you were wondering."

"Good."

"You said your dad is a fisherman?"

"That's right," he said, biting into his burger. "He goes out every day before dawn."

"Did he teach you how to fish?"

"He tried. I didn't care for it. It's too slow, and there are too many variables out of my control."

"But there is still a battle between man and fish.

Surely, that would appeal to your competitive instincts?" she teased.

"The few seconds when the fish takes the bait, and I try to reel him in, is the only exciting part. The minutes and hours in between I always found incredibly boring."

"What about your mom? Did she work before she died?"

"She was an elementary school teacher here in Angel's Bay. Her classroom was her second home. Every August, she'd take me to school and we'd hang mobiles and posters and alphabet letters to get ready for the first-graders coming in for the next year. She was a wonderful person."

"You must take after her."

"I would prefer that over my father, but the truth is I'm probably somewhere between both of them."

"You got the best of each."

"That would be better than the worst."

She smiled. "I'm going to use the restroom. Ashlyn, do you want to go with me?"

Ashlyn nodded and stood up, taking Mia's hand as they walked across the restaurant.

While they were in the restroom, he quickly finished his meal. He'd no sooner put the last bite in his mouth when Kent entered the café.

Kent wasn't in uniform today. Wearing faded jeans and a T-shirt, he looked much more like the guy Jeremy had grown up with. Kent stopped at the counter to order a roast beef sandwich to go, teasing Dina into giving him extra beef, and then headed over to Jeremy's table.

"Hey. Where's your better half?" Kent asked, grabbing one of the three empty chairs at the table.

"In the restroom."

"I'm glad I ran into you. I've got good news. Barton is

going to be in town tomorrow."

"Really? Why?"

Kent grinned. "He says it's his mom's birthday, but I think he wants to check up on you."

"I'm fine." He had mixed feelings about Craig Barton, his high school buddy and fellow Delta Force soldier, coming to Angel's Bay. It was one thing to hang out with Kent, who'd left the service a year ago and had another life now, but another thing to spend time with Barton, who was doing exactly what Jeremy wanted to do and might not ever be able to do again.

"How's the shoulder?" Kent asked, a speculative gleam in his eyes.

"Better than yesterday," he lied.

"That's good. Have you thought any more about my suggestion?"

"I'm not going to be a cop in Angel's Bay."

"There are worse things."

"Like dying of boredom?"

"We have crime here."

"Stolen bicycles and bar fights."

"It's not the big city, but there's still a need for a strong police force. We've had more serious problems to deal with than you might think, and I believe you'd fit in quite well. I know you want to save the world, but you've got a daughter to think about now. Plus, you're not getting any younger."

"Younger than you."

"By two months," Kent retorted. "I want you to meet some of the guys I work with. A bunch of us are going to Murray's Bar tomorrow night to shoot some pool. You should join us."

"I've got Ashlyn."

"I thought Mrs. Danbury said she'd be happy to

babysit for you."

"That's for when I go to therapy."

"A night out would be good therapy for you. Seriously, when's the last time you just had a beer in your hand and no worries in your head?"

He couldn't remember the last time.

"Just think about it," Kent added. "If Barton gets here in the afternoon, I'll make him come, too."

"I'll have to let you know."

"We'll be there around seven."

As Kent finished speaking, Mia and Ashlyn returned to the table.

Ashlyn hid behind Mia when she saw Kent. Kent had met Ashlyn the first day they'd arrived in Angel's Bay, but she either didn't remember him or just felt shy and awkward. Mia, however, greeted Kent with her usual friendly smile.

"Hello," Mia said. "I'm Mia Callaway."

"Kent Palmer," he said, reaching across the table to shake her hand.

"Nice to meet you. I think Ashlyn is being a little shy," she added with a laugh as she glanced over her shoulder at the little girl hiding behind her.

"And I thought all the ladies loved me," Kent drawled.

"In your dreams," Jeremy said.

"Not just in my dreams," Kent returned. "Jeremy and I go way back."

"High school?" Mia asked as she sat down with Ashlyn hiding behind her chair.

"Second grade," Kent said. "How do you know Jeremy?"

"I'm cleaning out my aunt's house, which is next door to his rental," she explained.

"Oh, you're Carly's niece. Which one are you? The artist?"

"I'm not really an artist, but I am involved with art. Did you know her?"

"Yes. She helped me through a dark period. She let me stay in her cottage after I got out of the service, and that time helped me get my head on straight."

"Did you paint while you were there?"

"All night long. I was suffering from some heavy-duty insomnia, but two weeks in that studio with that incredible ocean view, the blank canvases and the bright paints, not to mention the kindness of your aunt, changed my life."

Jeremy was a little surprised by the depth of emotion in Kent's voice. He'd really had no idea Kent had gone through such a bad time. It made him wonder what else he'd missed when it came to his friend.

"Your aunt used to bring me a snack every afternoon," Kent continued. "It was usually fresh tomatoes with mozzarella on top. She'd pour me an icy-cold glass of lemonade and we'd sit on the patio and talk about life. She was a very interesting person. I will miss her."

Mia wiped some moisture from her eyes. "I'm so glad she touched your life in such a positive way. It's nice to hear."

"Are you going to sell her place?"

"That's up to my mom, but right now I'm tasked with cleaning it out and getting things organized."

"I've seen the inside of that house," Kent said. "You have a lot of work ahead of you."

"Well, I have time. I'm not going to rush it." She paused. "Did you leave behind a piece of your art for my aunt?"

"Of course. It was all she asked for, and the least I could do to repay her for giving me a safe place to heal."

"What would you think of me displaying your piece in a collection at a local gallery or perhaps the museum?"

Kent hesitated. "It wasn't any good."

"Are you sure? I don't know which one of the paintings is yours, but a lot of them are excellent. But whether it's fantastic or not doesn't even matter. I want to pay homage to art, to its healing powers, to the freedom of expression that my aunt encouraged at her studio, and to the artists who found something within themselves during their time there. Would you be okay with it?"

"I might have to look at my picture again before answering that question," Kent said slowly.

Jeremy was surprised by Kent's hesitation. His friend had never been shy about showing off anything. "It can't be that bad," he put in.

"You'd be surprised," Kent replied, a shadow in his eyes.

"You never told me things were bad," Jeremy said quietly.

"We've never told each other a lot of things, and we both know why." Kent paused as Connie brought over a to-go bag.

"Dina says she gave you extra roast beef and two extra pickles," Connie said.

"Tell her I love her," Kent said with a grin. "And I love you, too, Connie."

The middle-aged waitress brushed the compliment off with a wave of her hand. "Sure you do. You love anyone who feeds you."

Kent pushed back his chair and stood up as Connie moved on to the next table. "I need to take off. I'll see you all around."

"Why don't you come by the studio one day and take a look at the paintings?" Mia suggested. "I'll make sure to pull yours out if you don't want it shown."

"I'll do that." He looked at Jeremy. "I hope to see you tomorrow night."

"I'll see."

As Kent left, Mia gave him a questioning look.

"He wants me to join him for pool at Murray's Bar tomorrow night."

"That sounds like fun."

"Maybe." He took out his wallet and put some cash into the billfold.

"Can I help?" Mia asked.

"This is on me. You watched Ashlyn all morning."

"Actually, I think she watched me, but thank you."

"Ready to go?"

"Yes."

As they walked out of the restaurant, Jeremy's gaze was drawn to the park down the street. He felt an odd wave of nostalgia. Some of his happiest memories were in that park as well as a very important reminder of his mother.

On impulse, he said, "Would you mind if we take a walk through the park, Mia?"

"No, of course not."

"Good. I want to show you and Ashlyn something."

"What is it?" she asked.

"You'll see."

They walked through the trees, past a massive fountain that several kids were playing in, weaving their way through a picnic area and past a huge play structure to a circle of benches at the entrance to the Angel's Bay Conservatory of Flowers.

He stopped in front of one of those benches and

pointed to the gold placard on the back of the bench. "This is my mom's bench."

"In honor of Tracy Holt, inspiring teacher, loving mother and wife," Mia read. "Did your family donate the bench to the park?"

"No, the families of her first grade class the year she died took up donations and put the bench in. She used to bring her kids here on field trips. At the time, there were no benches at all. She'd sit on the grass and read the kids stories. She always said that children needed to be outside to play, to explore the world, so she took them outdoors whenever she could."

"She sounds like a fantastic teacher."

"I think she was good." He looked at Ashlyn. "Tracy Holt is your grandmother—my mother. She would have loved to meet you. But she's in heaven now. She's an angel, just like your mom."

Ashlyn stared back at him with her big, dark eyes, and he wished he could read what she was thinking, but he couldn't.

"Can we sit?" Mia asked.

"Of course."

Mia took a seat with Ashlyn sliding in next to her and then he sat down. It felt both odd and kind of wonderful. He felt a connection to his mother he hadn't felt in a very long time.

For a few moments they sat in silence, the only sounds coming from the laughter of kids in the playground. As two little girls ran past them, their high-pitched voices squealing about who was going to get to the slide first, he looked down at Ashlyn and saw something that looked like yearning in her eyes.

"Would you like to play, Ash?" he asked.

She refused with a shake of her head, but it wasn't as

emphatic a refusal as he was used to getting from her.

"What about the swings?" Mia put in, tipping her head to the nearby swing structure that was empty. "Looks like you'll have the swing all to yourself."

Ashlyn's little mouth twisted as she debated the suggestion. She gave him a questioning look.

"Go ahead. We'll watch you," he said. "We'll be right here when you're done."

Ashlyn got up and walked across the path as slowly as she possibly could, stopping every now and then to cast a look back at them. Finally, she made it to the swing. She sat down, digging her toes into the sand, but she didn't push off.

"Do you think I should offer to push her?" Jeremy asked.

"I don't know," Mia said. "Maybe give her a few minutes."

"I can't believe she actually went to the swing. I thought she'd say no, the way she always does." He blew out a breath. "Isn't this ridiculous? I'm worrying about whether or not I should push an eight-year-old on a swing. I was solving much bigger problems than this a few months ago."

"I don't know about that, Jeremy. Ashlyn's problems seem rather large to me, and having your complete attention is going to be necessary to get her better. What you're doing here and now is important."

"But my attention doesn't seem to be producing any results. I feel helpless. I don't even know if I'm doing the right thing half the time. You met my old man. That's my role model. That's all I know about being a father."

"Then it seems like you have nowhere to go but up," she said lightly.

He glanced over at her. "He was always a son of a

bitch. People told me my mom's death changed him, but I don't remember him being any different than he is now, except maybe with her. He was softer when she was around, but he was still blustery and cranky when she was out, and he always thought he knew better than anyone else, especially after several cocktails. He's an alcoholic, but no one would dare say that to his face."

"Was he abusive?"

"Not in a physical way. He never hit me, but his words could cut like a knife."

"I'm sorry he wasn't a good dad, but you're not your father. And Ashlyn isn't you."

He shifted in his seat, and the creak of the bench made him feel as if his mother was listening in and telling him to wake up and listen to the woman by his side.

"My mom would have liked you, Mia."

"I hope so," she said with a smile. "But why do you say that?"

"Because you're kind and generous. My mother respected those traits more than any others."

"Thanks," she said, moisture filling her eyes. "That's a nice thing to say."

He was surprised by her emotional reaction. "If it was so nice, why do you look like you're about to cry?"

She dabbed at her eyes with her fingers. "I'm just coming off a rough couple of weeks, nothing close to what you've been through. In fact, after meeting you and Ashlyn, I realize how self-absorbed I've been, how I got caught up in things and people that were just not that important."

"What do you mean?"

"You don't want to hear about it."

"Actually, I'd love to talk about someone other than myself. What happened? I assume this has something to do with why you're unemployed."

"It does. Okay, here goes. I have to warn you that it's kind of embarrassing."

"I'll be the judge of that."

"I told you that I was sick as a child and that I spent a lot of time with books and paints. I excelled in school, so that was my comfort place. I couldn't compete with most of my siblings in any other area but grades, although my brother Ian is a freaking genius, so I couldn't beat him, but I was head and shoulders above the rest of them."

"So there was a lot of competition in the family."

"Definitely. My father is also one of six kids, and he was raised with the idea that you grow up and you give back. He did that as a firefighter. He instilled in us the idea that it was important to live a life that mattered. He wanted everyone to set their goals early, to figure out their plans and stick to them. He wanted us to push ourselves to be the best at whatever we were doing. So when it came time for me to make my plan, set my goals, I figured that I needed to stay where I was the most confident—academics. After I got a bachelor's degree, I went back to school to get a master's degree. I got as much education as I could possibly get. Then it was time to find the perfect job to fit all that education and that was as an assistant curator at the Kelleher Museum. I helped to curate the visiting exhibitions."

Jeremy nodded. "Okay, so where's the embarrassing part?"

"I'm working up to that." She paused for a moment, trying to remember where she'd left off. "The first year was all right, but the job wasn't what I thought it would be. It wasn't nearly as interesting as I'd imagined. I was doing paperwork and making a lot of phone calls. I found myself setting up hotel reservations for the people bringing the collections to the museum. I was getting farther and farther away from art. Then a new director was hired. Grayson Maxwell. He'd been working in Paris, and he was handsome, sophisticated, a little older than me, and very flirtatious. He definitely brightened up my days."

Jeremy saw the shadows behind her smile. "You fell in love with him."

"I did. I thought I was being careful. I didn't jump into bed with him. We went out for weeks before things got intimate." She cleared her throat. "I thought I knew him pretty well by then, but I didn't. To make this long story a little shorter, he turned out to still be married to the woman he'd left behind in Paris. She found out about us and threatened to take all the money she'd donated to the Kelleher Museum elsewhere. Grayson broke up with me and the museum laid me off on some technicality that we all knew was just a smokescreen for appeasing his wife and getting me out of the way."

"That's not right. He was responsible for what happened as much as you were, even more so, because he was the liar." He'd always hated men who were disloyal or unfaithful to anyone: girlfriend, wife, friend, family member. He'd never understood how anyone could betray someone they allegedly cared about. But maybe it was because those people usually cared more about themselves.

"That's true. But that's not the way the real world works, and to be honest, I didn't want to stay there anyway, not just because it would have been horribly awkward but also because I really didn't like the job."

"So what's next?"

"That's what I came here to figure out. Maybe what happened with Grayson was the best thing that could have happened, because I was forced out of that supposedly perfect job that I didn't really love the way I was supposed to."

"Do you know what you want to do career-wise?"

She shook her head. "I wish I did. I know I want it to have something to do with art, but I can't make money as an artist; I'm not talented enough, and that's not really my dream, either." She sighed. "I just feel like I've let everyone down. My family doesn't know as much as I just told you. They know that Grayson turned out to be married, but I sort of glossed over the getting fired part. They're all expecting me to work in another museum, to do something important with my life, because that's what Callaways do."

He smiled. "Here I thought not having a family was a bad thing. Maybe I'm lucky not to have anyone who cares what I do."

"My family would tell you that they support me in anything I want to do, but that's not really true. There's underlying pressure. I know all my siblings have felt it at one time or another. It more difficult for me, because I had to choose a field that's hard to stand out in, to do something important in. My firefighter brothers save lives every day. Ian is working on some scientific breakthrough and Kate wants to serve up justice wherever she can. Annie is a bit closer to me, but even her job is making her famous. She was featured in a national magazine last year." She paused. "Anyway, it's not that I'm not happy for their accomplishments; I just want to bring something interesting to the table."

"I'm sure you'll do that, Mia."

"I hope so. Aunt Carly was the one person in my family who really understood me. Before she died, we exchanged emails. She didn't know that I'd gotten myself involved with a married man, but she did know that I didn't love the museum the way I thought I would. It was shocking to me that something I'd worked so hard to get would turn out to be so disappointing."

"What did she say?"

"That I needed to follow my passion, wherever it led. That life wasn't about a bank statement or a job title or the respect of anyone else. She told me to quit, find a new job. I wish I'd followed her advice then, instead of looking to Grayson to inspire my life. That was a big mistake."

"I don't find regrets to be that helpful, Mia. It's what you do next that matters. When you fall down, you get back up. That's all you can do."

"And maybe try not to fall again," she said with a wry smile.

He tipped his head. "Definitely."

"Have you ever been in love, Jeremy?" she asked curiously.

He thought about that question. "No, not really. I never stayed in one place or with one person long enough to find out, though."

"A lot of soldiers get married."

"And that makes their life even more difficult. I never had to worry about anyone but myself. It was all about the mission. I was better at my job because of that single-minded focus."

"Well, that's not true anymore. You have Ashlyn now."

"Yes, I do. She's giving me a lot to think about."

"Like whether or not you go back to the Army?"

"It's definitely up in the air." He looked over at his daughter, who was still barely moving the swing, but she hadn't gotten up yet, so he would leave well enough alone. "I love my career. I don't want it to end, but I'm dealing with physical constraints that may prevent me from going back to Delta. I have to be at the highest physical level to do what I do, and if I'm not at one hundred percent, I'm no use to the team."

"That's harsh."

"It's the truth."

"What is Delta? It sounds like a spy group."

"You're not wrong. A lot of what we do is classified."

"Like a Navy SEAL?"

"Only better," he said with a cocky laugh.

She smiled. "But seriously—"

"That's really all I can tell you, Mia."

"So, if you can't go back to Delta because of your shoulder, what will you do?"

"I don't know. And it's not only the shoulder that might stop me from returning to my unit; it's Ashlyn. Who would watch her when I'm deployed? Sometimes I have one hour to grab my bag and go to wherever in the world I'm needed. I couldn't do that as a single father."

"You'd have to get a full-time, live-in nanny."

"So my daughter would be raised by a babysitter?"

"What other option would you have? Unless you can find a wife really quickly."

"I need fewer complications, not more," he said dryly.

"Then you might have to change careers, too."

"Looks like we both have some big decisions coming up."

"We do," she agreed. "Mine aren't as big as yours. There is no one depending on my choice, but you have Ashlyn, and in the long run she's going to be more important to your life than any job you do. She's your daughter. She's your family."

"I thought the Army was my family."

"But isn't war awful? Aren't there just horrific parts of your job?" she ventured.

"Of course. But I feel like I'm making a small dent in reducing the evil in the world every time I go out."

"Well, I admire your bravery, and I'm grateful there are men and women like you who are willing to take that job on."

"Thanks." He paused. "But when it comes to bravery, I think the battlefield is easier than this playground."

She gave him a sympathetic smile. "Why don't you see if Ashlyn will let you push her?"

"You'd probably be her first choice for that."

"It's easier for her to like me because she's not supposed to love me. I'm just a friend. You—she's still trying to figure out what it means to have a father. She probably doesn't understand where you've been all her life."

"Even I don't understand that."

"But you know what it feels like to want a father in your life. Just be the dad that you wanted your father to be."

"That's good advice."

"I hope so. And, Jeremy…"

"Yes?"

"I know what a good father looks like, because I have one. And he's a lot like you. Don't sell yourself short."

"Okay, thanks for the pep talk. I'm going in."

"Good luck."

He walked over to the swing. "Want to go a little faster, a little higher?" he asked.

She quickly shook her head, her hands gripping the chains of the swing.

"I won't let you fall, Ash. You can trust me."

She met his gaze, and for a moment he thought he

had her, and then she jumped off the swing and ran back to Mia.

A wave of disappointment ran through him. But he wasn't going to quit. He would win her over, no matter what it took.

Unfortunately, his daughter might have inherited his stubborn streak along with her dark hair and dark eyes. This battle would not be won in a day.

Seven

--->>><<<--

Mia felt bad for Jeremy when Ashlyn dissed his offer of a push and ran straight to her, but she didn't say anything. Jeremy and Ashlyn would have to find their way to a relationship; she couldn't make it happen for them no matter how much she wanted to.

As they walked through the park, her thoughts turned back to her recent conversation with Jeremy. She felt a little foolish for telling him about her affair with Grayson and the loss of her job, but in a way it had felt good to get it out. She hadn't told anyone the whole story and now that she had, she felt like she might be able to truly move on. She would find a job that she loved, something she could make enough money at to pay her bills, because that was the Callaway way, but she wasn't going to settle for something that wasn't right for her, no matter how perfect it seemed to everyone else.

"Would you mind if we stopped at the market so I could pick up some groceries?" she asked, as they got into the car. "I promise to be quick."

"You don't have to rush; I need to pick up a few things as well."

"That would be great."

"I don't know about great, but happy to help."

"I'll feel better once I have food in the refrigerator. Then I can settle in and really get some things done."

"As long as you don't let your neighbor and his daughter derail you," he said lightly.

She smiled. "I'm not keeping a schedule. I've done that for all of my life. I'm going to take these few weeks to work at my own pace, however slow or fast that might be."

"I like to control the pace, but right now I don't have that luxury. Someone else is calling the shots."

"I bet you never thought your life would be in the hands of an eight-year-old."

"I definitely did not," he agreed.

"You're a soldier. Don't you sometimes have to retreat so you can fight another day?"

"I prefer to have a solid enough plan before I go into battle so that retreating isn't necessary."

"I have a feeling you're a good soldier."

"I was trained to be good."

She had a feeling his talents went way beyond his training, but Jeremy definitely didn't talk himself up, and she liked that about him.

A few minutes later, they pulled into the parking lot of the market. They each grabbed a cart and split up to do their shopping. Of course, Ashlyn chose to stay with Mia. She decided to take one little minute to offer Ashlyn some advice.

"You know, honey, your dad is trying really hard to make you happy. You might want to think about letting him do that. Wouldn't it have been fun for him to push you on the swing?"

Ashlyn stared up at her, then shrugged.

Well, at least she hadn't said no or not reacted at all.

"Your dad loves you a lot. And he's not going anywhere, even if you try to push him away." It had occurred to her that Ashlyn might be consciously or subconsciously testing her father to see if he would get mad and leave. Ashlyn needed to know that her father was going to stay before she could trust him. "So maybe give him a break once in a while. You can do that, can't you?"

Ashlyn twirled a strand of her hair around on her finger as she considered the question. Then she pointed to the freezer section behind Mia. "Ice cream."

Mia smiled. "You can definitely talk when you want to." She opened the glass door. "Ice cream is actually a pretty good idea. There's nothing better than a hot summer night and a bowl of cherry vanilla ice cream."

"Chocolate," Ashlyn said, pulling out another container.

"Okay, chocolate isn't bad, either," she said, tossing it into her cart. "Now we need to get some vegetables so that I can justify eating the ice cream for dessert."

They met up with Jeremy ten minutes later by the checkout line.

"You stocked up," he said, eyeing her rather full cart.

"I had a little helper with me." She noted that he'd managed to get through the store with only a few items in his cart.

He laughed. "Ice cream?"

She nodded. "I had to say yes because she asked for it out loud."

His lips tightened. "Good. I'll pay you back."

"Don't be silly. You and Ashlyn just need to help me eat it later, or I'll be waddling out of Aunt Carly's house at the end of the summer."

"I seriously doubt that," he said dryly.

After checking out of the store, they headed back home, and Ashlyn reluctantly said good-bye to Mia after her father told her she needed to give Mia some time on her own.

Mia promised she'd see them soon, and then let herself into the house.

It felt good to fill the refrigerator and make herself a cup of tea. After the groceries were put away, she grabbed two large plastic trash bags and headed upstairs. While the studio was still her main focus, she did want to make the guest room more livable. It didn't feel as sad as her aunt's room, so it was much easier to start there.

She didn't know who the items in the guest room belonged to, but the drawers in the dresser were filled with an odd assortment of clothes, including a few men's shirts, which might possibly have belonged to one of Carly's lovers.

Mia smiled at that thought. She'd never actually met any of her aunt's male friends, but she'd heard some amazing stories. Carly had a way of making men fall at her feet and worship her. But no man had ever managed to get her down the aisle.

After debating for a few moments, Mia decided to put all of the gently used clothes in a bag for donation. Anything with a button missing or a stain, she put in the trash bag. She was about to tie off the second full donation bag when her cell phone rang. It was her sister Annie.

"Hey, Annie, hang on a sec." She put the phone on speaker and set it on the dresser as she knotted the ties of the trash bag and set it aside. "How's it going?"

"Good. I'm just leaving the hospital. Nicole and her beautiful daughter Amanda are doing very well. She's the sweetest baby with fuzzy blonde strands of hair on her head and the face of an angel."

"Thank goodness everyone is healthy." Nicole had still been in labor when she'd left San Francisco, and although she'd gotten several texts that baby and mother were fine, she felt better actually speaking to someone.

"So what's happening in Angel's Bay?" Annie asked. "What does the house look like?"

"It's filled to the brim."

"I told you."

"I'm up for the challenge. Taking care of Aunt Carly's things is what she'd want me to do. And I'll feel better for doing it. It will be my way of saying good-bye."

"Have you found anything good yet? I know she had some really interesting jewelry, and you might overlook that while getting caught up in some dusty old paintings," Annie teased.

"I will put anything aside that looks interesting, valuable or sentimental. Then you and Kate and anyone else in the family can take a look and see if you want it."

"I know. I trust you, Mia. I would help if I wasn't so busy right now."

"It's fine. It feels good to be here. I forgot how much I like the town. Everyone is so friendly and down-to-earth. It's a nice change."

"Well, I'm happy that you're happy. We'll talk soon."

"You've got it."

As she ended the call, her gaze was caught by something moving outside the window. She looked down at the backyard. A shadowy figure moved through the studio door.

Had Ashlyn come back?

She really hoped the little girl hadn't snuck out of the house again, but she wouldn't put it past her.

Setting the bag aside, she hurried down the stairs and

into the yard. She pushed open the door of the studio. "Ashlyn, are you in here?"

She stopped in surprise when she realized it wasn't Ashlyn in the cottage but a woman. She appeared to be in her early thirties and had brown hair and dark eyes. Her silk blouse, gray pencil skirt, and high heels suggested she held down some type of office job.

"Hello," Mia said, feeling a little awkward and uncomfortable. "Can I help you?"

The woman hesitated. "You're Carly's niece, aren't you?"

"Yes, I'm Mia Callaway and you are..."

"Christina Wykoff. I probably should have stopped at the house first."

Probably, Mia thought, wondering why Christina looked so nervous. "Did you need something?"

"I used this studio last year. I heard that you might be putting together a display of Carly's art, and, well, I'm not sure I want my painting to be part of that."

"Oh, right. I was going to try to contact the artists before I did anything." She couldn't help wondering how Christina had heard about her plan. It had to have come from Kara since she doubted Jeremy would have told anyone. Although, come to think of it, she'd mentioned her plan to Jeremy's friend Kent as well.

"This studio is more messy than I remember," Christina commented.

"I've just started cleaning things out."

"Yes, I saw the paintings on the patio, but mine wasn't out there."

"Why don't you describe it to me, and I'll keep an eye out for it? If you give me your number, I'll let you know when I have the display ready, and you can come by and see if your piece has come to light. I certainly won't display it without your permission."

"I suppose that will work," she said slowly, but she didn't look happy about it. "I would never want my art to be displayed in public. It was for me, and the piece I did for Carly was for her. You really should think about what you're doing. The people who stayed here over the last couple of years came for a reason and their art was personal."

Christina's words gave her pause. Mia hadn't really thought that anyone would leave something behind with Carly that was that personal. Wouldn't they have taken their emotional pieces with them when they left?

Christina opened her bag and took out a business card. "Please call me when you have things organized."

"All right." She read the card. "Are you an attorney?"

"No, I'm the business manager for Hamilton and Sloan."

"Okay. Was your painting a seascape, landscape, still life or a portrait?"

"I'll know it when I see it. Just call me when you've put all the paintings in one place."

"Of course."

"This mess is very—disturbing." On that note, Christina left the studio.

Mia felt a little disturbed, too; not by the clutter but by Christina. She didn't seem like the kind of woman who would spend days making art in a studio like this. So why had she stayed here? She had to have been one of the people who had come to the studio to work out some sort of problem, and Mia couldn't help wondering what that problem had been.

She stared down at the card again, but there was no answer on the foil-embossed card. Didn't she have enough to worry about? Why waste a moment thinking about a rather rude woman?

It bothered her that Christina had made no attempt to ring her doorbell. She'd just let herself into the studio. Maybe that's the way Carly had let the artists come and go, but Carly was gone and Christina knew that. It would have been far more courteous if she'd rung the bell and asked for permission to look for her painting.

Putting the card into her pocket, she debated whether to pull out more paintings in the hopes of getting that organized or finish turning the guest room into a more comfortable living space for herself.

She decided the paintings could wait for another day. Christina would just have to wait.

—➤◄—

Wednesday morning, Mia took her coffee out to the patio table and sat down, enjoying the beautiful vista. The morning sun bounced off the waves of the ocean beyond, and the horizon opened up her mind, making her feel like she was starting over, finding a new path. She had no idea where the path would lead, but she was eager to find out, and she was determined not to force herself to follow any signs or map things out too closely. She'd done that her entire life, trying to stay in control of every little thing and make every decision count for something big.

From today on, she was going to try to relax and not hold on so tight to what she thought was right or wrong. No more seeing life in such a black-or-white way. It was time to let the colors in.

She'd stayed up late the night before cleaning out the guest room and going through the kitchen cupboards to get rid of any trash. She felt a little better now that her personal space was more organized. She might have felt a special connection to her aunt, but she did not share Carly's love of clutter.

Her cell phone buzzed on the table, and she smiled at the text from her sister Kate.

Kate had attached a photo she'd taken from a plane, the skyline of Tokyo in the distance. The caption read, *"First assignment. Can you believe it?"*

She couldn't believe it. *"What are you doing in Japan?"* she texted back.

"Waiting to get off the plane. We landed 10 minutes ago! So annoying."

"What's the assignment?"

"Can't say, but I feel like my life is just beginning."

She could hear her sister's excitement. Kate had always wanted adventure and now she had it. *"Be safe."*

"How's Angel's Bay? Met any angels yet?"

"No, but there is a really sexy man living next door."

"What??? Is he single?"

"Yes, but he has a kid and a lot of baggage."

"You love baggage," Kate wrote back, knowing her all too well. *"And cleaning things up."*

"Not men. Too complicated."

"Life is complicated. Remember what Aunt Carly used to say."

"What?"

"The right man will make you question your sanity."

"Should we really be taking advice from our spinster aunt?"

"She had love. She just didn't get married."

"Maybe." She wondered if she'd find evidence of that love when she started going through her aunt's things. *"I'm not looking for love, maybe just some great art. Crazy feeling that Aunt Carly's art studio is going to help me re-launch my career."*

"Hope so. Go for it. The Callaway twins cannot be stopped!"

Her sister Kate was usually the one who couldn't be stopped.

"Gotta go. Finally opened the doors."

She sent back a smiley face and set down her phone. Even though she and Kate were very different, there was a bond between them that would never be broken.

Her phone buzzed again, this time with an incoming call from an Angel's Bay area code.

"Hello?"

"Hi Mia, it's Kara."

"How are you, Kara?"

"Good. I've called a bunch of people, and we're all set to do the coloring book party tonight at the quilt shop."

"Really? I can't believe you pulled that together so fast."

"It wasn't that difficult. I know it's short notice, but tonight worked the best. Otherwise, it would have to wait a week or two."

"Tonight is fine. My schedule is not booked."

"Wonderful. Everyone is excited to meet you. Will you have time to copy the patterns for the party?"

"Definitely. How many should I make?"

"I'm expecting around twenty people. We have plenty of markers and colored pencils, so don't worry about that. And we'll have food and plenty of wine as well. It's going to be fun."

"You're very nice to do this."

"Oh, please, I'm doing this for myself, too. It will be fun to have a night out. Come around seven."

"See you then." She got to her feet. Time to get started on the day.

Eight

⟶⟫⟪⟵

Jeremy found his daughter staring out the window of her bedroom at Mia's backyard. Ashlyn clutched the doll Mia had given her to her chest, and there was a yearning look in her eyes that sent a wave of pain through his soul. He didn't know if it was Mia that Ashlyn really wanted, or if it was her mother, and Mia just reminded her of her mom. But there was definitely something about their neighbor that had captured Ashlyn's interest.

He silently admitted it wasn't only his daughter who was interested in Mia; he found her quite fascinating himself.

He'd thought about her last night and had fought the urge to call her or go over there, knowing he needed to put some space between them. They'd shared a lot for two people who had only met a few days earlier.

He hadn't let a woman into his life in such a big way—ever. He'd told her things about his father, his mother, his past that he hadn't shared with anyone but his longtime friends. Somehow, with Mia, he'd found himself wanting to spill his guts.

He'd liked hearing about her life, too. She'd told her story with some ashamed regret and he'd found her openness incredibly appealing. It was nice to be with someone who was willing to admit mistakes. She was still figuring things out, but she was on the right track.

He forced himself to stop thinking about Mia and focus on Ashlyn. That was the most important relationship in his life.

Clearing his throat, he said, "Ashlyn. I made pancakes for breakfast."

She didn't turn around. He walked closer to the window and saw Mia puttering around the patio. She wore shorts and a tank top, showing off her beautiful curves, and his stomach tightened into knots.

Yeah, it wasn't just her kind heart and warm smile he was attracted to; her killer body had a lot to do with it, too.

Despite his very recent resolution to put some distance between them, he heard himself say, "Should we see if Mia wants pancakes?"

He'd barely finished the question when Ashlyn bolted from the room, her long hair flying out behind her. When he got to the hall, he saw the sliding door off the kitchen was open. He grabbed the plate of pancakes he'd covered in foil, the bottle of syrup and headed next door.

When he came through the gate, he saw Mia giving Ashlyn a quizzical smile.

"What do you need, honey?" Mia asked.

His daughter pointed to their house.

"You have to say the words, so I can understand," Mia said.

"Pancakes," Ashlyn bit out, then pointed again to the house.

As Mia followed his daughter's fingers, her gaze caught with his, and a jolt ran through his body. God, she was pretty with her golden hair and incredible blue eyes.

She didn't have on a speck of makeup, but her skin was flawless and warmly kissed by the morning sun. He'd like to kiss that face, too, every sweet inch of it.

"Good morning," she said.

"Breakfast," he replied shortly, having as much trouble now as Ashlyn had had to get out a comprehensible word. He lifted the plate in his hands. "I figured you're busy, so I brought the pancakes to you."

"They smell delicious."

"Did you already eat?" he asked, moving forward.

"I just had coffee."

"Can I tempt you?"

She hesitated. "Probably too much, Jeremy."

He had a feeling she was talking about more than pancakes, and he swallowed hard at that provocative answer.

Mia's cheeks turned red. "I can't believe I just said that. I'm going to get some plates and silverware."

"Do you want to eat inside?"

"Out here is good. Just clear a space on the table."

As she practically ran back into the house, he looked at the table laden with what he might call crap, but what he suspected she would call art, and he wasn't sure how to start clearing a space. "What do you think, Ash? What can we move?"

Ashlyn set down her doll and then started putting a collection of teacups into a nearby box. Soon, there was space for him to set down the pancakes and syrup and even a little room for the plates when Mia returned.

"Are those blueberry pancakes?" Mia asked.

"Yes and the blueberries are organic, picked at the local farm."

"By you?"

"No. By the person who runs the shack on the side of

the road."

"Close enough," she said with a smile. "I love breakfast, and yet I almost never make it; I'm often running late in the mornings. I can't remember the last time I had pancakes. What a treat!" She glanced over at Ashlyn, who was actually eating with enthusiasm. "You love pancakes, too, don't you, Ashlyn?"

The little girl nodded her head, chewing away.

Mia turned back to Jeremy. "Thanks for sharing your meal with me. It's very thoughtful."

"You're more than welcome," he said, thinking he could look into her eyes for a really long time and have no desire to look away.

"Jeremy," she said softly.

He could see the conflict in her eyes, desire warring with reason. There was an undeniable attraction between them, but what to do about it was a big question and one he couldn't answer right now. "Eat your pancakes before they get cold, Mia. I'm sure whatever you have to say can wait."

"You're right. It can wait." She picked up her fork, took a bite, then sighed with delight. "Wow."

He laughed, feeling ridiculously proud. "Really? That good? The mix came out of a box."

"The blueberries didn't, and you put it all together. I'm impressed."

He wanted to impress her in a lot of other ways, but as Ashlyn reached for another pancake, he was reminded that he had a chaperone. "So how are things going around here? Did you get a lot done last night?"

"I filled about six trash bags, half to go to charity and the other half to the trash. But to be honest, I feel like I'm chipping away at an iceberg with a bobby pin."

"There is a lot of stuff."

"What you see is about ten percent of it. The problem is that I keep coming up with a plan of attack and then decide to change it. First, I was going to do the studio. Then I decided I should do the house, so I could be more comfortable in the room I'm staying in."

"That makes sense."

"Then a woman showed up in the studio yesterday afternoon and told me she wanted her painting back. She said she didn't want it to be in whatever exhibition I was planning, and she was kind of rude about it. So then I started thinking maybe I should go back to the studio and focus my efforts there."

"What was the woman's name?" he asked curiously.

"Christina Wykoff. She works at an attorney's office, Hamilton and Sloan. Do you know her?"

"No, I don't. I wonder why she had such a strong negative reaction to her painting being shown."

"I assume she's embarrassed by it. She looked like a woman who is very put together. What I found really odd was that she just went into the studio without ringing my front doorbell or asking for permission. I know this is a friendly town, but she knows Carly passed away, and she knew I was in the house, so why not introduce herself to me?"

"Maybe if she stayed at the studio, she just always went straight back there, and she didn't think about going to the house."

"That makes sense."

"You might want to rethink the exhibition, Mia. Kent wasn't happy about his painting being shown, either."

"I don't really understand why either one of them is upset about it. Most artists love to have their work displayed."

"I don't know about Christina, but it sounds like Kent

created his art while he was going through a bad period in his life. Maybe that's why he doesn't want to show it; he doesn't want the reminder. Christina might feel the same way."

She nodded. "It's something to think about."

His phone vibrated, and he pulled it out of his pocket. It was a text from his longtime friend Craig Barton.

"Where are you? I'm ringing your bell."

"Next door," he texted back.

"Coming over."

He got to his feet. "A friend of mine is at my house." He'd barely finished speaking when Barton's loud voice rang through the air.

"Jeremy, where are you?" Barton called.

"Back here," he said, walking toward the gate.

It burst open a moment later, and Craig walked into the yard.

Craig Barton was a big man: tall, broad, and stocky, with legs like tree trunks and muscled arms that any body builder would be proud of. The massiveness of his body was intimidating, but it was offset by Barton's friendly grin and outgoing personality.

They shook hands, and then Barton pulled him into a short, rough hug and let go.

"Damn, it's good to see you, Jeremy."

"You, too."

"You look better than when I saw you in the hospital a few months ago."

"A lot has changed since then."

"So I hear." Barton looked past him. "Is that your kid?"

He nodded. "Come and meet Ashlyn." He walked Craig over to the table. "Ashlyn, this is one of my best friends, Craig Barton."

"Hi Ashlyn," Craig said.

Ashlyn jumped out of her chair and ran down the path and into the studio.

"I haven't sent a female running that fast in a long time," Barton said.

"She's shy," Jeremy said, downplaying Ashlyn's problems.

Barton turned his attention to Mia. "At least I didn't send you running."

Mia got up to shake his hand. "I'm Mia Callaway. It's nice to meet you."

"Likewise."

Jeremy saw the glint of appreciation in Barton's eyes, and he didn't like it. He'd seen Barton make a lot of moves on a lot of women, and it had never bothered him—until now.

Mia was his. Well, maybe not *his*, but definitely not Barton's.

"So this is where you're spending your time," Craig said with a knowing grin. "Can't say I blame you. The scenery is beautiful."

"The house has a magnificent view," Mia said.

"I wasn't just talking about the view," Barton drawled.

Mia grinned. "Good line."

He laughed. "Apparently not that good."

"We're having breakfast," Jeremy interrupted, giving his friend a pointed look to behave, not that that would matter. Barton had never met a rule he didn't want to break. "There are extra pancakes if you want some."

"Blueberry," Mia added. "Fresh from a local farm."

"That sounds good, but I just ate at Dina's with Kent, so I'll have to pass."

"What are you doing in town?" Jeremy asked.

"It's my mother's birthday this weekend, big party on Saturday night. I figured I might as well come and check up on you at the same time. Kent and I are getting together tonight at Murray's with some of the guys from his department. A little pool, a lot of beer—you in?"

"I don't know. I have Ashlyn."

"You can't find a babysitter for an hour or two?"

He hesitated. There was a big part of him that wanted to spend a few hours way he used to. "I'm not sure. I'll have to call her and see if she's available."

"Do that. We have some things to talk about, Jeremy," Barton said more seriously. "Like your future."

"We're not going to solve that over pool and beer."

"Maybe not, but we can start the conversation."

"I'll see what I can do."

Barton looked back at Mia. "So, you're the crazy art lady's niece?"

"Barton," Jeremy said quickly. "She just lost her aunt. Don't call her crazy."

"Sorry, I meant it in a nice way. Your aunt was a lot of fun. Carly was a real sweetheart to Kent when he was going through a bad time a few years back. I stopped by here a couple of times when Kent was using the studio. She would bring us lemonade and tell us stories about her travels. Kent and I thought we'd seen the world, but Carly had been a lot of places we'd never been, and certainly places more beautiful than the ones we were sent to."

"I know," Mia said. "I always looked forward to her postcards. Even though she died too young, I find some comfort in the fact that she lived every day to the fullest."

"That's all anyone can do. I'm sorry about her passing," Barton added. "Are you living here now?"

"Only temporarily. I'm cleaning out her house. My mom inherited the property. I think she'll probably sell it, but not any time soon."

"Maybe you'll discover something valuable tucked away. You can take it on one of those antique shows, and find out you're a millionaire," Barton suggested.

"Somehow, I don't think that will happen," she said with a laugh.

"You haven't seen anything that looks like it could be worth some money?"

"Not yet. But I've barely scratched the surface."

"Just remember. Some things that look like junk turn out to be priceless."

"She's an art historian," Jeremy put in. "If anyone knows what she's looking for, it's probably Mia."

"I've never met an art historian," Barton said.

Jeremy laughed. "The places you go to meet women—that's not surprising."

Barton shrugged. "I'm a simple man with simple tastes. Anyway, I have to go to my mom's house. I'll see you tonight, right?"

"I can't promise."

"Sure you can. You want something to happen, you make it happen."

"It's not that easy."

"Yes it is." Barton slapped him on the back, and Jeremy winced as pain shot down his arm. "Oh, man, I'm sorry," Barton said quickly. "You look so good. I forgot about your shoulder."

"It's fine. Don't worry about it."

"How's the rehab going?"

"It's going."

"And the ribs?"

"Only a memory."

"We'll talk later."

"Sure." After Barton left, Jeremy sat back down at

the table, massaging his left shoulder with his right hand.

"Your friend is right, Jeremy. It's easy to forget you were hurt," Mia said. "Every now and then, I see the pain in your eyes, but you cover it up very quickly."

"It's not that bad."

"I didn't know you'd hurt your ribs, too. You didn't just trip over something and fall, did you?"

He stared into her enquiring eyes and knew he owed her more of the truth. "There was an explosion. I cracked a rib and had some internal bleeding. They had to dig metal out of my shoulder. But I was lucky."

"That doesn't sound lucky."

"When you consider the alternative, it is."

"Did any of your friends not make it?" she asked quietly.

"Not that time, thank God."

"But you've lost friends?"

"Too many."

"And yet you want to go back. Why?" she asked, bewilderment in her eyes.

It wasn't an unusual reaction. Civilians didn't understand what it meant to fight, to be part of something bigger than yourself, to work on a team that was trained to kill and also trained to protect one another. He thought of how best to explain it.

"Because there are more battles to fight, and my team needs me."

As he said the words, he wondered if they were really true anymore. He'd been one of the best, but he was smart enough and realistic enough to know that he might not ever reach the physical strength he'd had before the blast.

He let out a sigh and looked out at the ocean. "I have to admit that part of my life seems very far away right now."

"I feel like my life is far away, too," she said. "Angel's Bay feels like not just a safe harbor but also a good place to start a new journey."

"I never thought of this town as a safe harbor. For me, it was a place I couldn't wait to leave."

"Was it the town you couldn't wait to leave or your father?"

"Probably my father."

"Have you ever tried to talk to him about the past?"

"I went by his apartment when I first got here. It was afternoon, so he was already on his third or fourth drink. I'd called first, hoping that he might postpone happy hour until after our meeting, but he didn't. I told him about Ashlyn. He said he wasn't surprised I'd be so irresponsible as to have a kid somewhere in the world that I didn't know about." He paused. "I wasn't irresponsible that night, Mia. I used protection. I don't know how Justine got pregnant."

"Protection isn't always foolproof, and you said there was a lot of alcohol involved."

"True. And maybe it was a little irresponsible, but that was a long time ago. And it was one night."

"You don't have to defend yourself to me. It's like you told me at the park yesterday. It's not the mistakes you make; it's what you do afterwards. When you found out you were a father, you went straight to Ashlyn. And you've been with her ever since. She's got a lot of issues, and it can't be easy, but you're trying. I'm quite impressed."

He couldn't help but be happy that she'd recognized the challenges he'd faced and was still facing.

"Maybe you need to find a chance to speak to your father when he hasn't had a drink," she suggested.

"I don't know when that would be. And you saw him at the café. He scared Ashlyn. I can't have him in her life.

He ruined my childhood; he won't ruin hers. I need him to stay the hell away from me."

"Is there anyone else in his life? A woman? A friend? Someone who could step in and let him know that he needs to tread carefully around Ashlyn?"

"He has friends. They've never stepped up to the plate before, not that I've ever seen. He could have a woman. Hell, I have no idea," he said, shaking his head. "We've spoken maybe three or four times the last ten years."

"It's sad that you're so disconnected."

"It's just the way it is. That's enough about my father. I should probably find Ashlyn," he said, getting to his feet.

"She's fine," Mia replied, as she stood up. "She can't mess anything up in the studio."

"She loves coming over here. She was standing at her bedroom window watching you earlier. Just so you know, even when she's not here, you do have an audience."

"She's trapped in her own head and she desperately wants to get out."

"I agree. I just wish I could release her from the prison she's put herself in."

"You will."

"Or maybe you will. You've gotten her to talk more than I have. She said the word pancake because her desire to include you in our breakfast overcame her desire to stay silent."

"That's going to happen more and more as she gets comfortable with you and with me." She paused for a moment, giving him a thoughtful look. "When is the last time you had a break from Ashlyn, and I'm not just talking about going to therapy?"

"I don't know. I haven't wanted to leave her while she's so fragile."

"You should go out with your friends tonight. I'd offer to babysit, but I have a coloring book party to go to at the quilt shop that Kara set up."

"I wouldn't ask you to babysit again. I can call Mrs. Danbury, I suppose. She said she's free a lot, and she misses her grandkids who just moved away, so she likes doing it."

"Then you should ask her. You need to take care of yourself, too."

He liked the concern in her eyes. "Thanks."

"Your friend Craig Barton is a character."

"Sorry he called your aunt crazy. He has no filter."

"I know it wasn't mean-spirited. So you and Kent and Craig all grew up together?"

"Yeah. We've known each other all of our lives. We joined the Army together right after high school graduation. We have a lot of history, most of it good."

"Were Kent and Craig in Delta with you?"

"They were. We weren't always together over the years, but we ended up in Delta four years ago. Kent got injured last year and left the Army. Barton and I were part of the same team up until about six months ago. He got a promotion and moved to a different unit, but we still occasionally worked the same problem." He paused. "Barton wants me to go back to Delta and Kent wants me to be a cop here in Angel's Bay."

"What do you want?"

"The real question is what can I have?"

"Maybe you have to know what you want in order to answer the second question."

"You might be right," he said slowly, thinking that what he wanted right this second was the barefoot, sexy blonde woman standing in front of him.

Her blue gaze darkened under his stare, and he knew

she was feeling the same pull of attraction that had him in its grip.

"There are so many reasons why I shouldn't kiss you right now," he muttered.

Her tongue darted out, as she nervously swiped her bottom lip. "Are you talking to me or to yourself, Jeremy?"

"Maybe both of us."

"What about all those reasons?"

"One kiss."

"Could we stop at one?"

"Let's find out." He put his hands on her waist and covered her mouth with his.

She tasted like blueberries and maple syrup, like sweetness and sex, and he was instantly lost. She kissed him back with enthusiasm and impatient need. He liked the way she flung her arms around his neck and brought his head back to hers when he thought to end the kiss. That was fine with him, because he could have gone on kissing her forever.

Actually, that wasn't completely true, because he wanted more than a kiss.

He wanted to taste more than her lips, run his hands along her feminine curves, and wrap her hair around his fingers. He wanted nothing between them: no clothes, no restraint, no reasons why they shouldn't be together.

But there were reasons, dammit. And one of them was not too far away.

He finally pulled away from Mia, staring down at her soft pink lips, and her beautiful eyes now sparkling with desire, and it was all he could do to take a breath and step back.

"That was..." she began. "I have no words."

He couldn't help her. His blood was still racing

through his veins.

She tucked her hair behind her ears and gave him a somewhat self-conscious smile. "I don't know what that was."

"All I know is that it was great."

"But...it probably shouldn't happen again. You know—for all those reasons you mentioned a few minutes ago."

"Hard to remember what they are now." He ran a hand through his hair. Kissing her should have taken the edge off, but it had actually only made him want her more.

"You have Ashlyn and a career to figure out," she reminded him. "And I have my own employment issues to consider. Plus, neither of us is planning to be here long-term. We're like two ships passing in the night. We should just be neighbors, friends, don't you think?"

She was right, so why did he absolutely hate the suggestion? "That would probably be wise."

She gazed back at him for a long minute, conflict in her eyes. "Why does doing the wise thing always feel so bad?"

"It's more fun to give in to temptation than to resist it."

"It certainly is," she said with a wistful sigh. "I didn't expect to come here and meet someone like you."

He smiled. "I didn't, either."

"So...friends."

"Sure." He cleared his throat, thinking if he was going to fulfill the *friend* promise, he should probably leave before he did something wonderful and stupid like kissing her again. "I should get Ashlyn and leave you to your cleanup."

"You can let her stay if you want, unless you have

something specific planned for her and you to do together..."

"No, she'd probably prefer to stay with you." He hesitated. "If you really don't mind, I could grab an extra therapy session."

"I don't mind at all. I do need to go into town to make some copies of some of the sketches I found for the coloring book party tonight. Do you mind if Ashlyn goes with me?"

"No, that's fine."

"I'll make sure she wants to go. Otherwise, I can do it when you get back. It won't take that long."

"She'll want to go. What did you say you were doing—a coloring book party? Isn't that for kids?"

"These sketches are for adults. My aunt was putting together a coloring book of her sketches. They're quite good. I guess it's the hot new craze to relieve stress through coloring. Kara suggested a group party with wine and coloring. She wants me to meet some of my aunt's friends."

"The wine sounds like fun. I'm not sure about the coloring."

"I'm not, either, but we'll see how it goes tonight. Now, go and do whatever you need to do."

"Thanks. And Mia—when you told me before that I had to know what I wanted so I could go after it..."

"Yes," she said warily.

"You know the first answer that came to my mind?"

"Was it the Army?"

He shook his head. "It was you."

Her eyes widened as she licked her lips again. "Maybe in that minute you wanted me, but..."

"But what? Maybe that minute or this minute is all that matters. Sometimes tomorrow doesn't come."

"But when it does come, it helps if you haven't made a mess of the day before. I'll see you later, Jeremy." She walked into the studio and shut the door.

He turned back to the table, grabbed the pancake platter and syrup and headed home, thinking that breakfast with Mia had been both an excellent and a terrible idea.

Nine

➡➤◄◄◄-

Mia's nerves tingled long after she heard Jeremy leave the yard. She couldn't believe the way he'd kissed her or the way she'd kissed him back. It hadn't been the usual tentative awkward first kiss between two people who didn't know each other very well; it had been a fiery explosion, which did not bode well for a friendship.

But as she'd reminded him, they wouldn't be living next door to each other forever. She'd leave as soon as the house was pulled together. She'd go back to San Francisco, start sending out resumes, and get back to her life.

Jeremy would do…something. He'd either go back to the Army or go somewhere else, but she doubted he'd stay in Angel's Bay. Or maybe he would. But even if he did, she wouldn't be here.

There was absolutely no good reason for them to get together now. Any relationship between them had heartbreak written all over it, and she didn't feel like putting herself through that kind of pain again.

Forcing Jeremy out of her head, she walked into the studio and climbed up the stairs to the loft bedroom. She found Ashlyn sitting on the bed with a bunch of vintage jewelry spread out around her.

Ashlyn gave Mia a guilty look as she put another necklace around her neck. It joined the other three necklaces and the dozen bangles she'd put on each arm.

"Well, don't you look pretty," she said with a smile, as she sat down on the bed with Ashlyn and picked up three more gold bangles from the bed. "I think my aunt brought these back from India. She sent some to me and my sisters when we were little girls."

"Sisters?" Ashlyn muttered.

Mia tried not to let on that she was excited Ashlyn had verbalized a question. "Yes, I have a twin sister named Kate and an older sister named Annie. I also have three older brothers. They're good guys for the most part, but they like to boss me around." She paused. "When I was a little girl, my sisters and I used to play dress-up. I always wanted to be a princess. Kate wanted to be a pirate."

Her words brought tears to Ashlyn's eyes. "What is it, honey? What's wrong?"

"My mommy played dress-up with me."

Her heart twisted at the pain in Ashlyn's voice. She was also a little shocked by the complete sentence. "I'll bet that was fun."

"She's in heaven."

"That means she's watching over you."

"I want her to come back."

"I know you do." She gave Ashlyn a hug, because she just couldn't stop herself, and surprisingly Ashlyn accepted the embrace. Her body was stiff and awkward, but she didn't push Mia away.

Deciding to press her luck a bit further, Mia said, "Your father loves you very much. He's not trying to take the place of your mom, but he wants to take care of you and make you happy."

"Mommy said he didn't want us."

She shook her head. "He didn't know about you, Ashlyn. Your mom didn't tell him. He didn't find out about you until after she died."

Ashlyn looked confused. "Mommy said I didn't have a daddy. She said she was Mommy and Daddy."

"I don't know why she told you that, but your dad is a good person, and he's trying really hard. Maybe you should talk to him a little bit. Get to know him. Let him get to know you." Ashlyn didn't look convinced, so Mia added, "I have a fantastic father. As a little girl, I looked up at him, and I knew he was big and strong and he would always protect me. Now that I'm a grown-up, I still talk to him about my problems, because even if he doesn't know the right thing to say or he says something stupid, because he's a guy after all, I still know I can count on him."

"Where is he?"

"He's in San Francisco with my mom. That's where I live when I'm not here."

"Are you going to leave, too?"

"Not anytime soon. By the time I'm ready to leave, you'll be sick of me. But your dad is never going to leave."

"He makes good pancakes," Ashlyn said.

Mia smiled. "I bet he does a lot of other things well, too." She paused to pick up some decorative bobby pins from the bed. "I have an idea. We should put these in your hair. They would look so pretty. But first we should probably brush your hair." Ashlyn's thick dark hair was a mass of tangles and from what she'd seen over the last few days, she doubted anyone had put a brush to it in a while. "What do you think?"

Ashlyn nodded in agreement.

"Good. Your dad went to the gym for a while, so it's just you and me." She looked Ashlyn in the eye. "We need to get something straight. I don't want you to go back to your house without telling me. I'm responsible for you, and your dad won't let you come over here, if I can't keep an eye on you. Understand? If you get mad at me, you talk to me; you don't run away. Do we have a deal?"

"Okay."

"Let's go into the house and do your hair. Have you ever had a French braid?"

She nodded. "Mommy used to braid my hair. He doesn't know how to do it."

"Well, Jeremy is a guy, and they just aren't good with hair. But I am really good." She climbed off the bed. The little girl took her hand, and Mia didn't mind the sticky syrup on her fingers one bit. She felt like she'd just won a bit more of Ashlyn's trust.

An hour later, Mia had gotten Ashlyn in and out of the shower, blow-dried her hair and put it into a beautiful French braid decorated by the pins they'd found in the cottage.

Then they got into the car to take Ashlyn's new look into town and to get copies made of the art patterns. On their way out of the copy shop, Ashlyn pointed to a children's clothing boutique across the street, grabbed Mia's hand and dragged her across the sidewalk.

"Okay, okay," she said with a laugh. "We'll go look at clothes." She was beginning to realize that Ashlyn had inherited some of her father's determination.

They stopped in front of the window of the store, and Ashlyn's eyes widened in appreciation as she looked at the yellow and white summer dress on the child-sized mannequin.

"Let's go inside," Mia said.

As they wandered around the store, Ashlyn looked at the clothes with a reverence that made Mia realize that the little girl was starting to come alive again. She didn't know if Jeremy would appreciate her buying his daughter clothes. On the other hand, he'd told her that Ashlyn never wanted anything, so if she wanted something, he wanted to give it to her.

"Do you want to try on some clothes?" she asked.

"Can I?"

"Of course. Let's pick out a couple of dresses and shorts and shirts and see what you like. It will be fun. I love to shop for clothes."

Ashlyn seemed to share her enjoyment, and it was clear her favorite clothes were very girly with cute buttons, flouncy skirts, and bright colors.

They spent a good thirty minutes trying on outfits, and Mia had never had so much fun. Ashlyn also enjoyed herself, smiling and parading in front of the mirror in the dressing room. A new hairstyle and a pretty dress had certainly taken her mood to a new high.

Finally, they settled on the yellow and white sundress from the front window, a cute pair of sandals to go with it, and pink shorts with a matching tank top. Mia had also thrown in a pretty chain with a silver heart that had captured Ashlyn's interest. She really hoped Jeremy would be okay with everything. If he could see Ashlyn now, she thought he would be.

In fact, she felt a little guilty that she was the one seeing Ashlyn come out of her cocoon of pain, but hopefully Jeremy would soon get to witness his little butterfly beginning to fly.

After leaving the shop, she decided to take the long way back to the car. She wanted to see more of the town. She remembered some of the stores from her summer visits, but there were also quite a few new businesses. As Kara had said, Angel's Bay was growing, and it was clear it had become a tourist destination. The sidewalks were crowded with people checking out antiques shops, sipping coffee and iced drinks at outdoor cafés, and visiting one of the many clothing stores that offered options from everything to high-end evening wear and bridal attire to whimsical dresses and ocean resort clothing.

"I like this town," she said to Ashlyn. "What about you?"

"Are there really angels here?" Ashlyn asked, as they paused in front of a hand-blown glass shop with dozens of glass angels in the window.

"There are definitely those kinds of angels," she replied, looking at the display.

"I mean the real kind. Like my mommy."

Mia squatted down so she was face-to-face with Ashlyn. "I think the angels are everywhere. They watch over us and protect us, and we can feel them even if we can't see them. And do you know what they feel like?"

Ashlyn stared back at her, doubt in her eyes.

"They feel like love. Look up at the sky."

Ashlyn reluctantly lifted her gaze to the cloudless blue panorama.

"Do you feel the heat on your face? That's love. That's coming from the heavens."

The little girl drew in a breath and then let it out and then looked back at Mia. "Mommy liked the sun. She didn't like when it rained. Or when it was dark."

"I like the sun, too, but I don't mind the rain. It's not just the sun that makes me feel love: it's everything in this world: the moon, the stars, the trees, the flowers, but mostly the people. Love is everywhere, Ashlyn. You just have to open up your heart to it. Then you'll feel everything that's important, including the angels."

As she spoke, Mia thought it might be a good idea for her to take her own advice. She'd closed her heart down after Grayson. She'd told herself she'd rather be alone than make another painful mistake, than get hurt again, but she couldn't let Grayson ruin the rest of her life. She couldn't let him turn her into a cold person who only felt the chill of life and never the warmth.

She stood up and smiled at Ashlyn. "I think we should buy one of these angels to remind us, don't you?"

Ashlyn gave a vigorous nod, and they walked into the store.

"Be careful not to knock anything over," she warned. "Everything is very breakable."

The glass was amazingly beautiful, intricate designs of animals and angels, flowers and tiny glass houses. As they walked to the back of the store, they stepped onto a platform and watched the glassmaker blow the glass into shape.

Ashlyn was entranced by the old man's work and couldn't take her eyes off the glowing fire.

A woman came up next to them. "That's my father," she said with a smile. "He's been blowing glass since he was ten years old. He's almost eighty now, but he's only gotten better."

"He's amazing. He did everything in this store?" Mia asked.

"I helped as well. I'm Shannon Kelly. My father is Frank Kelly. He learned the craft from his father and his grandfather, and he's passed it through the family."

"The work is beautiful. We'd like to get an angel."

"We have lots of those," Shannon said with a laugh, leading them across the room. "Which one do you like?"

"You pick, Ashlyn."

Ashlyn took the suggestion quite seriously, taking a few moments before settling on a small glass angel with a flowing dress.

"Perfect," she said approvingly.

Shannon carefully placed the angel in a box pillowed with tissue paper. "Here you go. I hope you'll come back some time."

"I'm sure we will," Mia said.

"Are you locals or tourists?"

"Somewhere in between," Mia said with a laugh. "We're here for a few weeks anyway."

"You'll love this town. It's a little piece of heaven on earth."

"I'm beginning to think so."

After leaving the glass shop, they cut down a side street on their way back to the car, but once again Mia got derailed when she saw the sign for the Eckhart Gallery, the one Kara had told her about.

"Let's stop here," she said. "I want to see if they might be interested in my aunt's collection of paintings."

They walked through a beautiful arched doorway into a gorgeous space of hardwood floors, ten-foot arched windows that brought in a great deal of natural light and white walls that served as a background for some really excellent paintings. An older man dressed in a black suit looked up from the mahogany counter that he stood behind and peered at her and Ashlyn through his thick-framed glasses.

He didn't look particularly happy to see a child in the gallery. "Please tell her not to touch anything," he said, without bothering to greet them first.

"She won't," Mia said.

"Children always have sticky little fingers," he said with disdain. "Is there something I can help you with?"

Judging by his snobbish manner, she doubted he would be at all interested in helping her, but Kara had mentioned something about a relationship between the owner and her aunt. "I was wondering if Mrs. Eckhart is in today."

His thin lips tightened. "Who shall I say is asking?"

"Mia Callaway. Tell her I'm Carly's niece."

His expression softened at the mention of her aunt. "Of course. Excuse me."

He walked down a hallway into what she presumed was the gallery office. While he was gone, she took Ashlyn around the main room, noting that there were several rooms off the central gallery with exhibitions by visiting artists.

"That's pretty," Ashlyn said, pointing to an oil painting of a wild garden next to a small farmhouse. The painting was by the Italian artist Pietro Muscolini.

Mia had always enjoyed his work and knew the painting was quite valuable. The fact that it was here spoke well for the reputation of the gallery.

She turned around at the sound of heels on the slick floor. A curvy, short woman in her sixties, with white hair and bright blue eyes, gave her a warm, welcoming smile. "You're Carly's niece?"

"Yes, Mia Callaway."

"I'm Didi Eckhart. I enjoyed your aunt's company so much. I was devastated by her death," she added, compassion filling her gaze. "She was too young to die and always so full of life. She cared a great deal for people. When my husband died several months ago, she was very, very kind to me."

Mia wasn't surprised. She had yet to meet anyone who hadn't loved her aunt. "That's nice to know. I'm sorry about your husband."

"Thank you." She looked at Ashlyn. "Is this your little girl?"

"No, Ashlyn belongs to a friend of mine. She's a little shy," she added as Ashlyn moved behind her.

"I was like that when I was a little girl. I couldn't understand why strangers wanted to talk to me," Didi said. "Did you just come by to say hello or were you looking for some art?"

"Actually, I wanted to run an idea by you. I'm cleaning out my aunt's studio, and I've found at least a dozen really good paintings that I'd like to put together into a collection and put them on display. As you know, Carly loved to encourage new artists, and I thought the collection would be a wonderful homage to her and also give the artists who used the studio a public display. I thought of calling the exhibition *Freedom*."

"That's a wonderful idea. I know Carly received many beautiful paintings by the artists who used her studio. I told her once she should bring some down here to the gallery."

"Was she interested in that?" Mia wanted to get a clearer picture of what her aunt had thought of doing with all the art that had been left to her.

"She was very interested, but at the time we spoke my late husband had complete control of the gallery, and he didn't like the art that she showed him. He thought it was terribly amateurish. My husband, God bless him, could be very arrogant when it came to art. But now that I'm in charge and feeling better about life, I want to change things up around here, and I think your idea is wonderful."

"I'm so glad. I just can't bring myself to stick the paintings into storage. Art should be appreciated."

"I agree. However, I would like to see the paintings before making a final decision."

"I'll need a few days to pull everything out and see what I have. Then I can bring the paintings by, or if you'd like to come to the house, you can do that, too."

"Why don't you give me a call when you're ready?" Didi handed her a business card. "Make sure you speak directly with me." She dropped her voice as the snobby man moved past them and entered an adjoining room. "Mr. Raleigh was hired by my husband, and he doesn't share my new vision."

"That might make life difficult."

"Yes. I'd like to be loyal, but this gallery is all I have left, and I want it to be good and to be mine."

"I completely understand."

Didi gave her a thoughtful look. "Your aunt said you worked in a museum. Or is that one of your sisters?"

"No, that would be me. I was recently an assistant curator at the Kelleher Museum in San Francisco."

Didi laughed. "Well, then, you know all about snobs."

She grinned. "I do."

"What are you doing now?"

"Considering my options while I clean out my aunt's house."

"I'm sure a smart young woman like yourself has plenty of options."

"I hope so. Thanks so much for your time."

"Of course. I look forward to hearing from you."

As they left the gallery, she squeezed Ashlyn's hand and said happily, "That went well. I think we just found a place to display Aunt Carly's paintings. Let's go home.

We'll make lunch and get back to work."

"Can I put on my new clothes?"

"Yes." She smiled at Ashlyn's hopeful expression. "You can show your father what we bought." Hopefully, Jeremy would consider their outing as successful as Mia did.

When they arrived home a little after one, Mia headed straight to the kitchen to make some lunch while Ashlyn ran upstairs to try on her new clothes. She'd just finished putting together turkey sandwiches and a bowl of fruit when the bell rang.

She wiped her hands on a towel and walked down the hall. Jeremy stood on the porch, looking as handsome and as sexy as ever in jeans and a T-shirt, his hair damp from what appeared to be a recent shower. Her heart did a little flip-flop when he gave her a slow smile, and, instantly, she was taken back to the kiss they'd shared earlier that morning. Her idea to keep things at the friendship level didn't seem quite that good anymore. It was all she could do not to walk into his arms and take the kiss she wanted.

"Hi," he said softly, a knowing gleam in his eyes. "How's it going?"

"Great," she said, trying to get a grip on her suddenly impatient libido. "I was just making lunch. Come in. Are you hungry?" she asked, as they walked down the hall and into the kitchen.

"I am, but you don't have to feed me."

"I have plenty. It's just turkey sandwiches and fruit."

"Where's Ash?"

"She's putting on some new clothes. I hope you don't mind. We went into town, and she really wanted to go into this kid's boutique, so we did some shopping. I probably way overstepped, but—"

"You didn't." He cut her off with a shake of his head.

"I'm happy she found something she liked. I've taken her shopping a few times, but I couldn't get her interested."

"I think she's starting to come out of her shell."

"I hope so."

Ashlyn ran into the room, wearing the yellow and white sundress and her new sandals. She stopped abruptly when she saw her dad, worry in her eyes as she waited for his reaction.

"Wow," Jeremy said. "Who is this beautiful little girl?"

A smile tugged at Ashlyn's lips. She didn't want to respond to her dad. She didn't want to show that she cared, but she did. The wall between Ashlyn and Jeremy was beginning to crack, and Mia felt a knot of emotion grow in her throat as she watched the silent exchange that passed between them.

"You look like your mother," Jeremy continued. "Justine was beautiful, just like you. Who did your hair?"

"Mia," Ashlyn said out loud.

Jeremy sucked in a quick breath at the verbal answer. Then he looked at Mia with gratitude in his eyes. "Thank you. I am terrible at even getting her hair into a ponytail. I know she's been frustrated with me."

"Well, I'm sure you haven't had a lot of practice. We found the jeweled bobby pins in the studio earlier. We had to put them to use." She paused. "Why don't you both sit down at the table? I've got lunch ready."

"Can I help?" Jeremy asked.

She handed him the bowl of strawberries, blueberries, and raspberries. "More berries, but they are in season."

"They look good." He took the bowl to the table, and she brought over the sandwiches.

"What else did you do today?" Jeremy asked

"We took care of all my errands. We made copies of

the sketches for the coloring book party. Then we stopped at a glass shop, and Ashlyn picked out a beautiful angel that she can show you later. After that, we went by the Eckhart Gallery and I had a very productive conversation with Didi Eckhart. She's interested in the collection I'm putting together."

"You accomplished quite a bit."

"Ashlyn was very good company, too," she said, giving the little girl a smile.

Ashlyn smiled back at her as she munched on her sandwich.

"How did your therapy go, Jeremy?"

"It was all right. I was still a little stiff from yesterday, so I don't feel like I made as much progress."

"Maybe you're pushing yourself too hard."

"You sound like my therapist. He wasn't happy to see me two days in a row, but he gave me some time."

"If you go too fast, you might actually set yourself back."

"That's what he said. But I know how hard to push myself. I've had to make it through some grueling challenges in my time. Sometimes it's just about how much you want it."

"But not always," she said. "You can't will this injury away. Not everything is in your control."

He frowned. "I know that; I just don't like it." He pushed his empty plate aside and glanced at his daughter. "You must have been hungry, Ash. I've never seen you eat a whole sandwich before."

Ashlyn didn't say anything.

Mia sighed, hoping that Ashlyn wasn't already heading back into her isolated world. It was as if her father's words had reminded her that she'd let down her guard for too long. She'd really hoped that Ashlyn would start to let Jeremy into her life the way she'd done with Mia. Maybe the two of them needed an outing.

"Darn," she said aloud.

Jeremy gave her an enquiring look. "Something wrong?"

"I just realized that I'm supposed to bring some dessert to the party tonight and I forgot to pick it up while I was in town. I heard there's a really good bakery—Sugar and Spice. I was going to get something there."

"I know the place. It's actually run by a woman I went to school with, Lauren Jamison. Actually, it's Lauren Murray now. She's married to Kara's brother."

"You probably know a lot of people here," she murmured, thinking that she kept forgetting that Jeremy had grown up in Angel's Bay.

"I've been gone so long, I doubt many would remember me."

"I doubt that's true. You're not a man easily forgotten."

He smiled at her words. "I like the sound of that. Why don't I pick up the dessert for you? I have to run into town anyway. I need to go to the ATM."

"An assortment of anything would be great. Ashlyn could probably pick out some good desserts for me."

"What do you say, Ash?" he asked. "Want to run an errand with me and help Mia out?"

Ashlyn hesitated, not looking too thrilled by the idea of going with her dad.

"I want to make sure your dad gets the best cookies," Mia told Ashlyn. "And I don't think he eats very many cookies, so he needs your help. Plus, wouldn't it be fun to go into town in your new dress?"

Ashlyn nodded.

"Great," Jeremy said, getting to his feet.

"I really appreciate it, Jeremy. Ashlyn, why don't you get the shopping bag and take it back to your house so you don't forget," she suggested.

As Ashlyn left the room, she said, "We also bought shorts and a T-shirt, plus the glass angel."

He nodded with approval. "Ashlyn looks as happy as I've ever seen her, not that she wants to show me that anything has changed."

"She's fighting it hard," Mia agreed.

"Why do you think she's so resistant to letting down her guard with me? What am I doing wrong?"

"Nothing. She wants to love you. She wants to let you in. I think she's afraid. It's not just that her mother died; it's that she doesn't know where you suddenly came from, so she doesn't trust that you'll stay. If she doesn't let herself like you, then it won't hurt as much when that happens."

"I'm never going to leave her. I've told her that, but I don't know how to get her to really believe me."

"It's going to take time. She's stubborn. I think she might have inherited that trait from you."

He tipped his head. "Quite possibly."

"You don't have to solve everything today. Go into town, get my dessert and walk around a little. When we were on Main Street earlier, I saw there was going to be a kids' musical performance in the park this afternoon. You might want to check it out."

"That sounds like a good idea. But I have a better one."

He walked forward, and before she could guess his intention, his arms were closing around her and his mouth was on hers.

Her eyes closed as she savored the seductive taste of his lips and inhaled the musky scent of his aftershave. She liked the way he took possession of her mouth with need and determination, not that she had any thought of refusing what she wanted as much as he did. But the sound of footsteps broke them apart, and she jumped back as Ashlyn returned to the kitchen, shopping bag in hand.

"Ready?" Jeremy asked Ashlyn, a brisk note in his voice.

"You can go out the back if you want," Mia said, leading them through the adjoining family room to the sliding glass doors.

Ashlyn left the house first, Jeremy lingering behind.

"To be continued," he said.

"We're supposed to be just friends."

He smiled. "I thought you were going to stop doing what you're supposed to do."

He had a point, but she hadn't intended on making that step with him. Thankfully, he left before she had to work too hard to come up with an answer.

Ten

At seven o'clock Wednesday night, Mia entered the Angel Heart Quilt Shop with her coloring book patterns and a bakery box filled with two dozen assorted cookies. Jeremy and Ashlyn had dropped the dessert off in the late afternoon. Jeremy had stopped in long enough to tell her that the music in the park had been a great idea, that they'd run into Kara, who had her two children and two nieces with her, one of whom was Ashlyn's age, and Ashlyn had actually left his side to sit next to the kids.

She was thrilled that the outing had turned out to be a positive experience, and she'd actually gotten a fair amount done while they were gone.

Tonight, however, she was not going to think about the rest of the work waiting at the house. She was excited to meet her aunt's friends.

"Mia?" Kara called with a welcoming wave. She came down the wide staircase at the side of the store. "I'm glad you got here a little early. Charlotte and Lauren are already here. The older crowd should be arriving soon."

"Is this the infamous quilt my aunt told me about?" Mia paused by the foot of the stairs to look at the glass display case on the wall. Inside was a colored, somewhat tattered quilt, each square lovingly sewn by a different person.

"Yes, it is." Kara came down the stairs to join her. "I'm sure she told you that the town was developed after a shipwreck off the coast. The survivors who made it to the bay each made a square in honor of the people who were lost, the angels watching over the bay. That's where the town got its name. While some people eventually left, a lot stayed right here, wanting to be close to their lost loved ones. I had ancestors on that ship, and you'll find out that a lot of the people in this town have bloodlines dating back to those survivors."

"It's really cool," she said, her love of history making her want to know more. "My aunt told me some stories when I was a teenager. Now, I wish I'd paid more attention."

"If you're really interested, you can go by the library. You'll find lots of books by local writers on the shipwreck and the legends, and the miracles that have occurred since then. But you'll have to leave that for another night. Come on up and meet my friends."

"I really appreciate you hosting this party," Mia said, as they climbed the stairs.

"I'm happy to do it. And I'm also happy to have a little break from my children and my nieces who are visiting for a few weeks."

"Jeremy told me he ran into you at the park."

"He did. I can't quite believe he's a father now. I never really saw him in that role, but he's good with Ashlyn, and she's rather challenging."

"She is."

"He told me a little about her history; I'm glad that he came home to raise her. He'll find a lot of support here."

She didn't think Jeremy considered Angel's Bay

home, but she let the comment pass. "Is your husband watching your kids? I thought he was part of the boys' night out at Murray's Bar."

"He is. My neighbor is watching all the kids. They're going to have a blast, so I don't feel in the least bit guilty."

As they entered the large multi-purpose room, Mia took a look around. There was a cozy seating area in one corner, with four loveseats surrounding a large rectangular table. The other side of the room had sewing machines set up on tables and what appeared to be a lot of quilting supplies. Three large circular tables filled the middle space and a long buffet table was set up against the wall with platters of food and bottles of wine and cans of soda.

Two women were chatting by that table, a pretty blonde and an attractive brunette. Both appeared to be in their late twenties, early thirties.

"This is Mia Callaway," Kara said, taking her over to the women. "This is my sister-in-law Lauren Murray and my good friend Charlotte Adams—I mean Charlotte Silveira," she added with a laugh. "It's not that I forget that you're married now—you're just always Charlotte Adams in my head."

"I know," the blonde said, extending her hand. "So lovely to meet you, Mia. Your aunt was a patient of mine. I'm an OB/GYN. She often brought me a trinket from one of her trips, but as pretty as those were, I enjoyed her stories even more."

"Your aunt also knew my father," Lauren interjected. "She was kind enough to visit him when he got Alzheimer's. He would spend a lot of time in my bakery, sipping tea at the table by the window, and she used to come in and chat with him. She'd remind him of the things he'd forgotten. He liked that. I was really sorry to hear of her passing. She was too young."

"She was," Mia agreed. "But she died having the time of her life, so what more can any of us ask for?" She set her box of baked goods on the table. "I think these came from your bakery, Lauren."

"I recognize the box, but I don't remember selling them to you."

"My neighbor and his little girl picked them up for me."

"Jeremy Holt," Lauren said with a nod. "That man has only gotten better with age."

"I'll say," Charlotte put in. "He's more handsome than ever and quite the hero. Kent told Joe that Jeremy saved his life."

"That wouldn't surprise me," Kara said. "Jeremy always stuck up for people."

"That's true," Lauren said. "He punched Randy Hawkins in the nose after he bullied a little kid in middle school. Jeremy didn't even care that he got detention for that. He said it was worth it."

Mia liked hearing stories about Jeremy, especially such positive ones. She thought he was a good guy, but it was nice to hear people who'd known him longer confirm that feeling.

"So you're living next door to him?" Lauren asked, a speculative gleam in her eyes. "Is he dating anyone?"

"I haven't seen any women around, but I've only been in town a short time."

"I doubt he'll lack for company," Charlotte put in.

"He seems more interested in just being a good father to his daughter," Kara said. "Although, he is going to Murray's tonight to shoot pool with the boys, so who knows what trouble they'll get into?"

"Joe said that Kent is trying to talk Jeremy into

joining the police force here. Joe is my husband," Charlotte added for Mia's benefit. "He's the chief of police."

"I can't imagine he'd find Angel's Bay exciting after what he's been doing," Lauren said.

"You never know—he might be ready for a change," Kara interjected. "Do you know his plans, Mia?"

"I only know that he said he has some decisions to make."

"What happened to his daughter's mother?' Lauren asked curiously.

"She was killed in a robbery. Jeremy didn't know about his daughter until after her death." She hoped she wasn't speaking out of turn, but she didn't want these women to think that Jeremy had neglected his child for the last eight years. "Ashlyn has some issues to work through."

"You've gotten pretty close to Jeremy and his daughter," Kara commented, a thoughtful gleam in her eyes.

"I don't want you to get the wrong idea; we're just neighbors," she said quickly, although the few kisses they'd shared had been more than neighborly.

"Are you single, Mia?" Charlotte asked. "Is there a boyfriend back home?"

"No boyfriend. I'm definitely single."

"Maybe not for long," Kara said with a teasing laugh. "If your neighbor has anything to say about it."

"You're bad," she said, shaking a finger at Kara's mischievous smile.

"Ignore her. She likes to matchmake more than just about anything else," Lauren said.

"I'm only here for a few weeks, so there's no time for matchmaking."

"It doesn't always take long," Kara said. "But let's open the wine and sit down."

"Already open," Charlotte said, pouring three glasses.

"You're not drinking?" Lauren asked as Charlotte passed the glasses to everyone else.

Charlotte smiled. "Not anymore. It wouldn't be good for the baby."

"What?" Lauren squealed.

"Are you serious?" Kara asked in shock.

Mia stepped back as Lauren and Kara took turns embracing Charlotte.

"I couldn't keep the secret any longer," Charlotte said. "I just passed the twelve-week mark, so things are looking good."

"I'm so glad," Kara said. "This is great. I cannot wait for my girls to have a little playmate."

"Is it a girl or a boy?" Lauren asked.

"I'm not saying," Charlotte replied. "Joe isn't sure he wants to know."

"But you know," Kara said.

"I do. Okay, it's a girl."

Mia laughed as Kara and Lauren squealed again. "Congratulations," she said.

"Thank you. I wasn't going to say anything, and we do not have to talk about this anymore. Tonight is about you."

"Please, it's fine," she said. "A baby on the way is always something to celebrate."

Charlotte nodded, her eyes beaming with happiness. "I wasn't sure it would happen for me. I had a bad miscarriage years ago when I was a teenager, and it scarred me both physically and emotionally, but sometimes miracles happen."

"Especially in this place," Kara said with a laugh.

"The angels are always listening." She paused as a group of women entered the room. "We'll talk about this later, Charlie."

"I'm not worried," Charlotte said. "Take Mia and introduce her to everyone. Lauren and I will host the bar."

For the next twenty minutes, Mia felt like she was in a receiving line. Her mind spun with introduction after introduction and she was truly touched by all the wonderful things that were said about her aunt. Carly had truly made a home for herself in Angel's Bay, a place where she was greatly loved by all.

Around seven thirty, Kara decided it was time to start the coloring book party. She asked Mia to explain what they were going to be doing.

"When I started going through my aunt's studio," Mia said, "I stumbled across an envelope of sketches that my aunt was putting together to compile a coloring book for adults, or several coloring books. The patterns are beautiful. There are jeweled peacocks and intricate wheels, wave patterns and ocean scenes, and lots of others. Kara thought it would be fun if I brought copies of the sketches, and we all colored."

"I have markers, colored pencils, and crayons," Kara added. "They're all on the tables. So let's gather round and try our hand at something other than quilting."

Mia sat down at the table next to Kara, her mother, and several other friends while Charlotte and Lauren each took one of the other tables. She could see how hard they were trying to make this a special night for her, and she was rather amazed by their efforts. She was a stranger to them, but they'd already made her feel like a friend.

With the wine flowing and the colored markers sliding across many a page, conversation also picked up. Mia found out a lot of gossip about people she didn't

know and heard many more stories about her aunt and a
certain gentleman in Angel's Bay, a doctor at the clinic,
who had been quite distraught by Carly's death. She could
only imagine how many other broken hearts her aunt had
left behind.

As she watched the women at her table color in
Carly's art sketches, she felt very close to her aunt, and
she really hoped that Carly was an angel, that she was
watching and smiling and appreciating that she'd left
something behind for everyone to enjoy. This was what
art was supposed to be, a way to creatively express
emotions and thoughts and even burn off some stress at
the same time. There was something quite cathartic about
coloring between the intricate lines.

She would turn these patterns into books the way
Carly had wanted, Mia promised herself. Then women the
world over could enjoy them as well.

"I'm going to get more wine from the back room,"
Kara told her.

"Do you want me to help you?"

"It's not a two-person job, I'll be right back."

As Kara got up, another woman slid into her chair.
She appeared to be in her forties with short, curly brown
hair that was tinged with gray at the temples and dark
eyes.

"I'm Rita Phelps," she said. "I'm an artist. I spent two
weeks in your aunt's studio last summer. It was an
amazing time for me."

"That's wonderful."

"Yes, I was able to free myself from the creative
block I'd been struggling with. I was having a career and a
personal crisis, having just gone through a bitter divorce. I
really think I was emotionally frozen, but your aunt and
the loan of her beautiful cottage changed everything for

me."

"I'm so glad. Did you leave a painting with my aunt when your stay was over?"

"Yes, it was one of my best paintings I'd ever done. I didn't want to leave your aunt anything but my best."

"I spoke to the Eckhart Gallery earlier today, and I'm thinking of putting together an exhibition of the paintings that were left to my aunt. Would you be all right with me showing your work?"

"Kara mentioned something about that," Rita said slowly. "I don't want to say no, but I'm a little unsure. It would depend on the quality of the other paintings. A lot of the people who used the cottage were amateurs working through personal problems, but I was a professional then, and I still am. I sell my art. I take great pride in it. I don't know that I want to be part of a show that doesn't reflect my standards."

"Well, I can tell you that most of the paintings are quite good, but I'd be happy to show you the entire group before they go up."

"I would like that." Rita hesitated, looking suddenly nervous. "This is kind of awkward, but would you consider returning my painting? I could probably get some good money for it, and it was for your aunt, not really for anyone else."

Mia had a feeling this was the real reason Rita was hesitant about the show. She wanted to sell her painting herself, not show it. She didn't quite know what to say. She hadn't expected any of the artists to ask for their work back. The art left to her aunt had been payment for a stay in the cottage.

"I'm not sure," she said slowly. "My aunt left everything to my mother. It's not really up to me. I'd have to discuss it with her."

"Would you do that? I'd appreciate it. I feel a little cheap for asking, but I'm an artist. It's not easy to make money on art."

"I understand."

Rita handed her a card. "Let me know as soon as you can."

"Of course."

She was relieved when Rita left and Kara returned.

"Everything okay?" Kara asked, giving her a curious look.

"My idea of exhibiting my aunt's collection of art is taking a few hits. Rita wants her painting back."

Kara frowned. "That's just wrong. It doesn't belong to her anymore. She gave it to Carly to pay for the studio time."

"I think that, too, but then maybe my aunt would want her to have her painting back. It's hard to know what to do. I wish she'd left instructions, but she didn't even have a will. She had a trust for the house and her bank accounts, but no other itemized list of what she wanted done."

"She was probably too young to think she needed that. What are you going to do?"

"I'll talk to my mom. She's the one who has to make the decision. I'm not going to worry about it tonight."

"You shouldn't." Kara paused. "The coloring patterns are a huge hit. I have to say I didn't think it would be that much fun, but it is."

"I agree. I'm going to find a way to make them into books."

"We could sell the books here in the store. I think we'd sell a ton."

"I'll look into how I can get them published. I think Aunt Carly would like me to finish them for her, although, I have to admit that my aunt was known for starting things and not finishing them. It used to drive my mother crazy. She liked to set goals and check items off a to-do list but Carly was always impulsively changing her mind."

"Who are you like—your mom or Carly?"

"I've been pretty good about staying on the right path, but I'm kind of in the mood for a detour."

"Sometimes side trips are exciting," Kara said with a sparkle in her eye. "You never know who you'll meet—maybe a really hot, single guy with a super cute daughter who just happens to live next door."

"Jeremy might be single, but I don't think he's available. He's caught up in a lot of emotional stuff right now."

"That won't be forever."

"I won't be here long enough to find out."

"Unless you stay on the detour."

"Unless I do that," she echoed, wondering if she could really not go back to the life she'd planned out for so many years.

———

A beer in his hand, his friends at his side, a loud bar with baseball games playing on three different screens, and Jeremy felt like his old self again.

"See, this is good, right?" Kent asked, sliding onto the bar stool next to him.

"It's not bad, I'll say that."

"I'm glad you came. My friends are on their way. And Barton is coming, too, but who knows when he'll get here."

"I saw him earlier. I'm sure he'll show up."

"Did he talk to you about getting back to Delta?"

"He knows that's a long shot. We didn't get into it."

"I know your heart is in the Army, Jeremy, but think about all the positives this town has to offer."

"Like my father?" he asked sarcastically.

"Forget about him. You'd never see him anyway."

"True."

"This is a good place to raise kids. And you have friends here—good friends. If you don't want to work on the force, we'll find something else for you."

"What else is there?" he asked with a shrug. "I'm a trained soldier. I don't know how to do anything else."

"Which is why you should be a police officer. You can do that job, and so what if it's not as exciting as what you're used to. Haven't you had enough heart-pounding, near-death experiences to make you want a little peace?"

"Some days I think so," he admitted. "But I'd miss the adrenaline rush."

Kent nodded, understanding in his eyes. "It took me awhile to get past that."

"How did you get past it?"

"A lot of sleepless nights and some really bad art."

"You should have called me."

"And whined about the fact that I couldn't sleep? I don't think so. I'm not a pansy ass."

"I wouldn't have thought that. You went through a lot, Kent. It's not at all surprising you'd have to deal with some fallout." Kent had been held hostage for twelve hours before they'd been able to rescue him, and Jeremy knew that he'd suffered a great deal during that time period. He still hated that it had taken them so long to get him out.

"Well, it's over now. I've made peace with my past, and I like living here. I get enough excitement on the job to suit my adrenaline needs, and the rest of the time I sleep well."

"Plus, there's a sexy doctor who gets your motor running," Jeremy said with a laugh.

"There is that," Kent agreed, clinking his glass to Jeremy's. "It's taken me over a year to get a date, though."

"She's making you wait."

"At first, she wouldn't date me because I was a patient, then I was too recent of a patient. Now, she's run out of excuses. I'm planning to see Eva this weekend."

"You and a shrink—not a bad combination."

Kent's face sobered. "I'm not sure about that. I wonder if part of Eva's resistance is based on what I talked to her about when I first came back here. It's not like we talk about what we've done with just anyone. I told her things I wouldn't tell a woman I wanted to date. Maybe it was too much, too heavy."

"I guess you'll find out." He completely understood what Kent was saying. It wasn't just that what they did was classified; it was that it was too painful, too horrible, to share with a civilian. It was easier to compartmentalize, lock those memories away where no one needed to go. It was how they survived. But sometimes, as in Kent's situation, the memories had to be unlocked in order to get past them. He didn't plan on going down that path. "Let's talk about something else. Why don't you buy me another beer?"

"You got it," Kent said, asking for another round from the bartender. "Speaking of beautiful women..."

"Don't go there," he warned.

"Mia is pretty, sexy and blonde, which means she fits all your requirements."

"She's my neighbor and a friend."

"Since when do you have friends who are that hot?"

"Since now," he said. "And I do look for a few more traits in a woman than the superficial ones you just mentioned. But all that aside, let's not forget I have a daughter who is my constant chaperone."

"So you're really not going to see what could happen with Mia?"

"She's leaving in a few weeks. I'm probably going to do the same. What's the point?"

"I don't know—how about a few weeks of great sex?"

"Do I need to mention my chaperone again?"

"That's what babysitters are for."

"Maybe in another life, but not the one I currently have…"

"You only get one life. You can't waste it. Seriously, Jeremy—"

He put up a hand. "No more serious talk. You promised me fun. That's why I came."

"Fine, sorry." He paused. "Here come the guys."

Jeremy stood up as Kent got up to introduce him to Joe Silveira, chief of police and two other officers, Colin Lynch and Jason Marlowe.

"We met earlier," Colin said, giving him a friendly grin. "At the music festival. That was fun, huh?"

"Ashlyn had a good time with your daughters and your nieces," he admitted.

"Let's grab a table," Kent said, and they headed across the room.

"Kent tells me you're in Delta," Joe said.

He sat down next to the chief. "I was. But I messed up my shoulder. My status is uncertain."

"Kent speaks very highly of you. If you're looking to change jobs, I'd be interested in talking further. We have an opening coming up this fall."

"I appreciate that. I'll definitely consider it."

"I hope so. We could use someone like you."

"Really? I never saw myself as a police officer."

"You're protecting a community, making the world a safer place. Isn't that what you've been doing in the Army?"

Joe had a point. "True."

"Angel's Bay has a way of clearing out the cobwebs and showing you what you really want," the chief added. He smiled. "Damn, I'm starting to sound like my wife."

"Charlotte was a good catch. I knew her growing up."

"Believe me, I am very aware of how lucky I am to have her in my life. She's something special."

"Hey, guys, a pool table opened up in the back," Jason said. "Let's go."

He'd just gotten up to follow the others across the bar when Barton came through the front door. As always, he moved quickly, almost as if someone were after him. Jeremy understood that. Walking slow in the places they'd been living in was one of the most dangerous things you could do.

"You made it," Barton said with an approving smile.

"Kent got a table in the back."

"Good, but do you have a second first?"

"I don't want to talk about coming back to Delta. It's not the right time."

"It's not about Delta. I've been approached by Jeff Kinsey to join his new private security firm."

"Seriously?" He was surprised that Barton would consider joining a private military contractor. "You hate those guys."

"Not Kinsey. He was a good soldier. I trust him to set up his company in the right way. Times are changing, Jeremy. We need more freedom to do what we need to do, and, frankly, I'd like more cash, too. We've risked our lives a thousand times, and what do we have to show for it?"

"How about the people we saved? We didn't join the Army for the money."

"No, we enlisted to get the hell out of here and see the world. Well, we did that. And maybe that was enough for the eighteen-year-old kid I was, but it's not enough now." He paused. "I want you to talk to Kinsey with me. He has offices in LA. At least drive down and hear what he has to say."

"I'm not ready to make any career decisions."

"You're not leaning toward staying here and working with Kent, are you?" he asked with a frown.

"I just told you I'm not making any decisions right now. I had to get Ashlyn out of San Francisco, and Kent found me a rental, so I came. That's why I'm here. And I'm staying because right now it's good for Ashlyn to be in a safe environment."

"Sure, this is a great town to spend the summer but not your life. There's a reason we all left, and your reason is still here."

"My father wasn't the only reason I left town."

"He was part of that decision."

"Look, I'll consider your suggestion, but right now I just want to have a good time. Let's shoot some pool, drink some beer, and not think about tomorrow."

"Now that sounds like the old Jeremy," Barton said with an approving nod.

"For tonight anyway."

Eleven

Jeremy left Murray's a little after ten feeling pleasantly buzzed and happy he'd decided to leave his car at the house and take a cab to and from the bar. The taxi dropped him off in front of his house. He started to move toward the front door, then hesitated, seeing the light on in Mia's backyard. He'd told Mrs. Danbury he wouldn't be back for another hour, and she'd told him any time before midnight was good with her, so he had a little time to kill.

He'd just check on Mia, he told himself. See how her night with the women went. Ashlyn would already be asleep. There was no reason not to stop by Mia's house.

Well, there was a reason—he just chose not to listen to the warning voice in his head that told him he was playing with fire.

When he walked into Mia's backyard, he was surprised to see her standing in the middle of the yard. She was facing the ocean, an easel set up before her, a set of paints on a stool next to her. She stroked her brush against the canvas as the dim light from the patio and the moonlight guided her way.

God she was pretty, he thought, her floral sundress swirling around her legs, her blonde hair tumbling past her shoulders, her feet once again bare. The woman never seemed to have shoes on.

A rush of longing ran through him as the breeze blew her dress around her body, showing off her curves. He wanted to touch her, kiss her, lay her down on the grass and make love to her in the moonlight.

He couldn't do any of those things.

Could he?

She suddenly started, whirling around.

"It's okay, it's just me," he said, moving out of the shadows.

She put a hand to her heart. "Jeremy. You scared me."

"What are you doing?"

"I'm painting."

There was a look of joy and pride on her face that he didn't completely understand. "I can see that, but it's late, and it's kind of dark."

"I know. I just couldn't wait until the morning. The coloring book party inspired me. It brought back my love of creating art. When I came home, I felt restless. I needed to do something, so I decided to paint."

He moved forward, seeing the splash of blues, the shadow of trees, and a bright moon on her canvas. She'd painted the scene in front of her and it wasn't bad. He could see where she was going with it. "I like it."

"It's not very well done. I've gotten rusty. I haven't painted in years."

"Then it's a good start."

"It certainly felt good. As soon as I put the paintbrush against the canvas, I felt like something unlocked inside me. It was like I'd been a bird in a cage and suddenly someone opened the door and told me to fly. I was uncertain at first and then I decided to trust in my instincts, believe in myself."

"And you flew," he said with a smile, seeing the happy glow in her eyes.

"I love painting. I used to do this with my aunt when I came to visit in the summers. I have such wonderful memories of those days. But after the summer, I'd go home and go back to school and my parents would remind me that painting is a hobby, not a job, at least for most people. As I got older, I didn't have time to come here. It was all about college and grad school and finding that perfect job. Look how great that turned out."

"Sometimes you have to get far enough down the road to know if you're lost."

"That's true. I don't know what I'm going to do for a career, but there has to be some part of it that I love. I know it's unrealistic to think I'll love all of it, but there has to be something. My job can't just be about making a living."

"That's a good goal. How was your party tonight?"

"It was amazing. The coloring books were a huge hit. I had many great conversations with my aunt's friends, who all spoke so warmly of her. It was really touching. Kara and Charlotte and Lauren were super nice. They have such a great friendship. I feel like they'll be friends when they're in their nineties."

"Well, they have a long way to go."

"What about you? How was boys' night out?"

"Maybe a little too much fun," he admitted. "It was good to shoot pool, drink beer, and just be around men. My house has been pretty girly lately."

She laughed. "That's what happens when you're a single dad of a beautiful little girl. It was good you got out for a while. You have to take time for yourself."

"I agree. When the cab dropped me off, I wasn't

ready to go inside. I saw your light on back here, and I couldn't stop myself from coming to see you."

"It's a beautiful night to be outside," she said lightly, but he could see her beginning to tense.

"You're what's beautiful," he told her. "Do you know how pretty you are in the moonlight?"

"I've always thought I looked better in the shadows."

"You don't see yourself the way I see you, Mia."

"Okay, I think a better question to ask might be how many drinks have you had?"

He moved closer to her, putting his hands on her waist, so she couldn't run away from him, not that she seemed that interested in running. "I've had a few drinks but not so many that I don't know what I'm saying or what I'm doing."

"And what are you doing?"

"I'm thinking about kissing you—maybe more. What are you thinking?"

"That we shouldn't kiss or…anything more," she said softly.

"I told you, Mia, that I don't like that word *shouldn't*. Didn't you just say tonight that you'd unlocked something inside you? The cage is open. The bird is free to fly."

"Not into your arms."

"Why not into my arms?" he challenged.

She took a breath, determination in her gaze. "I don't want to be with you, Jeremy."

He didn't believe that for a second. "Yes, you do. You can say no, but don't lie to me, Mia. We've been honest with each other since we met. Let's keep it that way."

She stared back at him, and the truth was in her eyes. "All right. I was lying. I'm tempted," she admitted. "I like you, and there's an undeniable attraction between us, but I don't want to make another mistake. I don't want to move too fast."

"Did moving slowly make your ex any less of a mistake? Didn't you say you spent weeks getting to know him and he was still able to deceive you?"

"You're right. It wasn't the speed that made things go wrong."

"It was the lies. But we're not lying to each other. We're not making promises we can't keep. We're just living in the moment. Isn't that what you came to Angel's Bay to do? Be more like your aunt?"

She let out a sigh. "You are very persuasive, Jeremy Holt."

"I want you," he said simply.

"And you always get what you want?"

"Usually."

"You can't tell me that you don't think us being together wouldn't complicate things."

"Maybe I don't care."

"Oh, Jeremy, you're going to kill me," she said, giving him a helpless shake of her head. "It's hard enough to fight myself; I don't know if I can beat you, too."

"I don't want to kill you. I have other, more pleasurable activities in mind. All you have to do is say yes, Mia. One simple word."

"It's so *not* simple," she breathed, as he leaned over and took the kiss he'd been dreaming about all day.

Despite her previous words of rejection, Mia opened her mouth to his and let him take the kiss to a deeper level. Her hands slipped under his shirt and moved up his back, and her fingers on his skin brought more heat between them. His body hardened, and he wanted her hands all over him.

He pulled her closer, moved his head one way, then

another, wanting, needing each taste, each kiss, to be better than the last. And Mia went along with him, all objections gone, nothing but desire raging between them.

She tugged at the hem of his shirt, and he fulfilled her need by pulling his shirt up and over his head and tossing it on the grass.

"Jeremy," she murmured, her gaze sweeping his broad chest as her hands came to rest on his shoulders.

"Like what you see?"

"Most of it, but not this..." She traced the long scar on his left shoulder, then her hand slipped down his chest to his abdomen where another raised scar ran below his rib cage. "Or this."

"They don't hurt anymore."

"Really? Not even deep inside?"

He met her questioning gaze, knowing that what he'd said recently was true; he couldn't lie to Mia, and he didn't want to. Even if he tried, she wouldn't believe him. Mia had an eye for detail. She always saw past his barriers to the man inside, the man he let few people see.

"Down deep—maybe," he conceded. "If you kiss them, I'll feel better."

Her bright smile made him blink. It was like a moonbeam hitting him in the face.

"I walked right into that, didn't I?" she asked.

"You did."

"Okay." She pressed her mouth to his shoulder and then lowered her head to trace a wet path along the scar at the bottom of his rib cage.

His jeans grew uncomfortably tight as he thought about where else he wanted her mouth to go. But he didn't want this night to be just about him. He grabbed her arms and pulled her up against him. "You still haven't said the word."

The heat between them practically sizzled in the summer night.

"If I didn't know better..." she said.

"What?" His pulse leapt at the possibility that she was going to say no.

"I'd say yes."

His breath caught in his chest. "But..."

She shook her head. "You're making this hard."

"You're making me hard."

Her tongue darted out to wet her lips. "I don't know what to say."

"I'm not looking for conversation. If you want me to go, tell me to go."

She hesitated for a long, tense minute. "Do you have anything—protection, because I wasn't planning on you or this..."

His heart jumped. He pulled a condom out of the pocket of his jeans. He'd put it there earlier, an old habit from whenever he headed out for a night with the guys, not that he'd actually thought he was going to use it.

"So you were planning..." she said.

"I was dreaming," he corrected. "And hoping." He paused. "But you still have to say the word, Mia. I'm not talking you into anything."

"Aren't you?" she asked with a helpless smile. "If it makes you feel better...yes."

His pulse leapt. "Are you sure? I thought you knew better."

"I thought so, too."

She reached for her back zipper, unzipped it and then stepped out of her dress. The material fell next to his shirt, and he watched in amazement and appreciation as she unhooked her bra and slid her panties down over her beautiful legs.

"Is this real?" he asked, feeling a little dazed.

She took his hand and put it on her breast. "Do I feel real?"

"You feel amazing," he said, his thumb caressing her nipple into a tight peak that was followed by a slight gasp of air coming through her parted lips.

He lowered his head and put his lips to one soft, full breast and then the other. Then he stripped off his jeans and pulled her down to the grass.

The cool ground quickly heated as they moved together. There were no more words. They spoke with their hands and their lips, as they let go of everything— except each other.

———

Mia lay on her side, her head resting on Jeremy's incredibly solid chest, her arm laying across his flat, muscled abs, her leg holding his to the ground. Above them, the moon shined bright, and the only sounds she could hear were the crashing ocean waves and Jeremy's heartbeat.

She felt sated and incredibly content, her body still tingling from Jeremy's touch.

If this was a mistake, at least it had been a good one. She would never forget this night. The painting she'd done had unlocked her heart, but Jeremy had made her fly.

What she *should* do, what she *should* think, had fallen to the wayside. Instead of listening to her brain, she'd paid attention to her body and her heart, and she might have just had the best night of her life.

Whatever happened next, she would have no regrets, she promised herself. She wouldn't let herself look back and judge what she'd done. Life was about living, not always trying to do the right thing.

As she looked up at the stars in the sky, she had a feeling that her aunt would have approved of her impulsive behavior. She smiled at that thought.

Jeremy shifted beneath her, and she lifted her head. "Am I weighing you down?"

He gave her a lazy, happy smile. "Not at all. You look happy, Mia."

"You might have to give yourself a little credit for that."

"Only a little?"

She laughed. "Okay, a lot."

"No, it wasn't me; it was all you—beautiful, gorgeous you. Your eyes are so amazing. They're like the sea. The colors change from light blue to dark blue to mysterious blue. And your mouth is so soft, so sexy. Damn, you're hot."

She laughed, flattered by not only his words but by the look in his eyes. "You're not so bad yourself." She pressed her fingers against his abs. "These muscles make me feel like I should get to the gym."

"I like you just the way you are," he said, running his finger down her cheek. "You never have to be anyone but yourself with me."

His words made her heart tighten. It felt like the first time she'd ever been with a man who saw her—the real her, which seemed a little crazy because she and Jeremy barely knew each other and yet she felt incredibly close to him. "The same goes for you," she murmured.

"We're good together."

"It did feel a little magical."

"I agree. You've put a spell on me."

"Or you've put a spell on me. I've never actually made love on the grass before."

"The bedroom wasn't even a thought. Too far away."

"So true. It's such a warm night. I don't even need clothes."

He laughed. "I like you without clothes."

She smiled down at him. "I'm not usually this uninhibited."

"You should be. You wear it well." He paused and let out a little sigh. "I really don't want to go home, but..." He raised his arm so he could look at his watch, then he groaned. "It's almost midnight. I told Mrs. Danbury I'd be back by twelve. I'm afraid I need to go."

"Then you should go." Reminded that reality was not as magical as the past few hours had been, she sat up and reached for her dress, pulling it over her head.

He grabbed his jeans and shirt and put them on. "I'd ask you to come over and spend the night with me, but I don't know if it would confuse Ashlyn."

"I understand," she said, not quite sure how to handle the sudden change in mood. Sometimes waking up from a dream took a moment.

He paused, a frown on his lips. "*Do* you understand? I feel like something just changed."

She saw the concern in his eyes and had to take it away. "Nothing changed. It's fine. We had a good time. We'll talk tomorrow."

"We *will* talk tomorrow," he promised, giving her a hard kiss, as if he needed her to feel him one last time.

Her lips burned as he walked out of the yard. If he thought she was in any danger of forgetting his kiss, he was very wrong. She blew out a breath, picked up her underwear, and headed into the house. It was a lot of fun to live in the moment. Unfortunately, the moment had passed, and she was back to real life.

Twelve

Mia didn't know when she'd expected to see Jeremy again, but it hadn't been at nine o'clock Thursday morning when she was tired, cranky, and needed a shower.

She hadn't slept well, a never-ending parade of images floating through her head, most of them amazingly good reminders of being with Jeremy. But the fact that she was sleeping alone and had no idea if there would ever be a repeat of those amazing images hadn't put her in the best of moods.

"Good morning, beautiful," he said with a smile.

She frowned. "It's too early for beautiful." She pulled her robe around her boxer short bottoms and clingy tank top.

He raised an eyebrow. "You're not a morning person? I thought you were pretty happy yesterday when I brought pancakes over."

"Well, that was later in the day, and I don't see any pancakes," she grumbled.

He leaned forward and stole a kiss. "I missed you, too, babe."

"I did not say I missed you."

"But you did." He gave her a pointed look.

"Maybe," she conceded, because his kiss had definitely brightened her day. "And I usually like mornings, but I didn't sleep well."

"Thinking about me?"

She had to smile at his cocky question. "Not at all. I have a lot of other things on my mind. So, what are you doing here? Where's Ashlyn?"

"She's at the house. She didn't have the greatest night, either."

His words distracted her from her own mood. "Really? What was wrong?"

"She has nightmares. I don't know if she's reliving what she saw the evening her mom was killed or what. Some nights seem to be worse than others. I try to comfort her, but she usually pushes me away. It's hard to watch her in so much pain and not be able to help."

"I'm sorry. Is there anything I can do?"

"I know you're busy with this house, but I wanted to do something fun with Ashlyn today, and, frankly, I think she'd enjoy it more if you were with us. I was thinking of taking her down to the beach. There's a sand castle competition starting at eleven. It's a pretty big event in Angel's Bay. I think the three of us could build an awesome castle."

"That sounds fun, but maybe it would be better if you and Ashlyn went on your own."

His brows knit together as he studied her face. "Are you saying no because of last night? Because we got too close, and now you need to push me away?"

Damn. Was he a mind reader?

"That's not it." She could see by the look in his eyes he didn't believe her. "Maybe that's a little bit it, but I also have a lot of work to finish around here."

"Ashlyn and I will help you clean stuff out this

afternoon. You said you wanted to enjoy a little summer in Angel's Bay. Have you even been to the beach yet?"

"No, I haven't."

"Then you need to say yes." He gave her a smile that made refusing him pretty near impossible.

His words also reminded her that she'd already said *yes* last night.

But who was she kidding? Of course she wanted to go to the beach with him and Ashlyn. "Yes."

"Good. We'll leave in an hour."

"Do you want me to bring some lunch?"

"No, just bring yourself. We'll stop at the deli and pick up some food on the way to the beach." He paused, stepping forward in a deliberate way. "Now, that we've settled that..." He kissed her with a tender intimacy that took her right back to the night before.

She sighed a little as he lifted his head. "You're addicting, Jeremy."

"Right back at you."

"But this—whatever this is—it's just a summer fling. We both know that." She felt like it was important to state that reminder out loud, so neither of them would forget, especially her.

"Do we need to put a label on it?" he challenged. "Do we need an end date?"

"I just want to make sure we're on the same page, that one of us doesn't have the wrong expectation." Again, she was talking mostly about herself, because Jeremy seemed to be fine with the way things were, but she was being a girl and already feeling far too much of an emotional attachment to him. It was just sex, a fling, a moment in time, she told herself. It didn't have to be more, and it really *shouldn't* be more.

"It's going to be fine, Mia. We're in sync, in all the

ways that matter." His sparkling smile was followed by another hot kiss. "See you soon."

She closed the door behind him and found herself smiling all the way up the stairs. Jeremy Holt had a charming side, and she was definitely charmed.

—➤◄—

Angel's Bay boasted several beaches, but today's event was being held on the main beach by the harbor. Jeremy knew from experience that the summer sand castle building competitions were a popular event in town. It didn't matter that it was a Thursday morning; there would be plenty of people happy to take a day off on this warm summer day.

As he'd predicted, the parking lot was almost full by the time they arrived, and they were lucky to get one of the last few spots.

They got out of the car, taking a moment to gather together a cooler, a large tote bag filled with shovels and pails, another overflowing with beach towels, and then the grocery bags packed with food that they'd gotten at the deli.

He swung the heavier bags over his good shoulder while Mia took the food and Ashlyn volunteered to carry two extra towels.

"I never realized that when you get a child, you also acquire a lot more stuff," he told Mia as they walked toward the beach.

She smiled back at him. "I have a feeling you used to travel light before this."

"Very light," he agreed, happy to see her earlier tension had evaporated. "What about you?"

"I haven't traveled much at all. With six kids, family

vacations were usually within driving distance: Los
Angeles, San Diego, Lake Tahoe, Russian River, those
kinds of places. I did go to New York with a college
roommate one year and spent two weeks in Paris during
grad school. I've also been to two bachelorette parties in
Las Vegas, but that's about the extent of my travels. That's
why I had to live vicariously through Aunt Carly."

"There's still time to see the world."

"I'll get to it. What about you? Are there any places
you haven't seen yet?"

"Many places. I haven't spent much time in Italy
outside of Rome, and I've never been to Ireland or
Scotland. I'd also love to bike through the French
countryside, maybe do a wine tour."

"That sounds like fun."

"Maybe we can go together. It seems a crime that an
expert in art history hasn't been to all the amazing
museums in Europe."

"I would love to spend a few months in Italy, travel
through Spain, hop over to Greece and eventually make
my way to Russia."

"Maybe you should travel before you get your next
job."

"There's a little thing called money stopping me from
that," she said.

"Is it just the money that's stopping you, or the idea
that traveling seems too frivolous for a practical woman
like yourself?"

"You're getting to know me a little too well."

"And you didn't answer my question."

"Probably both. So where do you want to set up?" she
asked, changing the subject.

"Close to the water, if we can find a spot."

"It's so crowded. I had no idea this many people

would be here. I didn't expect live music," she added, tipping her head to the small stage where two guitar players and a drummer were warming up. "Or trophies. This is serious."

"It is serious," he said, noting the table next to the stage filled with trophies and ribbons. "I hope your creative artistic side is ready to come out to play. We need to help Ashlyn make this castle better than any of the others."

She raised an eyebrow. "Are we seriously competing?"

"Of course. It's a competition. If we enter, we're going to try to win. Otherwise, why play?"

"Just for the enjoyment, the pleasure of the activity?" she suggested.

"You can have the pleasure of building a sand castle any time. This is a contest."

"Got it. We're going for the gold."

"Absolutely."

"Let's go over there." She led them down the beach another thirty feet.

They spread out a blanket and put the cooler and bag of groceries on top of it. Jeremy dumped the beach tools into the sand and tossed the towels on top of the blanket.

"I brought some sunscreen," Mia said, kicking off her flip-flops. "Did you put any on Ashlyn?"

"Not yet."

"Ash, let me put this on you," Mia said to the little girl, who had already stripped down to her two-piece pink and white bathing suit. Mia knelt down on the blanket and lathered Ashlyn up. When she was done with his daughter, she looked up at him. "Do you need some?"

"Absolutely," he said, relishing the idea of her hands on him.

She smiled at his enthusiastic response. "Maybe just your back. You can do the rest yourself."

"Fine." He pulled his T-shirt over his head and tossed it on the blanket. He liked the way Mia's gaze ran across his bare chest with a gleam of hunger in her blue eyes. The way she was looking at him now reminded him of the way she'd looked at him last night, just before they'd gotten naked and made each other crazy.

Mia cleared her throat. "Turn around."

He obediently turned, mostly because he needed to get his own reactions under control. They were on the beach surrounded by people, and one of those was his daughter. Despite the fact that he was looking away from her, Mia's hands on his back did amazing things to his body and he was almost happy when the painful but pleasurable massage was over.

"Thanks," he said, turning back to her. "What about you?"

"I'm good. I already put some on."

"Let me know if you need more. I'm here for you."

"You're in a good mood," she said with a smile.

He was in a good mood. He felt better than he had in months and that had everything to do with the beautiful blonde by his side. All of his problems, his nagging pain, disappeared under her warm gaze. A cautionary voice in his head urged him to slow down on the feelings, but it was probably too late to send that train back to the station. He already liked Mia more than he probably should. But he wasn't going to worry about anything today.

"Let's talk about our castle," he said. "I think we should go big and detailed at the same time. While the judges like the showy stuff, what they like even more are all the little things, like panes in the castle windows."

She raised an eyebrow. "How on earth would we

make paned windows with sand?"

"You pack the wet sand in really tight and then use the point of your finger to make a small square. I'll show you."

"You're going to do more than show me; you're going to actually do it."

He laughed. "Okay, but you'll still need to help with the turrets and of course the moat."

"Turrets and a moat?"

"It's a castle, Mia. You've seen those, haven't you?"

"I think you're a little ambitious."

"Go big or go home."

She laughed. "All right. I'm in. Ashlyn, are you ready to build the biggest and best castle this beach has ever seen?"

Ashlyn gave a vigorous nod.

"Great," he said, happy to have his team excited and enthusiastic. He looked at his daughter. "Have you ever built a sand castle before?"

She shook her head.

He was happy that this was something he could do with her that she'd never done with her mother. "Well, you are going to love this," he promised. "We can't officially start for another ten minutes, but why don't you get your feet wet and fill up a couple of buckets and we'll figure out the best place to build our castle."

As Ashlyn moved toward the water, he saw Colin and Kara approaching with their two daughters and the two nieces they'd had at the park the day before.

"Hey," Kara said with a wave as they came over. "I didn't know you guys were going to be here. Colin, this is Mia Callaway, Carly's niece."

"Nice to finally meet you, Mia," Colin said with a cheerful grin. "I hear you've hooked my wife on coloring

books. I can't say I'm unhappy about that. Now she can
color with the girls. They laugh at me when I try; I have
trouble staying between the lines."

"The coloring books for grown-ups are fun," Mia
replied. "And who are these darling girls?"

"The redheads are mine," Kara said. "The three-year-
old is Faith and the almost fifteen-month-old is Becca.
The blondes are my two nieces, Jeanette and Melody,
nine and seven respectively."

"Hi girls," Mia said.

"Let's set up right here," Kara told Colin. "Then the
girls can all play together. Ashlyn and Melody hit it off
yesterday."

"Sounds good," Mia said.

"We'll sit next to you, Kara," Jeremy interrupted.
"But you guys are building your own castle."

Kara laughed. "Fine. I forgot you take castle building
seriously." She looked at Mia. "Did you know Jeremy
won this competition like five times when we were kids?"

"I did not know that," Mia said, giving him a pointed
look. "No wonder you said you wanted to win."

"I think it was six times that I won," he said. "I grew
up here. There wasn't a lot to do."

"I grew up here, too," Kara said. "But I never looked
at sand castle building like it was an Olympic sport, but
then Jeremy was always an overachiever."

"I think I can give Jeremy a run for his money," Colin
said, stripping off his shirt. "Let's do this thing."

"You're on," he told him.

Colin laughed. "May the best man win."

"We already know who that will be," Jeremy replied.

"We'll see."

A shrill whistle ended their conversation. A man
stepped up to the microphone on the stage. He announced

the rules of the competition, encouraged good sportsmanship, and started the sixty-minute sprint toward the perfect sand castle.

Jeremy waved Ashlyn over, and Mia joined them at the water's edge, while Colin and his family started digging next to them.

For the next hour, he dug holes, built walls, molded sand together and encouraged Ashlyn and Mia in their efforts. While there was a part of him that still wanted to win, because he could never turn off his instinct to be the best, he did try to make sure that Ashlyn and Mia were having fun.

And clearly they were, because Mia played like a kid in the sand, splashing water on her and Ashlyn, getting mud in her hair and on her face and not caring one little bit about her appearance.

When the whistle blew at the end of an hour, they all sat down on the sand, tired and dirty, but with a pretty good-looking castle. It wasn't the best he'd ever built, and looking down the beach, he had a feeling they'd be lucky to get a ribbon, but he felt more satisfied than he ever had in the past, because he'd seen actual smiles on his daughter's face, and even the occasional word had tumbled out of her mouth when she forgot to be silent and sad. That was the best prize he could have asked for.

"Not bad," Colin said, coming over to them. "But you didn't have a 15-month-old trying to smash everything down as soon as you put it up."

"Very true," he said with a laugh as he watched Kara hold her toddler back from making another destructive pass through the castle.

Colin went over, grabbed the little girl and swung her high up in his arms. "We're going to look for some seashells," he said as they headed down the beach.

"Mommy, I have to go to the bathroom," Faith told Kara.

"Okay." She looked at Jeremy. "Can you guys watch Melody and Jeanette for a few minutes?"

"Sure," Jeremy said. "They're having a great time with Ashlyn."

Since the contest had ended, the girls were jumping in and out of the water, squealing every time it hit their calves. Fortunately, this part of the beach was very protected, so the waves were quite far away.

"I wonder if Ashlyn knows how to swim," he murmured. "There's so much I don't know about her."

"You'll figure it out," Mia said. "And you could always ask her. She's starting to talk more."

"Mostly to you or the other kids, but I know that's a start, and I shouldn't complain."

"She'll get to you, Jeremy."

He wanted to believe that. He stood up as the judges made their way down the beach. They paused by Colin's castle, made some notes, and then moved on to their masterpiece. He thought their castle got a few approving nods, but it was difficult to say.

When they left, he sat back down next to Kara. "I don't think I'll continue my winning streak."

"Ashlyn and I held you back."

"No, you didn't do that," he said, giving her a warm smile. "You made sand castle building the most fun I've had in a long time."

"It was fun." She pushed the strands of hair escaping from her ponytail behind her ears.

He smiled at the muddy streak going across her cheek. "You do know you have mud on your face."

"I think I have mud everywhere. I'm going to rinse off in the ocean." She pulled her tank top over her head, revealing a sexy red polka-dot bikini top.

His mouth began to water at the sight of her beautiful breasts filling those cups. Mia then stood up and slid her short shorts off her hips, and his heart started pounding against his chest.

She flung him a look. "Are you coming with me?"

She didn't wait for an answer, but started walking down to the water's edge.

He quickly followed, because he had no thought whatsoever of refusing. In fact, he was probably going anywhere she wanted to go.

He caught up with her when the water hit her waist and she jumped a little at the cold. The weather might be warm, but on this part of the coast, the ocean was always chilly.

"It will get better if you just dunk," he told her as she jumped up every time the ripples raised the water higher on her chest.

"Or it will get colder."

"You're not one of those girls who can't get her hair wet, are you?"

"Do I look like one of those girls?"

He laughed. "I guess not. Let's do it together." He held out his hand. "On the count of three, we both go under."

"We're supposed to be watching the girls," she said, looking back over her shoulder.

"They're sitting on the blanket now, raiding the cooler. They'll be fine for one dunk."

She put her hand into his. "Okay, one-two—"

He pulled her under before she could get the last number out. She came back up, spluttering and wiping the water out of her eyes. "I didn't say three."

"I was afraid you'd chicken out."

"If I say I'm going to do something, I don't chicken out."

"My mistake."

"You have to trust me, Jeremy."

"I do trust you," he said, answering in a more serious tone than her playful comment required, but he wanted her to know that he meant it.

Her gaze changed as it clung to his—many mixed and turbulent emotions moving between them and around them.

Why hadn't he met her at another time, another place? Why did it have to be now when everything else was up in the air, when he was a father with a kid who needed to be his first priority, when he didn't have the job that he loved and wasn't sure what the hell he would do with the rest of his life?

"We should go back to the shore," he said. He needed to get out before he got too deep, and he wasn't talking about the ocean.

"In one second," she said, reaching for his hand again. "There's something I need to say."

"What's that?" he asked warily.

"Three," she yelled, and then jumped on him, shoving his head under the water.

She was on her way to the beach when he came back up for air. "You better run," he said, as she sent him a laughing look.

"I owed you for that."

"What happened to trust?"

"Apparently, it doesn't extend to dunking each other in the ocean."

He couldn't refute that statement. By the time he got back to the blanket, Colin and Kara were back, Mia had a towel wrapped around her hips, and the kids all wanted to eat lunch. It was time to put on his dad hat. Flirtatious games with Mia would have to wait for another time.

The next few hours were filled with family-friendly fun. After lunch, they threw around a football on the beach. He also managed to coax Ashlyn farther into the water. In fact, she got brave enough to put her hand into his, and when the water hit her hips, she actually held her arms up to him, and he'd picked her up.

She'd been happy enough to stay in his arms while he went a little deeper, and he'd found himself reluctant to leave the water, not wanting the closest connection he'd ever had to her disappear.

But eventually they'd made it back to the beach.

More people from his past came by. He was surprised at how many of the kids he'd grown up with had either stayed in Angel's Bay or had come back after college. He'd always thought anyone who stayed in Angel's Bay was an unambitious loser, but that wasn't true. It wasn't the town that defined them; it was who they were.

Maybe it was time he figured out who he was, because he sure as hell didn't feel much like a soldier anymore. He'd just never imagined leaving the Army, leaving his family.

But as he looked around the beach, a picture began to take shape in his mind.

Perhaps there was another kind of family in his future...

Thirteen

—➤≫◄◄◄—

"Are you sad that our castle came in seventh place?"
Mia asked, as they drove home from the beach a little
after three.

Jeremy had been quiet since they'd left the beach. She
didn't know what was on his mind, but he'd certainly been
thinking a lot about something.

"Not at all. I'm proud of our castle." He flung a look
into the backseat, and then gave Mia a smile. "Ashlyn is
already asleep."

"I'm not surprised. It's been a fun and exhausting day.
I had a great time, Jeremy. Thanks for inviting me."

"Thanks for coming. It was more fun than I
expected."

"This town is starting to grow on you again. You
have more friends here than you realized. And you're
remembering the good times, not just the bad."

"That's true."

"Does your father still live in the house you grew up
in?"

"No, he sold that place after I graduated from high
school. He has an apartment by the harbor. I don't know
what he did with all the furniture. He probably sold it. He

was never much for material things."

"Take me by your old house," she said impulsively. "I want to see where you grew up."

"Really?" he asked doubtfully.

"Yes. When was the last time you went by your childhood home?"

"Ten years ago. It was on my first trip back. It felt strange, surreal. I almost couldn't remember living there. So much had changed. Or maybe I was the one who had changed."

"Have you seen your father over the years? Did you spend holidays together?"

"Not after the first two years when we shared a couple of awkward Thanksgiving and Christmas dinners at Dina's Café. After that, if I came home, I spent my time with Kent or Barton and their families, but most of the time I just didn't come home."

"Where did you go then?"

"Sometimes I was deployed during the holidays. Or I'd hang with one of my buddies somewhere or just stay at whatever post I was at."

"It sounds like there might have been some lonely days."

"Not really. I was never lonelier than when I was living here with my dad. That was the worst." He paused at a stoplight and gave her a dry smile. "This can't possibly be interesting."

It was interesting because she was interested in him. "I like learning about your life. It helps me understand you better."

"Knowing my past hasn't helped me understand myself," he said dryly. "Glad it's working out better for you."

"Perhaps I'm more intuitive."

"There's a good possibility of that."

"Or you're just too close to your own life to see it in its true light."

"Could be."

The light turned green, and he drove another half-mile, then pulled up in front of a modest one-story house at the end of a quiet block. "This is the place."

"Was the basketball hoop over the garage yours?" she asked.

He nodded. "I shot at least a million baskets while I was growing up. That was my favorite place to be at night. I'd stay out there until long after the sun had set, hoping that when I went inside my father would already be asleep. Most of the time he was. If he wasn't, he could be a mean bastard. Alcohol might have made him happy, but everyone around him was made very unhappy."

"Have you ever had it out with him? A no-holds-barred, hard-truth kind of conversation?"

"No. I haven't felt the need."

"Really? It seems like there's so much unfinished business between you. The other day when he came into the café, the air was so tense. It was like you both had things you wanted to say, but you didn't know where to start."

"I tried to talk to him when I first came here. I told you how that turned out."

"Maybe you should make another attempt."

"Why?"

"Because he's your father."

"So what?" Jeremy shook his head. "I know you're an optimist, Mia, and that's a nice trait, but I don't believe people change just because you want them to. They are who they are. And I learned what family was all about when I got into the Army. It's the people who stand by you and stand up for you that matter."

"I get that, but I do believe people can change, not because you want them to, but because they want to."

"My father doesn't want to."

"He might when he realizes he's not just missing an opportunity to be part of your life but also Ashlyn's life."

"I can't let him mess up her life the way he did mine. And she's frightened of everything. His loud voice would probably set her back."

"That will change. She's getting better."

"Well, I'm not going to deal with him right now, and I think we've seen enough of the old homestead." He put the car into drive. "Let's go home."

A few minutes later, he parked in the driveway.

"Do you need any help getting Ashlyn into the house?" she asked.

"No. I'll carry her inside and then come out and unload the rest of the stuff." He paused. "I know I promised that Ash and I would help you with cleanup, so as soon as she's had a nap, we'll come over."

"It's fine. Don't worry about it. There's always tomorrow."

"A deal is a deal. Besides, I don't know if I can go the rest of the night without seeing you."

She shook her head in bemusement. "How is it you're still single when you know just the right thing to say?"

"It's not a line, Mia. I'm speaking from the heart." His eyes turned serious. "You're amazing. I've never met anyone like you."

Her heart skipped a beat at his warm gaze. "Thank you. Anyway, I'm going to go. You know where I'll be."

"Okay, one second." He cast a quick glance toward the backseat, and then turned his gaze back to hers. "One kiss?"

She leaned over and kissed his mouth, wishing for far more than the quick, teasing taste of him. Then she got out of the car and quietly closed the door while Jeremy took his sleepy daughter into his arms and carried her into the house.

She smiled as she watched them go, thinking that in sleep Ashlyn was more than happy to put her arms around Jeremy's neck. She was slowly coming to trust him. That trust would only get stronger.

She opened her door and walked inside. As she paused by the hall mirror to set down her keys, she saw her reflection and couldn't help thinking that the light in her eyes and red in her cheeks had as much to do with Jeremy as it did with her long day in the sun.

What was she going to do about him?

He was weaving his way into her heart. She'd told herself that it was just a summer fling, something light and fun...but it felt like so much more than that. And Jeremy wasn't helping with his compliments and his unmistakable desire for her.

But where could this go? Both of their lives were completely up in the air.

Which was why she needed this to just be a summer romance.

She'd go back to her life; he'd go back to his. And they'd just have a great memory.

That thought was completely depressing, so she decided maybe she'd just stay living in the happier present for now.

She went upstairs, walked into the bathroom and stripped off her clothes. A shower would cool her down and clear her mind.

An hour later, she'd changed into clean shorts and a shirt and decided it was too nice of an evening to stay inside. Plus, what she really needed to do was start organizing the paintings and make sure she had everything out of the studio that might be part of her planned exhibition.

On her way to the stairs, she paused in front of Carly's open bedroom door. She'd glanced in the room a few times, but she hadn't been able to get herself all the way inside.

Maybe it was time to make that move.

She crossed the threshold and took a deep breath, inhaling her aunt's favorite scent—lavender. Carly had often sprayed it on her pillows and bed sheets and lined her dresser drawers with scented paper.

Mia felt a wave of emotion run through her as she thought about her aunt's smiling face, her joy for life, and her love of travel. She wanted to be more like her adventurous aunt and less like her normal boring self, and not just while she was here in Angel's Bay, but wherever she went next.

Making that silent promise to herself, she walked over to the closet and opened the door. It was a walk-in closet, and as she entered, she was overwhelmed once again by all the stuff; not only the clothes hanging on the rods, but the boxes on the shelves, the piles of shoes on the floor, and the laundry basket overflowing with sheets and towels. She was surprised to see that there were more paintings lined up six deep against the wall. She'd thought all the art was in the studio, but that wasn't the case.

She flipped through several paintings, noting that her aunt had signed some of them. These were Carly's personal paintings and through them she saw a picture of her aunt's life. Some were seascapes that looked very much like the view from the backyard. Others showed European settings, quaint towns, fountains, a river that looked like the Seine.

A rush of emotion swept through her. She was looking at Carly's life—or at least what was left of it.

She'd been right when she'd decided to leave Carly's personal bedroom space for later. It was just too sad to be in here right now. She left the closet and the bedroom, closing the door behind her.

Still feeling a little too emotional, she decided to grab a cold bottle of water from the kitchen and go out to the backyard where there were far less memories.

When she stepped onto the patio, something felt wrong.

Her gaze moved toward the studio, and she was shocked to see many of the paintings she'd taken out of the cottage earlier thrown haphazardly on the grass. In fact, some of the canvases had been slashed with a knife.

Her stomach turned over as a wave of nausea ran through her. Who would have done this?

She forced herself to walk past the paintings and open the studio door. The first floor was a mass of destruction. Everywhere she looked, she saw chaos. Boxes of jewelry beads had been dumped on the floor. Sculptures had been smashed and lay in pieces on the tables. Bottles of paint had been poured over every available surface, creating rivers of what felt like anger and devastation.

Shaking her head, she backed out of the studio. The shadows of the trees now seemed ominous. She no longer felt like this was her safe, peaceful backyard. Goose bumps ran down her arms and her heart thudded against her chest.

She told herself to get a grip; it was probably just a disgruntled artist. Or some bored teenagers. At least, they hadn't tried to get into the house.

On the other hand, the house had been locked up while the studio had been wide open. She'd never imagined someone would come into the yard and do this.

She needed to call the police—or someone. Jeremy would know what to do.

Jogging toward the gate, she ran up to his front door and rang the bell.

He opened the door a moment later, a smile spreading across his face when he saw her. He'd changed out of his bathing suit into jeans and a clean shirt. "Mia, I was going to come by and see if you wanted to get dinner with us."

"I have a problem, Jeremy."

His smile faded as he took in the expression on her face. "What's wrong?"

"Someone broke into the studio. They made a huge mess. I think I need to call the police."

"Hold on—what?"

"Come see for yourself."

As she finished speaking, Ashlyn slid past Jeremy and gave Mia a smile.

"Hi Ashlyn. Can I borrow your dad for a second?" she asked. "I want to show him something at my house."

"I'll come, too," Ashlyn said aloud.

"Uh, I don't know," she said, not sure she wanted Ashlyn to see the mess.

Jeremy frowned. "Is it that bad?"

"A bunch of paintings were destroyed."

"Ashlyn, why don't you wait here? I'll be right back," he told her.

Ashlyn shook her head and darted down the steps, running toward the gate leading into Mia's backyard before anyone could stop her.

"She's really quick sometimes," Jeremy said, pulling

the front door closed behind him as he stepped onto the porch.

"I can't imagine who would have done this," she said, as they hurried next door. "I'm just glad they didn't get into the house."

As they walked into the yard, she saw Ashlyn picking up one of the slashed canvases. Jeremy walked over to his daughter and took the picture out of Ashlyn's hands. He glanced back at Mia, a grim expression in his eyes now.

"I told you it was bad."

"You were right." He looked at his daughter. "Ashlyn, I need to go into the studio with Mia and you need to stay out here. I mean it."

"There's broken glass inside," Mia added. "We don't want you to cut yourself. Why don't you sit at the table and wait for us?"

"Okay." Ashlyn walked over to the table and sat down.

Jeremy strode toward the studio, preceding her into the room. His gaze swept the room, his jaw tightening with anger. "I'm calling the police."

"It was probably just some bad kids, right?"

"I don't know, but this looks like more than kids to me."

While Jeremy called the police, she walked outside and went over to the table. Ashlyn looked a little worried.

"It's all right," Mia said reassuringly, sorry she'd involved Jeremy and Ashlyn. This was the last thing Ashlyn needed. She tried to downplay the problem. "Someone made a mess in the studio, so we'll have more to clean up, but it needed to be cleaned up anyway, so it's not the worst thing."

"They're sending someone over," Jeremy said as he joined them at the table.

"Good. This must have happened while we were at the beach."

"I'm glad you weren't here," he said grimly.

"It probably wouldn't have happened when I was home. I didn't lock the studio door when we left. I didn't think it was necessary."

"I wouldn't have thought so, either."

"You should go home. I'll wait for the police."

"I'd like to stay with you, but..."

"You should take Ashlyn home."

He looked toward his daughter. "Yes. Let's go figure out what we're going to have for dinner, Ash."

Ashlyn slid off her chair and walked over to Mia. She slid her hand into Mia's and said, "You come, too."

"I can't right now, honey. I have to clean up, but I'll see you later."

"Come now."

"Mia has some things to take care of," Jeremy said.

"I'll walk you back to your house," Mia said, sensing that Ashlyn was about to throw a fit. There were storm clouds brewing in her eyes, and she had a feeling the uncertainty of what was going on was bothering Ashlyn more than she and Jeremy could understand.

She held Ashlyn's hand firmly as they walked through the gate and down the side of the house.

As they neared the front yard, a police car sped down the street, coming to an abrupt stop in front of the house.

As the uniformed officer stepped out of the car, and headed toward them, Ashlyn let out a shockingly long scream of terror. She let go of Mia's hand and ran toward her father, her arms outstretched, begging for him to lift her up, to hold her.

Jeremy swept her up in his arms. "It's okay, baby," he said.

"Don't let them take me away," she yelled, tears streaming down her face. "Don't let them take me, Daddy. Please, please, don't let them take me away again. I won't be bad anymore. I promise."

Mia's heart tore a little more with each terrified, panicked word, especially the one that turned Jeremy's face white. Ashlyn had called Jeremy *Daddy* for the very first time.

"No one is taking you anywhere," Jeremy said firmly. "You and I are always going to stay together."

"You should take her inside," Mia said.

"I will." He gave Kent a nod and then took Ashlyn into his house.

"What's going on?" Kent asked in confusion. "What happened?"

"A few things," she said. "I think your police vehicle and your uniform scared Ashlyn. I don't know if you're aware of her background, but her mother was killed in a robbery. I assume the police must have arrived at the scene and were possibly the ones to take her away from her mother."

"Damn," he muttered. "Poor kid."

She nodded, hoping this event wouldn't be a setback for Ashlyn.

"So what's the other thing? Why did you call for the police?"

"The studio was vandalized. I'll show you," she said, leading him into her backyard.

As she showed Kent the cottage, Mia got angry. "Why would anyone do this?" she asked.

Kent studied the destruction with a sober gaze. "I don't know. It's a mess. This place looks nothing like it did when I stayed here a year ago. Then it was a safe, warm haven."

"Well, I don't think it's been that for a while. There was a lot of junk in here when I arrived, but someone came in here and deliberately destroyed things." As she spoke, she wondered if that person had been in the studio before, perhaps one of the artists who didn't want their work to be shown. But she doubted Christina Wykoff or Rita Phelps would do this, and Kent certainly didn't look like he was guilty.

It was possible some of the other artists had heard about the upcoming exhibition, perhaps someone she hadn't met yet. "Do you think this was done by someone who stayed here?"

"I don't want to believe that. Carly offered this studio up for free to give people a chance to recover from whatever they were going through. Coming here was the best thing that I could have done. The two weeks I was here changed my life."

"How so?"

"I needed a place where I didn't have to answer the well-meaning questions of my family; I didn't have to keep assuring everyone I was all right. I didn't have to worry that if I couldn't sleep at night that I would wake anyone else up if I turned on the lights or went for a walk at two in the morning. I got better here," he said. "I painted my demons and surprisingly enough, they went away once I put them on paper." Kent finally turned his head to look at her, and there was an apology in his eyes. "Sorry, this isn't about me. I got lost in the past for a moment."

"That's why you didn't want me to show your art, because you painted your demons."

"In crazy bad, big brushstrokes. They don't deserve to be displayed."

"I understand." She finally got it. It wasn't the quality

of the work Kent was worried about; it was giving his demons public attention.

"I never thought about what Carly would do with the painting I left her," Kent said. "I assumed she would throw it away; it wasn't good. But maybe she would have put it in a gallery with the others she'd collected. I guess I should have asked her if she had that intent. Perhaps she had the same idea you did. It was her right. The painting belonged to her." He paused. "Carly was a wonderful woman. She helped me turn my life around. I wish I could say we'll find out who did this and punish them, but I don't think it will be easy. We're still looking for the vandals who broke into the high school last month. They messed up a couple of classrooms."

"Like this? Maybe it was the same person or persons."

"It's possible."

"You can't get fingerprints or anything from in here?"

"A lot of people have been in this place. Even if we could get prints, I doubt they would pinpoint who did this. Was the studio locked?"

"No," she said with a sigh.

"Once you get this cleaned up, you might want to make it a little more difficult to get into the yard and into the studio."

"I know. I should have been more careful. I wasn't planning to go out today, and then Jeremy asked me to build sand castles with him and Ashlyn. I should have locked up first. But Angel's Bay has lulled me into a false sense of security."

"It is a safe town, but you still have to take ordinary precautions." Kent paused. "Jeremy didn't win the competition again, did he? You know, he won like ten years in a row, right?"

"I thought it was six."

"Close enough."

"No, we didn't win. We came in seventh."

Kent whistled under his breath. "Jeremy must have been pissed."

"He handled the disappointment well. His main goal was to get closer to his daughter, and that happened. Ashlyn had a great time, so from that standpoint it was a win."

"I'm glad to hear that. You know before this happened," he said sweeping his hand toward the mess, "I was thinking Jeremy should try his hand at some painting. It helped me get rid of my frustrations. It might work for his."

"You think he's frustrated?"

"Don't you? He has a kid who won't talk to him, and his career is up in the air."

"True. I'm aware of what's going on."

"You are, aren't you?" he said, giving her a thoughtful look. "You and Jeremy are getting tight."

"He's a good guy," she said simply.

"One of the best," Kent agreed. "Jeremy was always better than me and Barton. Whatever he did, he always had the edge, whether it was academics or sports or just being a natural-born leader. It used to drive Barton crazy. I just accepted that Jeremy was blessed with a few more gifts than I was."

"You want him to stay in Angel's Bay, don't you?"

"Yes. I know he has issues with his dad, and he's always said he'd never live here again, but this would be a good place for him to raise his daughter and to be with his friends. Leaving the Army will be extremely difficult for him. I know what it's like to have to reinvent yourself. I can help him navigate that course."

"You don't think this town would be too quiet?"

"I think he could use some quiet, some peace, a daily reminder that there are still beautiful places and good people in the world. It's easy to lose your way when all you see is evil."

His words sent a shiver down her spine. Despite Kent's easygoing manner, it was clear that he'd been to hell and back. Had Jeremy made that same trip? She suspected the answer to that question was yes.

"I should get back to work," Kent said. "If you have any more problems, give us a call."

"You don't think they'll come back, do you?"

"I can't imagine why. Whatever they wanted to do, they did."

She thought so, too. "I'll walk you out."

When they reached his car, Kent looked over at Jeremy's house. "I hope Ashlyn is all right. Do you think I should try to talk to her before I go, let her know I'm a good guy?"

"I think you should let Jeremy handle it for now."

"I hope I didn't make his life more difficult."

"Me, too." She also felt torn between trying to help and giving Jeremy and Ashlyn some space. But she'd told Kent to let Jeremy handle his daughter; she needed to take her own advice.

Fourteen

--->>>>>>>><<<<<<<<---

"It's okay, Ash," Jeremy said, stroking Ashlyn's hair. Since coming back to the house twenty minutes earlier, he'd sat down on the couch with Ashlyn's arms still wrapped tight around his neck, her body shaking with the weight of the sobs pouring from her mouth.

It was the most heartbreaking sound he'd ever heard. But he hoped that the flood of tears might provide some much-needed healing.

"No one will ever take you away from me. I'm your father. We're family."

As he said the words, his chest tightened again at the memory of her calling him *Daddy* for the first time. She might have been hysterical and terrified, but she'd called for him. She'd run to him and let go of Mia. She'd chosen him to be her safe harbor, and he was proud and humbled at the same time.

He was not going to let this child down. He might not have known her for the first eight years of her life, but he would be there for her every day going forward. He would be worthy of the trust she'd just placed in him, and they would get past all the pain.

Finally, her sobs started to slow and falter. His shirt

was soaking wet, but he didn't give a damn. He would hold her as long as she needed.

It was another ten minutes before her hold on his neck finally lessened, and she lifted her face, her tear-stained cheeks, breaking his heart one more time.

He gave her a reassuring smile. "It's going to be all right, honey."

"They took me away before."

"Who did? The police?"

She nodded. "They said I couldn't see Mommy, that I had to go with them."

"That must have been really scary," he said carefully.

"A bad man hurt Mommy."

"Yes, he did." He wasn't sure whether he should keep her talking or tell her not to think about the past. But she'd been silent for weeks and that hadn't been helping. Maybe she needed to get it out.

She stared back at him. "I wanted milk. She took me to the store to get milk."

He suddenly understood why she'd refused to drink the milk he'd offered up at every meal. He let out a breath as she stared directly at him. He'd wanted her eyes on his for weeks, but now the intensity and the pain was almost overwhelming. He didn't want to screw this up. He wasn't a psychologist, but he was a father, and he sensed that Ashlyn needed to say it all.

"Can you tell me what happened?" he asked.

"We went to the store. Mr. Robinson was working. I went to pick out a candy. He said I could have whatever I wanted. Mommy went to get the milk. Then the bad man came in. He hit Mr. Robinson and then he started shooting. It was so loud. I covered my ears and got on the ground. I wanted to run to Mommy, but I didn't know where she was." Ashlyn swallowed hard. "When I found her, she wouldn't wake up."

It was all he could do to keep it together, her words painting a horrific scene in his mind. "I'm so sorry, baby."

"They wouldn't let me stay with her. The policeman made me get in his car."

So much had suddenly become very, very clear. Ashlyn had not only witnessed the robbery, she'd seen her mother die, and she felt guilty for wanting milk, for not being with her mother when the shooter came in, for not being able to stay with her mom and make her feel better.

"The police officer was protecting you until I could get home and get to you," he said. "He was trying to help you, Ashlyn."

"I wanted to go home, and no one would let me go back to my room. They made me stay in a house that smelled bad, and I didn't like the other kids."

"You're never going back there. It's you and me now."

She stared at him, measuring his words. "What if the bad guy finds us again?"

"That won't happen. He's in jail. He's never getting out."

She let out a breath. "Never?"

"Never," he said, hoping that was true, but while the man was currently in jail, he had not yet been to trial. Still, the police in San Francisco had assured him that they had eyewitness accounts, the gun and DNA evidence. There was no way the guy was getting off.

Ashlyn looked relieved by his confirmation.

"What did your mom tell you about me?" He needed to get as much information as he could just in case Ashlyn shut down again.

"She said I didn't have a daddy. Why didn't she tell me about you?"

"I don't know. I wish she had. I'm in the Army, Ashlyn. I'm a soldier. I fight for our country, and I've been doing that since before you were born. I didn't stay away from you because I didn't want to be your dad, or because I didn't love you. I didn't know about you. I guess your mom couldn't find me," he said, deciding it was better to give Justine a break for Ashlyn's sake. "I wish I'd known about you sooner, but we're together now, and that's all that matters."

"Are you going back to the Army?"

Her question was a difficult one to answer. He opted for the truth. "I don't know yet, but before I decide anything, you and I will talk about it. You'll be part of the decision, okay? Whatever we do from here on out, it's going to be you and me."

She nodded. "Okay."

"Are you hungry? Do you want some dinner?"

"Can Mia come over?"

"I don't know what she's doing, but we can ask her."

"Is the policeman gone now?"

"Yes, he is."

"Can we go to Mia's house?"

"We can," he said, as she crawled off his lap. "Why don't you wash your face and then we'll go?"

As Ashlyn ran up the stairs, he blew out a breath, feeling as if a weight had just come off his back. Ashlyn had accepted him as her father. She was talking to him like a normal kid, and maybe now that she'd spoken about her mother and what she'd seen, the nightmares would go away.

—➤➤◄◄—

What a mess, Mia thought, as she cleared out one

corner of the studio. She'd already filled two huge trash bags with splintered frames, broken pottery, and empty paint containers. She was making a little headway, but it was slow. Whatever wasn't broken, she had taken out to the patio and started making a pile of things she could save.

The paintings that hadn't been damaged went into that section as well, and she'd managed to find eight pretty good paintings that had not been destroyed. She'd also discovered some rolled-up canvases in a large cardboard tube at the back of the studio closet that hadn't been touched.

It was a start. Plus, she still had the paintings that she'd found in her aunt's closet. Maybe she could put those in the show, too.

Frowning, she tied off each of the trash bags and then dragged them out to the curb. Tomorrow was trash day, so at least she could get rid of some of the mess.

Jeremy and Ashlyn came out of their house as she walked back down the driveway. Ashlyn had her hand in Jeremy's, and there was a smile on her face that Mia was more than happy to see.

"Hi guys," she said, pausing as they came over to her. "Everything okay now?"

"Everything is great," Jeremy said with a look of intense happiness in his eyes. "Ashlyn and I had a long talk."

"I'm so glad. At least something good came out of all this."

"We've come to help you clean."

"Oh, you don't have to do that."

"We want to."

"Then I won't say no. I would love to get a few more trash bags filled before pickup tomorrow."

"That's a good idea," he said, as they made their way back into the yard. "What do you want Ashlyn and me to do?"

She walked into the studio and looked around for a good job for Ashlyn. "I would love it if you could find all the loose paint brushes and put them into this box," she said, handing her a cardboard box. "There are a bunch over there." She pointed to the far corner of the room.

"Okay," Ashlyn said, happy to have an assignment.

"Jeremy, if you could help me move the sewing machine to the patio, that would be great. It's pretty heavy."

"People sewed in here, too?"

"Apparently there was a textile artist in the cottage at some point. I found quilting squares and lots of scraps of material. Maybe I'll have Ashlyn collect those next."

"I think she's game." Jeremy tipped his head to Ashlyn, who was happily collecting brushes.

"Despite the swollen red eyes and red nose, she looks a lot better than when I last saw her," Mia said quietly.

"She definitely is." He picked up the sewing machine. "Where do you want this?"

"I'll show you." She led the way to the section of the patio where she was putting the usable items. "Right there is good."

He set the machine down on the bricks. "What's next?"

"Before we go back inside, can you tell me what you and Ashlyn talked about? Or is it too personal?"

"No, I want you to know. Ash told me about the night of the robbery. She had told her mother she wanted milk, so they walked to the local store to get it. Ash went to get candy in another part of the store when the man came in and started shooting. By the time she got to her mother,

Justine was bleeding and not waking up."

Mia put a hand to her mouth at that image. "That's awful."

"She wanted to stay with her mom, but the police officer took her away in his car."

She nodded with understanding. "I was afraid the car had triggered some memory in her head."

"She was terrified she was going to be taken away from me."

"She loves you, Jeremy. She called you *Daddy*."

His jaw tightened as his gaze filled with emotion. "Best word I ever heard. She cried her heart out for almost a half hour. I wasn't sure she was ever going to stop. I just held her. I didn't know what else to do."

"That's all she wanted you to do."

"Hearing her sob just about ripped my heart in two. I wish I could have spared her all that pain and guilt, too. She's been carrying the burden of asking for that milk all these weeks. That's why she's always refused to drink it."

"Hopefully, she can let the guilt go now that she's told you what happened. She decided to give you her problems to carry."

"Which is all I want to do."

She smiled, feeling a wave of affection for this wonderfully strong and yet tender man who was both a warrior and a father. "You're going to be a great dad."

"I hope so. I feel better now that she's talking to me." He paused. "I told her that I was a soldier in the Army and that her mom probably couldn't find me, that's why she never told her about me."

"That was a nice lie."

"I don't want Ashlyn to think her mom tried to keep us apart. I'll never know why Justine did what she did, but she gave me a beautiful little girl, and she died too young, so I'm not going to tarnish her memory. Plus, it's possible that Justine did try to find me. I was deployed around the world, and I wasn't always the easiest man to find."

She thought Jeremy was being very generous, because she just couldn't understand why Justine would have deprived her daughter of her father, why she wouldn't have tried to find out if Jeremy was a good man, if he was someone she wanted to be in her daughter's life. But as he'd said, they couldn't change what had happened, so what was the point of going around and around on possibilities they'd never be able to prove?

"Well, I'm glad you and Ashlyn have come together," she said.

"So what happened with Kent?"

"He didn't seem too confident they could find out who did this. He mentioned that some classrooms at the high school had recently been vandalized. It could be the same people or person."

"Possibly," Jeremy said, not sounding too convinced. "What do you think, Mia?"

"It doesn't feel like kids to me. And the slashed paintings bother me the most. It feels like someone got really angry and didn't just want to take things—they wanted to break them."

"That's pretty much what vandalism is."

"I guess that's true."

"I think you should stay at my house tonight."

"I'll be fine here, Jeremy. I didn't lock the studio door; that's how they got in. The house was fine."

"I know, but I still don't think you should be here alone. It's almost seven, and we haven't had dinner yet. Why don't we save the rest of this for tomorrow and go back to my place? We'll make some food and hang out with Ashlyn."

"You said last night that having me to your house overnight would confuse Ashlyn."

"I feel like she'd be less confused now."

"Why?"

"Because she adores you. She couldn't wait to come back here."

"Let's start with dinner, and then we'll see," she said. "I'm going to run inside and change clothes. I feel very dusty."

"Great. I'll help Ashlyn finish getting the paintbrushes while you do that."

"Thanks." As she went into the house, she found herself smiling, and she wondered if there was any possible way she could actually ever say no to him. At this point, that didn't seem likely.

"What are we making for dinner?" Mia asked, as they entered Jeremy's kitchen a half hour later. "And should I have brought some food?"

"No, I've got food. And I can actually cook."

"Really. So is there anything wrong with you?"

He laughed. "I'm sure there's a list somewhere."

"Do you want to see my room?" Ashlyn asked her.

"Of course, but maybe we should help your dad first."

"No, you two go have fun," he said. "I've got everything under control. And if it all goes bad, we'll order take-out."

Judging by his confidence, nothing was going to go bad, so she followed Ashlyn up the stairs to her room.

The first thing that struck her was the massive number of stuffed animals and toys. The room was not messy, but it was full. Jeremy had obviously tried to bribe his way into Ashlyn's affection. Mia couldn't blame him. He had a lot of missed years to make up for.

The doll she'd given Ashlyn sat prominently on the neatly made bed. Mia wondered if Jeremy's military training contributed to the house being so well organized, or if it was just his normal way of doing things.

"So what's your favorite toy?" she asked, taking a seat on the bed.

Ashlyn picked up the doll she'd given her. "This one."

"Why do you like that one so much?"

"Because she looks sad."

"And she needed a friend," Mia finished.

Ashlyn nodded. "I'm her friend. Do you know her name?"

"I don't."

"It's Allison."

"I like Allison."

"Her name starts with an *A* like mine."

"And my name ends in an *A* so I'm cool with the As. What's your second favorite toy?"

Ashlyn set the doll down and grabbed a soft brown teddy bear that was on the foot of the bed. "This is Charlie. He likes to sleep with me, because sometimes he gets scared."

It was interesting that Ashlyn had given her stuffed animals and dolls many of her own traits and fears. But seeing as how she'd been wrapped up in her head since her mother died, that was probably a good thing. She'd been able to release some of the negative emotions by helping her dolls through the bad feelings.

"I heard you and your dad had a good talk," Mia said.

Ashlyn nodded. "He says he's not going to go

anywhere. We're going to live together forever."

"He loves you very much."

"I always wanted to have a daddy. But I wish I could have my mommy, too."

"I know," she said, giving Ashlyn a sympathetic smile.

"Do you have a mommy?"

"Yes, she's really nice. Her name is Sharon. I also have two sisters and three brothers and a great dad. I'm lucky. But there was a time when I thought it would be more fun to be an only child like you. Then I would have all the attention."

"I guess."

She saw the ribbon they'd won at the sand castle building competition pinned to Ashlyn's bulletin board. "I had fun today at the beach; did you?"

Ashlyn nodded. "I wish we could have gotten one of the trophies, though."

"Well, there's always next year." She paused as Jeremy called their names. "Dinner must be ready. That was fast."

Ashlyn took her hand, and they walked together down the stairs.

The kitchen smelled of garlic and onions.

"Spaghetti," Jeremy said with a shrug. "It's not fancy, but I think you'll like it."

"It smells wonderful," she said. "And salad, too?"

"Gotta get the veggies in." He handed her the bowl of salad, bright green lettuce, topped with cherry tomatoes and sliced cucumbers. "I'll grab the garlic bread out of the oven."

Mia sat down at the table next to Ashlyn and thought how much had changed since the first night she'd arrived and shared a pizza with the two of them. She'd come to care so much about Ashlyn and her very handsome father, and it felt absolutely right to be sitting down to another meal together.

Summer fling, she reminded herself silently.

Don't get carried away. Don't start thinking past tonight.

"Are you okay?" Jeremy asked, giving her a quizzical look as he passed her the bread.

"Yes. I just realized how hungry I am."

He didn't look like he believed her, but he let the lie go as they all dug into the meal.

After dinner, they watched a movie in the family room. Ashlyn sat between them, curling up against Jeremy's shoulder when her eyes started to droop, but she insisted on watching all the way to the end. When the movie came to a close, Jeremy took Ashlyn upstairs and got her into bed. While he was doing that, Mia went into the kitchen and put the dishes into the dishwasher and wiped down the counters.

"You didn't have to clean up," Jeremy said when he came back.

"You cooked. It seemed like a fair trade." She put the dishtowel back on the rack by the sink. "I should go home."

"Or you should stay." He moved so quickly she was trapped between his body and the counter. He put his hands on her hips and pulled her even closer. "Ashlyn is already fast asleep. I barely got through the second page of her favorite book."

"She could wake up. She could need you."

"And I'll go to her if she does."

She was tempted. Man was she tempted, especially when he gave her a tantalizing and inviting kiss. She drew in a breath, which was a bad idea, because his musky scent only turned her on more. "I don't know."

"Then let me make the decision for you. Come to bed with me, Mia. You won't regret it."

Maybe not for the next eight hours, but what about tomorrow—what about next week?

"Does any woman ever say no to you?" she asked.

"It's happened once or twice."

"Cocky and charming—a dangerous combination."

"Not as dangerous as sweet and sexy," he said, covering her mouth with his.

Jeremy led her to bed and took her to pleasurable heights she'd only dreamed about. When Mia fell asleep in his arms, she thought life was pretty much perfect. She just hoped the sun wouldn't bring that perfection to an end.

Fifteen

Mia woke up in Jeremy's bed alone, but the delicious ache in her body reminded her of the night they'd shared.

Rolling on to her side, she saw it was after eight. She didn't usually sleep this late.

Scrambling out of bed, she hopped in the shower, dressed and then headed downstairs.

Jeremy and Ashlyn were at the kitchen table. Ashlyn was eating cereal and watching the small television on the wall, and Jeremy was reading the paper and eating oatmeal. It was a cozy family scene, and she both wanted to be a part of it and wanted to run far away, because she really couldn't let herself start thinking that she belonged at that table, in this family.

Jeremy lifted his gaze and saw her hovering in the doorway. His intimate smile made her shiver, and for a long silent minute, they both relived the pleasure they'd found in each other's arms.

"What can I make you for breakfast?" Jeremy asked.

"Nothing. I'm going to go home. I'll get something there."

Disappointment filled his eyes. "Are you sure? You don't have to leave so soon."

"I need to really focus on the cleanup today."

"We can help you later. Ashlyn has an appointment with Dr. Westcott this morning, so we're tied up for a while."

"I want to go to Mia's house," Ashlyn protested.

Mia could see a storm brewing in Ashlyn's eyes. She had a feeling that yesterday's breakthrough might be both a good and a bad thing for Jeremy because now that Ashlyn was talking, she might have a lot to say that Jeremy didn't want to hear.

"You can come by later," Mia told her. "I need to take care of some stuff this morning. But we'll get together this afternoon, okay?"

Ashlyn didn't look happy, but she nodded and went back to her cereal and her television program.

"Thanks," Jeremy said, getting up to walk her out. "I think you just averted a tantrum."

"Ashlyn is going to test you," she warned. "She's trying to figure out where the boundaries are and what might push you away from her."

"Nothing will push me away, and, frankly, anything is better than the silence."

"I might have to remind you that you said that."

He smiled and took her hand in his. "I'm glad you stayed, Mia."

"Me, too." She felt an overwhelming wave of affection for him. He looked so ridiculously attractive even before a shower, his hair still mussed from her fingers, his cheeks with morning beard, his lips so perfect for kissing.

"You should not be looking at me like that," he warned her. "Not if you actually want to go home alone."

"The last thing I want to do is go home alone, but I can't keep getting into bed with you."

"Why not? It's working out pretty well so far."

"You know why not. We're both leaving…"

"Sometime. Not today or tomorrow. Let's not look any further ahead."

"Okay."

"Call me if you have any problems at the house, and Ashlyn and I will come over later to help you."

"Sounds good. And I'm sure I'll be fine."

He pulled her up against his chest. "One for the road."

His kiss was so long and so good she really wanted to take him with her, but somehow she managed to get herself out of the house and back home.

Her cell phone rang as she walked into the kitchen. It was her mom. Sitting down at the kitchen table, she said, "Hi, Mom. How are you feeling? How's the foot?"

"Much better, thanks. How are you doing?"

"Well, I'm making a little progress, but it's not fast. Aunt Carly had a lot of stuff."

Her mom laughed. "I know. I was actually a little relieved when you volunteered to go instead of me. I loved my sister, but she could be quite the pack rat. She hated to throw anything away. It all had sentiment attached to it."

"That's what makes it difficult. I feel guilty when I throw anything into a trash bag. I've started putting things together to donate to charity, which makes me feel better, but anything that's stained or torn or broken or chipped, I feel like I should toss."

"Of course you should. I know that you'll do everything with respect to your aunt, so don't make yourself crazy, Mia. And I should be able to get down there in a few weeks. I can finish up whatever you don't get to."

She sensed her mother was working the conversation toward a new point—a point that had to do with her future. She wasn't wrong.

"I know you're going to need to start looking for another job soon," her mom said. "I don't want you to feel like you have to stay in Angel's Bay for me or for Carly."

"I can send resumes out from here," she said, even though she had done absolutely nothing in that regard.

"That's true. Everything is online now. Are you applying to other museums?"

"I'm thinking about all my options. I didn't love the museum work the way I thought I would."

"Well, no job is ever going to be fun one hundred percent of the time."

"I know, but it should be fun more than ten percent of the time, shouldn't it?"

Her mother's sigh was quite distinct. "I just feel like your generation sets its expectations too high. Work is work."

"But you love being a nurse. And Dad loved being a firefighter."

"You're right. We both did choose careers that we loved. I thought you loved art. I just don't want to see you set back in your career because of a man."

"It's not about Grayson."

"Isn't it? You've been very close-mouthed about that relationship, but I know that he lied to you about being divorced and that you were the one who ended up leaving the museum when his wife found out, which I think is totally unfair. They should have fired him."

"It doesn't matter anymore. I made a mistake. I

trusted the wrong person. But I can't change what happened. What I need to do now is figure out where I want to work that will pay me a living and make me happy. I have time to look. I have money in the bank. I'm a good saver, you know that."

Her mom laughed. "That's true. You've never been one to overspend."

"And it's not costing me anything to be here, so it's all good. I really like Angel's Bay, Mom. I can see why Aunt Carly wanted to live here. The people are wonderful. Kara Murray Lynch threw me a party so I could meet all of Aunt Carly's friends. They said the most wonderful things about her. When you come down, you'll have to meet them, too."

"I'd love to."

"By the way, did Aunt Carly talk to you about publishing a coloring book for adults?"

"She did mention that, but I thought it sounded a little crazy."

"It's all the rage. It's fun, easy, and you can drink a lot of wine while you're doing it," she added with a laugh. "The pictures she drew are really well done. I'm going to see if I can publish the books in her name."

"That sounds like another project that will take you away from your own life," her mother said gently. "What's really going on, Mia?"

She sighed, knowing her mother deserved more of the truth. "I feel like I spent a lot of years in school to end up doing something I didn't like that much. Since I came here, my world has opened up again. There's so much I can do with art. Maybe being in a museum is the wrong place for me."

"What are your other options?"

"I could work in a gallery or teach art. Maybe I could

paint."

"You're going to be a painter now?"

She heard the doubt in her mother's voice. "I'm not that bad."

"I'm sure you're not, honey. I just don't know that it's practical."

"Well, I've been practical my entire life, so it's time for a little impractical. I just feel so inspired since I got here, like I have options I haven't ever considered. I can't really explain it. Maybe it's Carly's spirit guiding me in some way."

"Are you sure this inspiration doesn't have something to do with the attractive man next door?"

"You talked to Kate."

"She mentioned something about your neighbor. What's he like? Is he single?"

"He's a single dad, and he's very attractive. He's a soldier, although I'm not sure what he's going to do next. He was injured a few months ago, and he's still recovering."

"That's terrible."

"He's going to be all right. He can live a normal life; he's just not sure he can pass the extreme physical tests for his unit. Plus, his daughter needs a father. Her mother recently passed away."

"That sounds very sad and complicated. Are you sure you want to get in the middle of that?"

It was a good question. Unfortunately, it had come a little late. "I'm already involved, but Jeremy isn't the reason I'm reevaluating my career plans."

"Are you sure about that?"

"Yes. He's a great guy and I like him, but we aren't making serious plans. We both have things to figure out. It's fine. You're going to have to trust me to run my own life."

"I know. You're not the first of my six children to tell me that, but you are my baby, and I've always felt a little more protective of you. You gave us such a scare when you were little. I've always worried more about you."

"I'm the picture of good health now, and I'm actually having a great time here, so don't worry, okay?"

"All right. I'll let you go. Love you, Mia, take care of yourself."

"I will. Love you, too."

She ended the call and set down her phone. She didn't usually keep things from her family, and she felt a little guilty about not telling her mother about the vandalism in the studio, but there was nothing her mother could do about it. Plus, she would have wanted Mia to come home, and she wasn't ready to leave.

She could handle things here. Whoever had broken in had had plenty of time to take what they wanted. There was no reason to think they'd come back.

She needed to move on with her plans, clean up the house, set up the paintings for the exhibit, and even though she'd lost some pieces, she still had others she could use, including the ones upstairs.

As she thought about her aunt's paintings, she decided to take a closer look. She got up from the table and went upstairs. She pulled the paintings out of the closet one by one and stood them up around the bed so she could see what she was looking at. As she reached for the last painting, the ragged edge of the frame cut her finger. She winced and sucked the blood off her finger as she glanced down at the frame.

It was pulling apart at the corner. When she tried to pull the two edges into place, she just made things worse, and the corner of the painting came loose from the frame.

Carrying it over to the bed, she set it down so she could take a better look at it. This particular painting didn't really look like the others. It wasn't a scene or a portrait. It was just a mass of brushstrokes in bold colors. It didn't look like something her aunt would have painted.

As she tried to tuck the edge of the canvas under the frame, her eye caught on the frayed edges of something underneath.

Frowning, she pulled the corner of the canvas up, stunned to see what appeared to be another painting underneath.

Her pulse began to race and after a few seconds of trying to gently remove the broken frame, she just gave it a ruthless pull until it came away from the canvas. Then it was easy to pull up the top picture to reveal the hidden painting.

Her breath caught in her chest. This painting was not the work of an amateur. The exquisite brushstrokes, the attention to detail and light, the subject matter—Moulin Rouge and Paris nightlife in the nineteenth century—reminded her of the French painter Henri de Toulouse-Lautrec. He was one of the most talented painters in the Post-Impressionism period.

Her pulse jumped and blood raced through her veins as she studied the painting, turning it one way, then the other, knowing without a doubt that she was holding art in her hands that was very old and probably very valuable. She'd studied the works of the masters for years. If this painting wasn't by Henri de Toulouse-Lautrec, then it had to have been done by someone who had studied under him.

Or—it could be a forgery, a copy. She didn't remember this particular scene. She knew it was different than the painting entitled *At the Moulin Rouge* by

Toulouse-Lautrec, but there were quite a few similarities.

She sat down on the bed, her legs feeling suddenly weak. She'd been hoping to find a treasure in her aunt's house, but what if the treasure had been stolen? If the painting had not been hidden away, her mind wouldn't go to that possibility. She would have thought that her aunt bought it somewhere or that it was a copy, not worth anything more than the pleasure it gave from studying it.

But someone had carefully put another really terrible piece of art in front of it. If the frame hadn't broken, she never would have discovered it.

And the painting had been hidden away in her aunt's closet, where she kept her personal paintings, which led her to believe that it hadn't been left behind by one of the visiting artists, although she couldn't be sure.

In truth, she didn't really know what her aunt had painted and what she'd gotten from others.

Her stomach began to churn. She felt a little sick. Her aunt couldn't have been an art thief, could she?

Her gaze drifted to the other paintings she'd pulled from the closet. What if there were other masterpieces hidden by what appeared to be amateur art?

Another thought occurred to her…

Had the paintings she'd found slashed in the yard been ripped apart to see if they held this treasure?

Her heart was beating so fast, she felt dizzy. She needed to talk to Jeremy. She needed him to calmly tell her that her imagination was running away from her. But he wasn't home. He had things to do this morning. Still, she had to reach out.

Picking up her phone, she punched in his number. It went to voicemail. "Call me or come by when you get back," she said. "I've found something in my aunt's house that's a little…odd."

Jeremy dropped Ashlyn off for her therapy appointment and then drove down to the harbor to meet Barton at the Java Hut. He knew Barton wanted to talk to him more about working for Kinsey Private Security, but it didn't really hold any interest for him at the moment. Everything about his previous life seemed suddenly very far away.

When he'd woken up in the hospital two months ago, all he could think about was how soon he could get back to his team, but now there were other things and people in his life that mattered more—Ashlyn and Mia.

Mia kept telling him they were just having a summer fling. She wanted to define it so she'd be okay when it ended, and he understood her self-protective instincts. It was easier for him to think of their relationship that way, too. But the idea of summer turning into fall without her living next door was not something he wanted to contemplate. However, he'd told her not to think too far ahead; he needed to take his own advice.

He arrived at the Java Hut before Barton, which wasn't surprising. After getting a coffee from the barista at the counter, he sat down at a table by the window. From his vantage point, he could see the boats bobbing in the harbor and the sign for Buddy's Bait and Tackle. His father was probably out on his boat this morning.

He'd hated fishing, every single thing about it: the waiting, the gutting of the fish, and the stink that never left your clothes. He didn't know what his father loved about it, but then his father had always been better with fish than with people.

The door opened and he saw Barton walk in with Hal Conroy, one of his father's fishing buddies and longtime friends.

Barton tipped his head and went up to the counter to order while Hal walked over to the table.

"Hello, Jeremy," he said. "Mind if I sit for a minute?"

"Go ahead," he said, bracing himself for what he was sure would be a conversation about his dad.

"How are you enjoying being back in Angel's Bay?"

"It's better than I expected."

Hal nodded approvingly. "Cameron said you have a daughter, that cute little girl you were with at the café."

"Yes. Ashlyn is eight years old."

Hal stared back at him and drew in a breath, then let it out.

"Say whatever you want to say," Jeremy told him. "I can see you have something on your mind."

"I know you and your dad haven't gotten along in the past, but don't you think it's time to mend fences? Now that you're a father, don't you have a better sense of how difficult it is to be a parent, especially a single parent?"

"It is difficult to be a single father, but I try. My father gave up after my mother died. His relationship with her was over, so our relationship was over. I was eleven years old. My friends' parents were the ones who showed up for me at baseball games and school events. They looked out for me. They helped me with my homework. My father was drunk or asleep or gone."

"I know it was bad," Hal acknowledged. "Your father was so guilty about your mom's death that he could barely breathe."

"Guilty?" he asked, surprised by the choice of word. "She got cancer. He didn't cause that."

"No, but he was gone the first two months she was sick, remember?"

"Vaguely. He was always coming and going."

"He'd joined a crew in Alaska to earn some extra money. She didn't tell him she was sick right away, because she didn't want him to come home. By the time he got back, she had only a couple weeks left to live. I don't think he ever forgave himself for not having more time with her, for not being there with her when she first heard the news."

Jeremy didn't know what to say. If someone had told him this before, he had no recollection of it, but then the time around his mother's death had passed in a hazy blur.

"Your dad drank to ease the pain," Hal continued. "He wasn't the father you needed. He knows that down deep. He just doesn't know how to get past it. He thinks you hate him."

"I can't say he's wrong."

"Can't you?"

"No, I can't. I went to see him when I first got back. When I told him I had a kid I'd just found out about, he ranted about how irresponsible I was. He didn't ask about her at all. He didn't ask how I felt about things. He just shouted. Does that sound like a man who's worried about whether or not I like him?"

"You took him by surprise. When you called and said you were coming to town and you wanted to talk to him, he had an anxiety attack. He slipped up, took a drink, and then he couldn't stop. He felt bad about what he said to you. He felt even worse for falling off the wagon."

"What wagon? When has he ever been on the wagon?"

"He's been sober for five years, Jeremy. I should know; I'm his sponsor."

"What the hell are you talking about?"

"Just what I said. He stopped drinking five years ago. He hadn't had a drop to drink until last week. I think he was afraid to see you when he was sober. Then he'd have to deal with actual conversation, maybe admit he'd screwed up with you. I wish in a way that you'd surprised him, just shown up. Knowing you were on your way to see him just set him off. He panicked."

Jeremy stared at Hal in disbelief. He could not wrap his head around the idea that his father had quit drinking five years ago. "You seriously want me to believe he stopped drinking completely five years ago? Why? Why would he do that?"

"He crashed his car into a tree. He woke up injured and sick and finally realized how low he'd sunk. I took him from the hospital to rehab. He came back to town a month later and he's been on track ever since."

"So it's my fault he slipped up, something else for him to blame me for," he said bitterly.

"He doesn't blame you; he blames himself." Hal paused. "I know you think this isn't your problem, and I can't say that it is, but your father has tried to change, and I wanted you to know that. He would love to get to know his granddaughter."

"I can't have him around Ashlyn."

"You can make sure it's a good experience. He's back on track, Jeremy. He's going to meetings every day. He's trying. This is a pivotal moment for him. He needs you to give him a second chance."

"A *second* chance? He's on about twenty now."

"Then let's call it twenty-one. If you can't do it for yourself, do it for your daughter. She has a grandfather, and from what I hear she doesn't have much else in the way of family. Neither do you. I don't think it's too late for you to fix this relationship."

"That would take a miracle."

Hal smiled. "We are in Angel's Bay, a place where

miracles happen."

"Not any that I've seen."

"There's still time."

Jeremy shook his head. "I know you're my father's friend, and you want to help him, but I have to protect my daughter. If he wants to change things, it's on him. If he can show me he's sober for more than a few days, maybe I'd consider talking to him again, but I can't make any promises."

"All right. I had to try. Good luck, Jeremy." He got up and gave his seat to Barton.

As Barton sat down, he said, "I was going to rescue you, but I didn't want to get in the middle of that conversation. It sounded heavy."

"I don't blame you," Jeremy said, sipping his coffee. "Hal says my father got sober five years ago, that he didn't fall off the wagon until I came back to town. He wants me to give him another chance."

"What is it with people needing a million chances?" Barton asked, no sympathy in his voice. "Your dad is an asshole. Sorry, but that's the truth. If he wants to change things, he should stop being an asshole."

"That's what I told Hal." He appreciated that Barton actually saw the relationship the way he saw it.

"In fact, I think you should leave this town and move to Los Angeles. I talked to Jeff Kinsey again this morning. He wants a meeting with you. He's ready to pay you more money than you ever dreamed of and let you call your own shots. If you need time to be with your kid, he'll wait until you're ready. It's the perfect job for you, Jeremy."

"Is it? Private military contractors are more about profit than patriotism. We've both seen that."

"It doesn't have to be one or the other. Kinsey is an

honorable guy. You like him. You know him."

That was true, and if he was going to go into private security, Kinsey would probably be the best choice. He just didn't know if he wanted to make that move. "I told you I'd think about it. That's all I can give you right now."

"What else will you do? Your future won't be in Delta, Jeremy. You know that. Your shoulder will never be able to handle the demands of our job. And even if it could, you've got a kid now. You can't leave her with an hour's notice."

"You're not telling me anything I don't know. Just give me some time. I've got a lot on my plate."

"All right, I'll back off," Barton said, putting up his hand in surrender. "So on another note, what's happening with you and the hot blonde next door?"

"Nothing," he said, but the word didn't come out as convincingly as he would have wanted.

Barton gave him a knowing smile. "Yeah, right. You're into her. Have you slept with her yet?"

"That's none of your business."

"I'll take that as a yes. And I'm happy for you."

"Don't read anything into it. She's leaving in a few weeks, just as soon as she finishes cleaning out her aunt's house."

"Leaving in a few weeks makes her the perfect woman in my book. Are you taking her out tonight?"

"We haven't made plans. I'm thinking about taking Ashlyn to the movie in the park."

Barton smiled. "They still have those? Man, this place never changes. It is as hokey a small town as any you'll ever find."

Jeremy had always thought so, too, until recently. "You should come."

"I have no interest in that, and, even if I did, I have

my mother's birthday party tonight. It's her sixty-fifth, and the entire family is coming, so I have to be there. She told me she'd leave me out of the will if I didn't make it. Not that she has any money to leave me," he joked.

Jeremy smiled. Barton was as far from a mama's boy as anyone he'd ever met, but if there was one person who could make him do something he didn't want to do, it was his mother. "Wish her well for me."

"I will, but if you stick around here, you should go by and see her. She always thought of you as her extra kid."

"I always thought of her as my second mom."

"Maybe you should take Mia to the movies."

"She's got her hands full with the house and some other issues."

Barton nodded. "I ran into Kent earlier; he said someone broke into her studio yesterday and made a huge mess."

"It's bad," Jeremy acknowledged. "I hope Kent can find out who did it."

"He doesn't seem to have much hope of that." Barton paused. "You know this is exactly the kind of crime you'd be handling if you became a cop here. Small-town vandalism would be the highlight of a boring day."

Jeremy grinned and shook his head. "You never give up."

"Not when I want something."

"You don't need me to join Kinsey's operation."

"We've always been a good team. We watch each other's back. That's why I want to work with you."

"I can't believe you really want to leave Delta. It was your dream as much as mine."

"I'm tired of following orders, and I want the money. I've earned it. So have you." Barton shoved back his chair. "But I'll let you think about it. Just don't think too long.

I'm driving down to LA on Monday. You and Ashlyn should come with me. We'll get a hotel with a pool. Maybe your beautiful blonde would like to join us. She can watch Ashlyn and tan by the pool while we take care of a little business."

As much as the idea of seeing Mia in a bikini by a hotel pool was enticing, he doubted she'd go along with Barton's plan, but all he said was, "We'll talk before Monday." Then he stood up and followed Barton outside. They said good-bye in the parking lot. Jeremy was about to head to his car when he saw his father's boat bobbing in its harbor slip. He debated for a long minute and then changed directions.

He could not believe what he was about to do...

Sixteen

"Jeremy," his father said warily as he boarded the boat a few minutes later. "What are you doing here?"

His father's face was ruddy from the wind and the sun, but Jeremy saw the lines of age around his eyes and mouth, reminders that time kept passing. Was Hal right? Was it time to let the past go? Try to start over?

"I came to talk to you," he said briskly. "The other day when you saw me in the café, you scared my daughter. I don't care how you talk to me, but I won't let you intimidate her."

"I just asked why she didn't have your last name."

"Because I wasn't around when she was born. I told you that last week. Her mother named me on the birth certificate but gave Ashlyn her name. The social worker tracked me down after Ashlyn's mother Justine was killed in a robbery. My daughter was traumatized by her mother's death and by the arrival of a father she'd never heard about. I brought her to Angel's Bay because she needed to be in a place where she would feel safe, where she could heal. She's having a rough time getting past everything that happened, but I'm finally starting to see some progress. I can't let you set that back. We're going to run into each other; it's inevitable in this town. We need to come to an understanding."

His father stared back at him for a long minute. "I'm sorry, Jeremy."

He had to admit he was a little shocked to hear those words come out of his father's mouth. He didn't know if his father was apologizing for his words at the café, for being drunk last week or for a lifetime of sins, but maybe it was just enough to know that his dad felt some regret for something.

"All right," he said. "Look, we don't have to talk about the past. It's long over, but we need to come to an agreement about the present. I don't know how long I'll be here, but while I'm here, I'd rather not have any problems between us, at least not in front of my daughter."

"My granddaughter," his father reminded him.

He stared back at him. "If you want to be her grandfather, you're going to have to show me I can trust you not to be drunk around her, and you sure as hell can't ever talk to her the way you talk to me. I won't stand for that."

His father's lips tightened. "You should have more respect for me. I am your father. I provided for you."

"You did put a roof over my head, and I did have food to eat, that's true, but we both know you checked out after Mom died."

"I was destroyed by her death, Jeremy. I know I didn't do right by you. It was all I could do to get through the day."

"You weren't suffering alone."

"I know," his dad admitted. "You were hurting, too. I know you probably won't care, but I quit drinking five years ago. I was sober until a few days ago when you called me and said you were coming by. I didn't know what you wanted to talk to me about, so I had a few drinks to calm myself down. I went back to AA the next day. It's a daily struggle, but I'll get back on track again. I know you can't forgive me, and I probably wouldn't forgive myself if I was in your shoes, but I do want you to know I'm sorry." He took a breath. "Your mom made me feel sane. She helped me fit into the world. I didn't know who I was before I met her, and I didn't know who I was afterwards. I guess I'm still trying to figure that out."

Jeremy swallowed hard, emotion putting a knot in his throat. He really hadn't thought he needed to have this kind of conversation with his father, but it was surprisingly good. Maybe Mia had been right. They had had unfinished business between them.

"I'd like to know your daughter—my granddaughter," his father continued. "I'd like to be someone you'd want to introduce her to. I know your mother has probably been furious with me all these years for screwing up with you. She'd want me to try harder, and I want to try harder."

"Okay." If his father was going to make an effort, he could try to meet him halfway. "I'm going to take Ashlyn to the movie in the park tonight. If you're there, and you're sober, we'll say hello. But if you do anything I don't like, I will protect Ashlyn, and there won't be any more chances."

"I understand. You know something—I did one thing right, Jeremy."

"What's that?"

"I raised a better man than I could ever be."

Jeremy drew in a breath and blew it out. He didn't know what to say, so he settled for, "I'll see you later."

As he walked off the boat, he wondered if a miracle had just occurred. But only time would tell if his father would make good on his promise to be sober.

After leaving his father's boat, Jeremy drove to the Redwood Medical Center to pick up Ashlyn. On the way, he pulled out his phone and saw he had a missed call from Mia. Her voicemail was rather interesting, too. He wondered what she'd found in her aunt's house. Despite her use of the word *odd*, she didn't sound upset, so he'd just go by there when he got home.

"How did it go?" he asked Ashlyn when she hopped into the car.

"Dr. Westcott said I'm really good," she told him with a proud smile.

"I'm happy to hear that."

"I told her about Mommy." She hesitated, her eyes concerned. "Was that okay?"

"Absolutely okay. I want you to talk about your mom whenever you want to. Where do you want to go now? We can get lunch, go to the park, the beach, whatever you want."

"Can we pick up sandwiches and go see Mia?"

"We can do that," he said, happy that Ashlyn's plan for the day meshed perfectly with his.

They picked up sandwiches, chips, and cookies at the deli and then went straight to Mia's house. She opened the door with a gleam of excitement in her eyes.

"Come in," she said. "I can't wait to show you what I found."

"Is it treasure?" Ashlyn asked.

"It might be," Mia said, taking them into the kitchen.

Spread out on the kitchen table was a painting, the four corners anchored down by salt and pepper shakers.

"Look at this," Mia said, as he set the food down on the island counter.

"Is it a famous painting?" he asked, not sure exactly what he was looking at. "I know nothing about art, so that's probably a stupid question."

"It's not famous, but it's very old, and it's possible that it was painted by Henri de Toulouse-Lautrec, a French painter who worked in the Post-Impressionist period with artists like Cézanne, Van Gogh, and Gaugin."

"That sounds like a good thing," he said, feeling way out of his depth. "How do you know if it's his painting?"

"It's not signed, so I'd have to take it to an expert to get it appraised and make sure it's not a really good forgery, but my instincts tell me this is valuable."

"How valuable?"

"Well, one of his paintings was recently auctioned at Christie's for 22.4 million dollars."

"That's a lot of cash. Where did you find it? Was it in the studio?"

"No, it was in my aunt's bedroom closet."

"She's pretty," Ashlyn said, pointing to one of the female figures in the painting. The woman wore a dark red dress with a black and red hat on her head and long, lacy gloves up to her elbows.

"She is pretty," Mia agreed, giving Ashlyn a smile.

"Can I paint something?" Ashlyn asked.

"Of course, maybe after lunch," Mia said. "Judging by those bags, I'm guessing you brought food."

"You haven't eaten, have you?" he asked.

"No, I've been too caught up in this. I've been trying to research the painting online, but I haven't had any luck. It's possible it wasn't painted by Henri, but my gut tells me it's his work."

"I'd trust your gut."

"Can I have my sandwich, Daddy?" Ashlyn asked, sliding off the kitchen chair.

He didn't think he would ever get tired of hearing her call him *Daddy*. "Yes. Why don't you sit at the counter, so we don't mess up this painting?"

They walked over to the counter, and Ashlyn got on the stool while he opened up the wrapped sandwiches and handed her one.

"Do you need any drinks?" Mia asked.

"We brought some," he said. "I've got turkey, roast beef, or a vegetarian wrap."

She smiled at the spread. "That's a lot of food."

"What doesn't get eaten now, we'll save for later. What would you like?"

"I'll take the wrap," she replied.

He passed it to her. "So you said you found the painting upstairs in a closet?"

"Yes, but that's not the strangest part. It was hidden behind another painting."

"What do you mean?"

"I pulled out a framed painting and the frame was broken. As I was trying to put it back together, I noticed that there was something underneath the rather ugly picture in front. I peeled the top canvas off and found this underneath."

His gut tightened. "You're saying someone deliberately hid this painting?"

She met his gaze. "That's exactly what I'm saying, and why I'm convinced it's valuable."

He stared back at her, seeing not just excitement in her eyes but also a little worry. "You're wondering if your aunt knew it was there."

"How could I not? It was in her bedroom." She drew in a breath and let it out. "I need you to tell me to slow down and not jump to conclusions. My aunt didn't know the painting was hidden in that frame, right? She didn't steal a piece of valuable art. She didn't accept stolen art from some other thief. None of that happened—right?"

He saw the need in her eyes, and while he liked to fulfill every need Mia had, he wasn't sure he could satisfy this one. "I don't know, babe. There are a lot of things to consider."

She frowned. "That's not what I wanted you to say."

"Is there any way to find out if this painting was actually done by this artist you told me about? Isn't there some itemized list of his work somewhere?"

"Not all paintings are listed, especially if the work was not put forth by the artist in a public way. It could have been a painting that he didn't care for, that he didn't want to sell or display. Artists can be very temperamental. But I am going to look into his work and see what I can find. I have a friend in Paris who knows a lot about French art; I have a call into her. I also texted a photo of the painting to my sister Kate. She might be able to tap into the FBI's database of stolen art."

"Was it wise to call the FBI so soon? If your aunt did have something to do with this—"

"I'm sure she didn't," Mia said quickly. "Aunt Carly had so much respect for artists; she wouldn't steal someone's work. I know she wouldn't do that. I was just tripping before, letting my imagination go crazy. Besides, Kate will be discreet. I can trust her. She wouldn't want to put a black mark against Aunt Carly's name and reputation anymore than I would." She paused. "It's possible this painting was stolen during WWII. Hitler was a frustrated artist, you know. He looted Paris of many treasures, and while some were returned, many were not."

"So even if it was stolen at some point, your aunt might not have known that."

"Exactly."

"Or she didn't know she had the painting at all, since it was hidden away. Unless, she was the one who hid it away."

"I don't want her to be a thief, Jeremy," she said, worry in her blue eyes. "I've trusted people who I shouldn't have trusted, and I've been let down. I don't want Aunt Carly to be someone other than the person I think she is. I don't think I can handle that."

"Then maybe you shouldn't look for answers, Mia. Let your aunt be who she is in your mind, in your memories."

"That's the logical thing to do, but I can't do it. I have too much curiosity to just let this go."

"Even though you found the painting in your aunt's bedroom, it might not have belonged to your aunt," he suggested. "A lot of artists have been through the studio. Maybe one of them stole the painting and covered it up with another. Maybe it was one of the paintings left to your aunt as rent payment for the studio."

"That's possible. I like that idea better."

He wasn't sure he liked the idea at all. His body tightened as he remembered the slashed paintings strewn across the lawn the night before. But he didn't want to talk about that in front of his daughter. "Ashlyn, why don't you take your sandwich outside? It's a nice day."

"Okay," Ashlyn said happily. "Can I play in the studio when I'm done?"

Jeremy gave Mia a questioning look.

"Everything is fine outside," Mia said. "You can play in the studio, Ash."

After Ashlyn left the room, he turned back to Mia. "Is it possible this painting is what your vandal was looking for?"

"I had the same thought, Jeremy. The way the

paintings were ripped apart made me wonder if someone was looking for something hidden behind another painting."

"Have you told anyone else you found this?"

"Only you, my friend in Paris, and my sister."

"Let's keep it that way."

"You don't think they'll come back, do you?"

He frowned at the question. He hadn't thought so before. Now he wasn't as sure. "Maybe we should talk to Kent."

"Let me find out more about the painting first. I don't want anyone else leaping to the conclusion that my aunt was an art thief. I should hear back from my friend or Kate in the next few hours."

"All right. Why don't we take our food outside?"

"That would be perfect. My eyes are tired from looking at that painting. I could use a break from it."

They sat at the patio table to eat. Ashlyn had already abandoned her lunch and ran back and forth between the studio and the table, showing them new items she'd discovered.

"I kind of like this," Mia said with a smile. "I just sit here and Ashlyn does all the work."

"She does have a lot more energy these days."

"How did her therapy session go?"

"Very well, I think. She told me that she spoke to Dr. Westcott about her mother. I think she's on the right track, Mia. She's getting better."

"I think so, too, Jeremy. She trusts you now. She gave you her secret to hold for her."

"I would much rather carry her burdens than watch her struggle to walk."

"Spoken like a true father. You're going to be a good dad."

"I hope so. I don't want to fail her. I feel like I have a lot of missed time to make up for."

"But there's so much more time ahead of you."

"That's true. I'm taking her to the park tonight. They show a movie on the wall of the rec center on Saturday nights in the summer. Tonight it's the *Sound of Music*."

"That sounds like fun."

"It's something to do. Everyone brings blankets, lawn chairs, food, and drinks. It's one of many Angel's Bay traditions. I'm hoping you might want to join us."

She hesitated. "I really shouldn't keep putting off the cleanup. I haven't accomplished much since I got here."

"You have all afternoon to clean, and you'll have two helpers. You'll want to relax tonight."

"Okay. I'd love to go to the movies with you and Ashlyn."

He felt remarkably happy at her words. "Good. I have to warn you that my father might show up at the movie."

"How do you know that?"

"I stopped by his boat while Ash was at her therapy appointment. You were right, Mia. We did have unfinished business."

"Did you finish it?"

"I said what I needed to say for us to be able to be in this town at the same time. He was surprisingly receptive. Apparently, he hadn't had a drink in five years until I called him last week and told him I was coming home and needed to speak to him. That shook him up so much, he went off the wagon."

"Because he wants to have a relationship with you, and he's scared."

"Why he thought getting drunk would be a good start, I don't know. But he actually apologized for the past."

"That's something big," she said, surprise in her eyes.

"I was shocked," he admitted. "I told him I'd consider letting him get to know Ashlyn, but if he steps out of line once, he's done. I think he believes me, but we'll see."

"I'm glad you went to see him. I didn't think you would. What changed your mind?"

"I ran into one of his friends in town. He persuaded me to talk to him again. But mostly I just wanted to prevent another awkward encounter. Ashlyn is doing better now; I don't want anything to set her back."

"You're doing the right thing, Jeremy."

"I hope so. We'll see what happens. It's going to take a long time for me to trust him."

"Trust can be a slow build," she agreed.

As she said the words, he realized that time wasn't always necessary. Sometimes trusting someone was instinctive. He knew without a doubt he could trust Mia and he'd known her for only a week. A lifetime with his father hadn't built any kind of trust.

"You're staring at me," Mia said, wiping her mouth with her napkin. "Do I have something in my teeth?"

He smiled as she showed off her pretty white teeth. "No, I just like looking at you, Mia."

She smiled back at him. "I like looking at you, too. But let's not forget your daughter is nearby." She crinkled up her empty sandwich wrapper. "Time to get to work."

"All right. As long as you promise to play later."

Her cheeks flushed at his words. "You have to stop saying things like that, Jeremy."

"No, I don't. It's still summer, and you said this was a summer fling. I plan on enjoying the hot days and the even hotter nights as long as I can."

Seventeen

As they walked toward the center of Central Park a little after seven, Mia was surprised at how many people were gathering for the eight o'clock movie. There were at least fifty families with every generation represented, from the older crowd sitting in their stable lawn chairs to the middle-aged parents sipping wine with their friends at picnic tables and the young moms and dads running after their kids.

"Mia," Charlotte said with a wave. "Come sit over here. Kara, Colin, and kids are on their way."

Mia glanced back at Jeremy. "What do you think?"

"Sounds good to me."

"I want you to meet my husband Joe," Charlotte said, as they approached the picnic table where Charlotte and a very attractive dark-haired man were standing.

Mia shook hands with Joe, noting his strong, firm grip. "It's nice to meet you, Joe, and congratulations."

"Congratulations?" Jeremy asked, giving Charlotte and Joe a speculative look.

Charlotte smiled. "We're having a baby, Jeremy. I spilled the beans the other night at the coloring book party."

"That's great news," Jeremy said. "I'm very happy for both of you."

"She's doing the hard part," Joe said with a laugh, putting an arm around Charlotte. "But thanks for including me."

"You had a lot to do with the fun part," Charlotte told Joe with a mischievous smile.

Mia found them both delightfully charming. Like Kara and Colin, Charlotte and Joe seemed madly in love and also quite respectful, admiring and caring about the other person in their partnership. Theirs was the kind of relationship she wanted for herself, and she found her gaze moving to the strong, handsome man by her side.

Summer fling, she told herself again.

She stepped back as Kara and Colin joined the group with their four kids in tow. As Kara set down a plate of cookies on the picnic table, she said, "Remind me never to have any more children. Four is crazy."

"How long will your nieces be here?" Charlotte asked with a laugh.

"Three more days. I love them to death, but it's a lot of work. I don't know how my mother did it."

"I've often wondered that about my mom," Mia said. "I'm the youngest of six, and my mother worked as a nurse, too."

"Did the older ones help?" Charlotte asked.

"My sister Annie watched me a lot, but the boys were usually gone." She paused as another couple joined their group—Kent and a pretty blonde.

"This is Dr. Eva Westcott," Kent said. "I think you know most everyone, Eva."

"Except probably me," Mia said, giving Eva a friendly smile. "I'm Mia Callaway."

"I've heard a lot about you from Ashlyn," Eva said,

giving the little girl a smile. "How are you today, Ashlyn?"

"Good," Ashlyn said, then wandered over to join Kara's crew of girls, who were lining up some dolls for the upcoming movie.

"She's doing so much better," Jeremy told Eva. "I wanted to thank you for your help."

"I don't think I had a lot to do with it." Eva paused. "Both Ashlyn and Kent told me that his police vehicle triggered her breakthrough. We never know what will make the wall crack."

"I'm just glad she turned to me," Jeremy said.

"You're her father. That's going to happen more and more." Eva nodded to a couple waving at her from across the path. "If you'll excuse me for a minute."

"Of course," Mia said as Eva walked over to her friends.

"So you finally got her to go on a date with you," Jeremy said to Kent.

"I wore her down," Kent said with a proud smile. "It's nice to see you all out here. Any other problems at the house, Mia?"

"No," she said, not wanting to get into the discovery of the painting in front of everyone. She glanced over at Jeremy and he gave her a nod, silently telling her he would follow her lead. "However, I have cleaned out the studio. I think I've found all the paintings. Let me know if you want to come by and see if yours is there. I'd be happy to give it back to you." She'd decided that was the easiest thing to do rather than get into a battle with any of the artists.

"That sounds good. I'll come by and take a look tomorrow."

"Perfect."

"I'm going to catch up with Eva. See you around."

As Kent left, she smiled at Jeremy. "Kent seems smitten by Ashlyn's therapist."

"It's taken her a year to decide if she wants to date him, so we'll see."

"He doesn't give up, does he?"

"No, but it usually doesn't take him this long to convince a woman he's the perfect man for her."

She had a feeling that neither Jeremy nor his friends had ever had trouble finding women. They were good-looking alpha warriors. Who could resist that?

"Ashlyn is having a good time," Jeremy commented, tipping his head toward his daughter, who was in the middle of the group of girls. "I can't believe the change that has occurred in the past few days." He turned back to her. "It started with you, Mia. Once you climbed onto that roof and yelled for help, everything changed."

She made a face at his teasing smile. "You need to forget about that."

"Impossible. I can't forget anything about you."

"You should try, and we should set up our chairs. It's getting close to eight."

"I think Ashlyn has already chosen her seat," he said. "Why don't you and I sit behind everyone else? Then we can make out during the boring parts."

"There are no boring parts in the *Sound of Music.* Making out will have to wait."

"But it will eventually happen, right?"

She liked the hopeful gleam in his eyes. "If you play your cards right, there's a good possibility of that."

"You just made this movie we're about to sit through even longer."

She laughed, loving how easy it was to joke around with Jeremy. When she'd first met him, she hadn't imagined he'd have such a good sense of humor, that he could not only be serious but also playful. She also loved the way he looked at her. Even in a crowd, she could feel his admiration, his desire, and it was a heady feeling. She'd never felt so wanted before. She was just afraid that it wouldn't and couldn't last.

Twenty minutes later, the crowd had settled into chairs as the movie began to play. It was a beautiful warm, starry night—the temperature around seventy degrees, the perfect background for an evening of family entertainment.

Mia felt relaxed and happy, and even happier still when Jeremy took her hand midway through the movie and wrapped his fingers around hers. She couldn't remember the last time a man had just held her hand. The connection was more special than she would have imagined.

When the movie was over, they chatted with Kara and Colin, Charlotte and Joe and a bunch of other people whose names she couldn't remember. Finally, they began to pack up a little before eleven. While Jeremy took some stuff to the car and Ashlyn ran around with her friends, Mia took some trash to the large garbage bins set up near the bathrooms.

On her way back, she was surprised to see Kent standing under the shadows of a nearby tree with Christina Wykoff, the woman who had come to her house a few days earlier. They appeared to be having a rather heated discussion. Kent said something, then Christina waved her hand in the air in frustration. Kent said something else, and she gave a vehement shake of her head.

Then Christina suddenly turned around and walked away, stopping abruptly when she saw Mia.

Mia started, realizing that she'd been caught staring at them.

Christina moved toward her. "I'm glad I ran into you. Have you pulled out all the paintings from the studio? I'd really like to find mine."

"I was actually going to give you a call. I do have the paintings available for you to look at."

"Good. Will you be around in the morning?"

"Yes, I should be there all day."

"I'll come by around ten."

"Great," she muttered as the woman walked away without even bothering to say thank-you.

Kent came forward as Christina left. "Hey, Mia."

"Hi," she said. "What happened to Eva?"

"She got a call from a patient; she had to leave. How do you know Christina?"

"We met the other day when she came to my aunt's house to look for her painting," Mia answered.

"That's right. I forgot she painted there last year, too."

"She'd also like to get her painting back."

"That makes sense. She stayed there after a bitter divorce. I'm sure she had some demons to paint away, too."

"I told her to come by tomorrow and take a look." She paused. "You don't think Christina could have broken into the studio, do you?"

"No," he said, shaking his head, not a doubt in his eyes. "The damage that was done there was not perpetrated by a woman who hates to break a nail."

"I have to admit she doesn't seem the type." She really wanted to ask Kent what he'd been arguing with Christina about, but that seemed a little too nosey.

"Kent, Mia," a man called.

She turned around to see Barton walking toward

them. "Hi. It's Craig, right?"

"Call me Barton, everyone does," he said. "I guess I missed the movie?"

"Yes, it ended awhile ago," she said.

"I figured."

"Like you came here to watch the movie," Kent teased. "Who is she and where is she?"

Barton laughed. "I don't cruise the park for women, Kent."

"You'll cruise anywhere for a woman."

"You've got me there."

"I have to run," Kent said. "I'll see you both around."

"Bye, Kent," she said.

"So where's Jeremy?" Barton asked.

"He's putting our chairs in the car."

"What's going on with you and him?" he asked with an interested grin.

Apparently, Barton didn't share her concern about being too nosey.

"Tonight, it's just a movie," she said lightly, seeing his speculative gaze.

"What about tomorrow?"

"Who knows?" she said with a shrug.

"He's a good guy—Jeremy. One of the best men I've ever known."

She saw the sincerity in his eyes. "I believe that."

"You should. He's the kind of person who will stand by you no matter what. Once he's your friend, he's your friend for life."

She appreciated the admiration in Barton's gaze. "Good to know."

"I think you're good for him. When I saw him in the hospital after he got hurt, he was a shadow of himself. That blast had changed everything for him. His luck had finally run out." He paused. "I didn't expect him to find out he had a kid. At first, I thought it was the worst thing, just another horrible setback for his career, but now it seems like it was the best thing that could have happened. He can't go back to Delta, but he still has a lot to live for."

"Of course he does. He's more than a job, no matter how good he was at that job."

"I want him to work in private security with me. There's a position down in L.A. that would be perfect for him."

"What does he want?"

"He's thinking about it," Barton said with a smile. "That's Jeremy. He always has to think things through. I'm more of a jump-first, think-later kind of guy, which is probably why Jeremy had to save my ass on occasion."

"I have a feeling you returned the favor."

"We've been through a lot together, but Jeremy has always been one step ahead of me."

She was curious about his comment, but she didn't have time to ask what he was referring to when Jeremy interrupted them.

"Barton, what the hell are you doing here? I thought it was the big birthday bash tonight," Jeremy said.

"It was, but Angel's Bay birthday bashes end by ten, especially with my mom's crowd. I'd ask you to hit a bar with me, but I have a feeling there's a kid nearby."

"Ashlyn is with Kara, and we're headed home, but you have fun," Jeremy said.

"I always do," Barton replied.

"Daddy, Daddy," Ashlyn interrupted, running over to them with excitement in her expression.

"What's up?" Jeremy asked.

"Faith's mom is going to have a sleepover at her house tomorrow night, and she said I can come and play with everyone. Can I go?"

"Sure, I guess so," Jeremy replied, looking as surprised as Mia was by Ashlyn's request to spend the night elsewhere. "That sounds like fun. We'll talk about it when we get home."

"I'll tell them I'm coming," she said, running back to the group.

"Looks like the kid is coming out of her shell," Barton commented.

"I can't believe it," Jeremy muttered. "I'm happy she wants to play with other kids. I'm not sure about a sleepover, though. Do you think she's ready to be away from me, Mia?"

"There's probably only one way to find out. You have to trust what she wants to do."

He nodded. "I'll talk to her more about it tomorrow."

"Hey," Barton said, a mischievous gleam in his eyes. "Maybe you and Mia should have a sleepover tomorrow night, too."

Jeremy shot his friend a dark look. "Not cool, Barton."

"I'm just joking. Mia knows that, don't you, Mia?"

She smiled and gave a nod, doubting that Barton ever thought before he spoke, but he had no malicious intent. "It's fine. But Jeremy and I don't need your help to plan a sleepover. We can do that ourselves."

He laughed. "I like your style, Mia. A straight shooter." He patted Jeremy's good shoulder. "Lucky guy. I'll see you later."

"Sorry about Barton," Jeremy said, as his friend left. "He doesn't know when to shut up."

"He's entertaining, that's for sure. Ready to go?"

"After you."

It was close to midnight by the time they got home.

Ashlyn had once again fallen asleep in the car.

"Do you want help carrying things inside?" Mia asked.

"I can make a few trips."

"Are you sure?"

"Unless you want to bring some things inside and stay awhile—maybe all night?"

"I think I should stay at home tonight," she said, forcing the words out of her mouth, then regretting them immediately. But her practical side, the side that told her she better be careful or she was going to fall completely in love with this man, and he was going to break her heart, was making her cautious.

"Really?" he asked with disappointment.

"I could use some sleep, and we don't do much sleeping when we're together."

He smiled. "That's true. All right. Let's talk about tomorrow night. Since Ashlyn has plans for herself, what do you think about going on a date with me?"

"A date, huh?"

"Yes. I take you somewhere nicer than a pizza parlor or a diner, and we have an adult evening." He gave her a sparkling smile that sent butterflies dancing through her stomach. "Say yes."

"Yes," she said, realizing that once again she'd had another opportunity to say no to Jeremy and had chosen the affirmative instead. "I'd love to have dinner with you and have an adult evening."

"Good. I'm still going to miss you tonight, though."

"I'm going to miss you, too."

"You can change your mind."

"It's tempting, but I have a lot to do tomorrow."

"What's on the schedule?"

"More cleaning, and more research. I'm surprised

Kate hasn't gotten back to me yet or my friend. I thought one or both of them would have contacted me by now. In the meantime, I'm going to move on with the gallery exhibition. I spoke to Didi Eckhart at the gallery earlier today, and she's going to come by tomorrow afternoon to see the paintings. I also told Kent and Christina they could come by and look for their art. I still need to contact one other woman. But it should be a busy day." It felt good to have a plan of things to do other than sleep with Jeremy.

"Sounds like it. I hope the artists let you keep their paintings. It seems wrong for them to take them back. I get that it's personal for them, but they still gave their art to your aunt, so it couldn't have been that personal."

"I feel the same way. I'm surprised by the negative reactions." She paused. "By the way, Christina was with Kent in the park after the movie. Kent told me that Eva had to leave to see a patient and that Christina was an old friend, but they didn't look too friendly. They were having a heated argument when I saw them. You said you didn't know her, right?"

"No, I don't know her, but Ken has been back here for over a year now. He knows lots of people I don't."

"I got the feeling their friendship went back longer than a year."

"Maybe. Kent has always had more friends than me. He was a lot more outgoing than I was when we were growing up. Barton was the same. I was the quiet one when I was with those two." He paused, giving her a thoughtful look. "It sounds like you think something strange was going on."

"I just had an odd feeling when I saw them arguing; I don't really know why."

"Do you want me to ask him?"

"Of course not. It's none of my business. Forget I said anything."

"You know, Mia, it occurs to me that some of the artists who stayed here might not be completely sane. It might not be safe for you to stay alone in the house."

She smiled at his latest attempt to convince her to stay with him. "I'm not worried about crazy artists, Jeremy. I think you just want to get me into your bed."

"Well, I do want that, but I'm also concerned about the vandalism and the odd reactions you're getting from the artists."

"I appreciate that, but I'll be fine. I'll lock all the doors, and I'll put my phone by my bed. If I hear anything, you'll be my first call."

"I better be."

She leaned over and gave him a kiss. "Goodnight, Jeremy. I had a great time."

"So did I."

She got out of the car and forced herself to walk across the lawn. When she reached the porch, she waved to Jeremy, who was watching to make sure she got in okay. Then she locked the door behind her and mentally kicked herself for choosing a night alone instead of a night in bed with one of the sexiest men she'd ever been with. But it was the smart choice, wasn't it?

Her brain said yes; her body said hell, no.

But it was better this way. She needed to get some distance, some perspective, some plan for how she was ever going to say good-bye to him.

Eighteen

At ten o'clock, Christina Wykoff walked into Mia's backyard, once again choosing not to ring the bell.

Mia had anticipated her arrival and had spent the past hour cleaning up the patio and putting the entire group of paintings in one spot so that Christina could easily take her painting and go.

Christina was dressed more casually today in skinny white jeans and a sleeveless blouse. But there was still a cool air about her. Most of the people in Angel's Bay were warm and friendly, but not Christina.

"Hello, how are you this morning?" Mia asked.

"Fine. Are these all the paintings?"

"Yes. Is one of them yours?"

Christina looked at the paintings on display and frowned. "No, mine isn't here."

"Really? What did it look like?"

"An abstract maze. I drew squares and rectangles; it was a metaphor for my life at the time. Have you seen it?"

"I'm sorry, I haven't. It's possible my aunt did something with it or that it was unfortunately destroyed during some vandalism that occurred in the studio a few days ago."

"A few days ago?" Christina asked, raising an eyebrow. "Since I was last here?"

"Yes. Some of the paintings were ripped apart."

"You couldn't salvage them?"

"No, I could only throw them away." She could see that Christina was not happy about her reply. "I will say, though, that the description of your painting doesn't ring a bell. I don't remember seeing anything that looked like an abstract maze."

"Well, what would your aunt have done with it?"

For a moment, she thought about the paintings she'd seen in her aunt's closet, but none of them fit Christina's description. "I have no idea. I'm sorry. If it comes to light, I'll contact you, but you can certainly be assured it won't be part of the show I'm putting together, so you don't have to worry about that."

Christina didn't look satisfied by her words. "Are there any paintings in the house?"

"No."

"Really? Not one painting? Your aunt was an art lover. I can't believe her walls are bare."

"Your painting isn't in the house," she said, lifting her chin as Christina sent her an angry look. "You're going to have to trust me on that. And, frankly, your painting was payment for your stay here. It belongs to my aunt's estate. However, I am trying to be sympathetic to your feelings. If I see anything that looks remotely like it, I will let you know, but I can tell you right now that I've been through everything, and I don't believe it is anywhere on this property."

Christina stared back at her through angry, frustrated eyes. "All right. I guess I'll have to live with that."

After Christina left, Mia blew out a breath, feeling unsettled by their conversation. She didn't like the interest

Christina had expressed in getting into the house, but she reminded herself that the locksmith had changed the locks so the house should be secure. If someone wanted to come back here and steal everything in sight, she couldn't stop them. But she also couldn't worry about it anymore. There was nowhere else to put anything. Hopefully, once she spoke to Didi Eckhart, she could take the paintings to the gallery and move on with the showing.

"Hello? Hello? Anyone back here?" A woman's voice rang through the air. A moment later, Rita Phelps walked into the yard, wearing a flowing, colorful maxi dress and sandals. "Mia, there you are. I rang the bell."

"I didn't hear it; I'm sorry."

"I thought I might retrieve my painting."

"Of course. You were on my list to call. Here are the paintings I pulled out of the studio."

Rita made the same trip around the patio that Christina had taken. "It's this one," she said with relief, pointing to the oil painting of a seaside landscape. It wasn't the best painting in the group; in fact it might have been one of the worst, but Mia kept that opinion to herself.

"May I take it with me?" Rita asked.

"Yes, please. I'm glad you found it."

"I really feel that Carly would have wanted me to take it back and sell it myself, and then use the money to continue my art."

She nodded, not sure of any of that, but she wasn't up for arguing with any more possessive artists. "I'm sure you're right."

"What are you going to do with the studio, if you don't mind my asking? Will you open it up again to other artists?"

"I don't know if we'll keep the house or the studio.

My mother will make that decision."

"It would be sad to see it go. This place has been an inspiring refuge for so many people."

Mia felt a little sad at the thought as well, but it wasn't realistic to think her parents would want to keep this property. It was far away, and they could probably use the money that would come from a sale.

She looked up as the gate opened once again, and Kent walked into the yard. Everyone was coming at the same time. It was just as well. She'd get through the three reluctant artists first.

"Thanks again," Rita said.

"You're welcome." She gave Kent a smile. "Good morning."

"How are you today?"

"Getting a lot done."

"That's always good. So are these all the paintings you could find? I don't see mine."

"Well, you know that some of them were destroyed the other day. Maybe yours was one of them."

He nodded. "I guess I should have looked more closely when I came in that day. But, whatever, it probably belonged in the trash anyway. Jeremy told me I was an idiot for caring about this."

"I understand that you painted from a very personal place."

"I did. I never stepped outside when I was here. I couldn't face the sun or the beauty of the view. I painted in the dead of the night, sometimes by candlelight, and it was all just washes of color, darkness and evil, and the images that wouldn't leave my mind." He stopped talking abruptly, as if he'd just realized she was there. "Sorry, that was a little heavy, wasn't it?"

More than a little heavy for a guy who usually acted

like he was the happiest man on earth. But there was obviously another side to him. "I'm sorry for what you went through, Kent."

"I signed up for it. I just didn't think the enemy would look the way it did."

"What do you mean?"

"My team was ambushed by a bunch of kids. They couldn't have been more than fourteen or fifteen. Children should be children, not pawns of war, but in other parts of the world, the indoctrination starts early." He drew in a breath. "Sorry again. I don't know what is wrong with me. I guess being back here makes me remember that time in my life. I'm proud of the service I did, but I'm happy to be living a normal life again."

"Do you think Jeremy could ever be happy away from the Army?" she impulsively asked.

Kent gave her a thoughtful look. "I know the answer you're looking for, but the truth is I don't know if I can say he would be happy. I don't think he would have ever quit if it had been left up to him, if he hadn't been injured, if he hadn't discovered he was a father. Those changes have turned his life upside down. You should have seen him when he first got here; he was a pale shadow of himself. He's come a long way in a few weeks, just like his daughter has." Kent smiled. "I have a feeling that has a little to do with you."

"Probably more to do with time," she said.

"You're being modest."

"I like Jeremy. I'm sure that's not a surprise to you. But we're both in a transitional period, and Jeremy has a lot of decisions to make that don't include me; and I do as well."

"Maybe you'll start factoring each other into those decisions."

"That seems like a crazy idea."

"Crazier than walking away from each other? It's so hard to find someone you really click with, Mia. Do you want to throw that away because of geography or career choices?"

It was a good question. Too bad she didn't have an answer.

"I think Jeremy should stay here," Kent continued. "Angel's Bay is a good place for him to start over. And Ashlyn would have a great childhood here. But I'm not sure this town has enough to offer him. Jeremy has lived on adrenaline for a long time. He's used to danger, excitement, and adventure."

"You were used to that, too."

"But I was ready to move on. Once I started sleeping through the night, I appreciated the fact that I could sleep without worrying about surviving until morning. There's something to be said for peace. Jeremy and I have been fighting for peace in the world, but at what point do you ask for some peace within yourself? For me, I reached that point. Jeremy's tipping point is still to be decided. He'll figure it out. And you'll figure things out, too. Angel's Bay is a good place for soul searching."

"It's funny, because coming to Angel's Bay for me was an exciting adventure. I got to step away from my real life and see what else is out there. Who knows what's next?"

"The sky's the limit, Mia."

"That's what Aunt Carly would have said."

"Good luck with the exhibition. Sorry for being a pain in the ass about my art."

"You've been nicer than some of the others."

"Did Christina find her picture?"

"No, she came by earlier. She was pissed off that it

wasn't here. I wouldn't be surprised if she asked you to get her a search warrant for the house. She really wanted to go inside, but I have to draw the line somewhere. I'm trying to be understanding, but there's a point where people have to accept that if you give something away, it might not come back."

"Now, you're making me feel guilty for trying to get my painting back."

"Sorry, I was talking more about Christina, because she was really rude to me. I don't have the best impression of her."

"She has a hot temper," he conceded.

"It looked like the two of you were arguing last night in the park.

"That usually happens when we're together," he said. "She's just one of those people who pushes my buttons, and I push hers."

Mia nodded, thinking that he still hadn't said what they'd been arguing about.

"I'll see you later, Mia. And let me know if anyone else gives you any trouble. You don't have to let anyone into your house, and you shouldn't."

"Thanks."

After Kent left, Mia went back into the house. She still had some time before Didi Eckhart arrived, and she wanted to spend it looking into her mysterious painting.

She spent the next two hours on the computer. She'd studied Henri de Toulouse-Lautrec in school, but she hadn't had much to do with his artwork in recent years, so it was good to refresh her memory. She learned a lot about his life in Paris and his love of the Parisian nightlife. She thought many of his paintings were exquisite and several reminded her of the one on her kitchen table. She became more and more convinced that he was the artist or that someone had copied his style.

It wasn't unusual for artists to copy the works of the masters, sometimes as a method of studying and learning, other times as a way to pay homage to the classics. And, of course, there were forgers interested in passing off their work as the real thing for lots and lots of money.

While it was frustrating not to be able to find the exact painting online, she did enjoy the research, which took her back to her college days. She'd always loved to learn. It was when she'd graduated and started working that she'd stopped learning new things. That was going to change no matter what she decided to do.

Around one, she made a salad and ate her lunch in front of the computer. Her mind occasionally drifted to Jeremy. Since she'd arrived, they'd spent all their time together, and it felt strange when hours passed without him calling or coming by. But they had a date tonight, and that would be fun.

So much of their relationship had involved Ashlyn, except for the steamy nights, of course. It would be fun to spend time with him alone, to get to know him even better.

She shivered a little at the thought of spending the night with him again.

Last night had felt long and lonely and while she'd chosen to sleep alone, hoping she'd actually catch up on some sleep, that hadn't really happened. She'd spent most of the night thinking about Jeremy, about being the woman in his life past the summer. And she thought about Ashlyn, too. The little girl had already stolen her heart. She needed a mother. And someday Jeremy would probably give her one. Mia felt a little jealous at the thought of that unknown woman who would take her place with Jeremy and Ashlyn, the one she'd been really enjoying the past week.

She tried to remind herself that she'd only known him a short time, that it was a summer romance, that she was getting way ahead of herself, but she'd always been one to look to the future, and a future without Jeremy seemed rather dismal.

Her computer pinged, and she focused her attention on the screen as she realized she'd finally gotten an email back from her friend in France, Danielle Malone.

According to Danielle, the painting was thought to be one of Toulouse-Lautrec's unfinished paintings.

She smiled a little proudly, happy that she'd already guessed that.

Danielle believed that the painting had been part of a collection of paintings discovered in an attic after his death in 1901. It was said that he had put paintings there that he deemed unworthy of his talent. But everyone in the art world thought they were stunning.

The paintings had then been purchased as part of a collection for a museum in Paris. Unfortunately, that museum was looted during World War II, and the painting had not been seen since. Some of the artwork from that museum had shown up in various parts of the world, but the location of that particular painting was still unknown.

Mia blew out a breath as goose bumps ran down her arms at the knowledge that the painting in front of her was not only very old but had also been stolen—maybe more than once.

Danielle suggested she get in touch with the museum to see if they had any further information.

She noted the name of the curator, his email, and phone number. Danielle said she'd attempted to contact the museum, but it was closed until Monday. She would be off on a business trip, so Mia would have to do it herself.

Mia wrote back a quick thank-you and told her she'd take it from there and would keep her posted on what she found out. She was thrilled that Danielle had confirmed her suspicion that the painting had been done by Toulouse-Lautrec, and she couldn't wait to hear what the curator at the museum in Paris would be able to tell her.

There was still a possibility that the painting in her possession was a forgery, but based on the circumstances surrounding her find, she didn't think so. Who would take such care to hide a fake?

However, she would need to send it to an expert to determine if it was an original work. She didn't have the tools to test the paint or age of the paper or study the brushstrokes in enough detail to be certain of its authenticity, but she had plenty of contacts in San Francisco. She just wasn't ready to leave Angel's Bay to do that, and she didn't want to let the painting out of her sight. Nor did she want to alert the world that her aunt was in possession of a stolen painting until she'd had a chance to figure out how it had gotten into Carly's closet.

The doorbell rang interrupting her thoughts. She closed her computer, rolled up the painting and stuck it in the kitchen pantry, then walked down the hall to open the door.

Didi Eckhart was on the front porch, dressed in a blue sleeveless sheath dress and heeled sandals, a large purse hanging over her shoulder.

"Mrs. Eckhart. Thank you so much for coming."

"I'm excited to see what you have. And please call me Didi." She glanced around as she stepped into the entry. "I haven't been inside this house in a long time. Carly has acquired more art since the last time I was here."

"Art and junk," Mia said with a helpless shrug. "She loved what she loved; it didn't always have to have value."

"A sentiment I share." She paused in front of a portrait of a young girl sitting at a piano, her hands resting lightly on the keys, her gaze turned toward the window and not the instrument she was about to play. "Carly purchased this one from the gallery. It's by a local artist named Roger Henry. He's quite good."

"I do like it," Mia said. "Why don't we go out to the patio? I have the paintings set up out there. Can I get you some lemonade?"

"That would be lovely. It's such a warm day."

Mia had made some lemonade earlier, so she grabbed the pitcher and two glasses from the kitchen and ushered Didi into the backyard. She poured the lemonade while Didi looked at the paintings.

"It's certainly an eclectic mix of oil, acrylic and watercolors," Didi said, walking back to the table.

"It's definitely a mix," Mia agreed, as she handed her a glass of lemonade. "Please sit down. Sorry for the mess, but I'm still sorting everything out, and it was easier to do it out here than in the studio. I needed the space to see what I had."

"I completely understand." Didi gave her a warm smile. "It's so nice to sit with you, Mia. Your aunt spoke of you often, how proud she was that you were moving forward in an art career. She told me that she'd given you your first set of paints."

"That's very true. She taught me to paint and she inspired me in many ways. I spent several summers here when I was a teenager. They're some of my fondest memories. I wish now I'd made more of an effort to get back before this tragedy."

"Well, Carly might not have been here. She did a lot of traveling the last few years." Didi sipped her lemonade and then said, "Your aunt inspired me as well. After my husband died, I was just going to let the gallery run the way it had always run, but Carly talked to me about making it into a business that I really cared about. At first, I thought it might be disloyal to my husband to make huge changes. I'd always left the big decisions in our lives to him. But the more I thought about it, and the more time I spent at the gallery with Harrison Raleigh, the more I realized that I wanted a gallery with my last name on it to be reflective of my personal choices."

"That makes sense."

"You probably wonder why it took me so long to get to that conclusion, but I'm in my sixties, and I grew up in a world where women deferred to men. I'm still fighting some of the old traditions in my head. But you're a young woman. You would never let a man decide your life for you, would you?"

"I would try not to," she said. "But it's easy to get caught up in love."

"Are you in love with someone, Mia?"

"Possibly," she said slowly.

Didi laughed. "I don't know everything, but I do know one thing about love. When the answer is *possibly,* it just means you're fighting your instincts or maybe keeping some walls up."

"You're right about that. I've made some mistakes in the past when it came to men, or at least one man."

"Don't let that one man influence the way you think about other men."

"It's hard not to do that."

"Well, no one said love was easy. You know what I

sometimes ask myself when I'm trying to make a decision now that my husband is gone?"

"What's that?"

"What would Carly do?"

Mia smiled. "Good question."

"What would her answer be for you, Mia?"

"Probably to go for it. That love isn't practical. That it makes you crazy and that's the fun of it. But it's not that simple. I've met a man here in town, and I won't be staying in Angel's Bay past the summer. I have to go back to San Francisco and find myself a job."

"I thought you were already working in a museum."

"I was. That man I was referring to—the one I made a mistake with—kind of messed that up. But I'm not sorry the job ended; it wasn't really for me. It was more paperwork than art, and since I've come back here, I've been reminded that art is so much more than the famous paintings displayed on the walls of a museum. I want to be able to have more freedom to work with artists and open art up to more people. I love that Aunt Carly used her studio for art therapy, that she let people stay here for free while they painted their problems away. I hate to see that end."

"Does it have to end?"

"It's not my house. My parents own it now, and I'm sure they'll sell it."

"Maybe to you."

"Out of my price range. And there's still the problem of a job."

"You know, I might have an idea for you," Didi said, a gleam in her eyes.

"What's that?"

"You could come and work for me. You could take Harrison's place as soon as I fire him."

She was shocked by Didi's suggestion. "That's a very generous offer, but I don't think I could do that. And Mr. Raleigh has worked at the gallery a long time. Can you really fire him?"

"I don't want to fire him out of loyalty to my husband, but he fights me at every turn. If I want to take control of the gallery, he has to go. Just think about it, Mia. Put it on your list of *possibilities*."

She smiled at Didi's choice of words. "I will do that. But you don't know that much about me."

"I know enough. I'm sure you're very qualified, and I love your idea for the exhibition. Why don't you bring the paintings to the gallery next week? We'll set up a date and make our plans."

"Do you want all of them?"

"I'd love for you to pick eight that you think are worthy of a spot in the gallery. We'll figure out the rest of the details later."

"I do have one other concern," she said. "My aunt asked every artist to leave her a piece of their art as payment for their stay in the studio. I assume that all these paintings belong to my aunt's estate. But a couple of artists have already expressed concern about their art being publicly displayed. I don't quite know what to do about it. I've resolved the issue with those artists who have contacted me, but I have no idea who painted these works of art."

"Well, this is a small town and news spreads fast. I'll let the artists I work with know about the exhibition. We'll make up a flyer, and we'll see who comes out of the woodwork. As far as I'm concerned, the paintings belong to your aunt's estate. I'm not a lawyer, but I could certainly consult an attorney to make sure we're on the right track."

"That would be great. I don't want to make any problems for you or for myself."

"Consider it done." Didi got to her feet. "Thank you for the lemonade. It reminded me of Carly. We shared many a glass of lemonade on this very patio. We talked about men and work and life and the world. I miss those days."

Mia wished she'd had more days like that with her aunt to miss.

She walked Didi out to her car, debating if she should mention the mystery painting and eventually deciding against it. Didi seemed like a good friend of Carly's, but how well did Mia really know her? It would be better to get the painting out of Angel's Bay and give it to an objective party who knew nothing about her aunt or anyone else in town.

After she said goodbye, she went back into the house and unrolled the painting once more. "Tell me your secrets," she said, as she spread it out on the table once more. Unfortunately, the painting wasn't going to give her an answer. She would have to find it somewhere else.

Nineteen

---※───

Jeremy pulled up to Kara's house a little after five. He'd spent the day with Ashlyn getting her ready for the sleepover. She'd told him she needed new pajamas, a new sleeping bag, and a new backpack to carry her toothbrush and teddy bear in.

While Ashlyn seemed pretty happy about the upcoming event, he was worried that she was getting ahead of herself. What if the nightmares returned when she was at Kara's house? What if she scared the other kids with her screams, or woke up crying and couldn't be comforted? It seemed too soon to let her go.

On the other hand, she really wanted to go, and she'd told him that she'd gone to a sleepover for her friend's seventh birthday party last year, which meant she wasn't a complete novice at being away from a parent.

As that thought crossed his mind, he realized that he was forgetting the month she'd spent in foster care completely alone. But that had been different. That had been scary and sad.

He turned off the engine and turned to Ashlyn. "If you change your mind and you want to come home at any point, you know you can call me. I'll come right over and pick you up."

"I know," she said.

"It doesn't matter what time it is. If it's the middle of the night, I'll still come, and I won't be mad."

"Okay, Daddy."

His heart caught at her response. He still wasn't used to hearing that word come out of her mouth.

"It's going to be okay," she told him. "I'm going to have fun."

He smiled, wondering when the tables had turned. Now she was worrying about him. "I know you'll have a good time."

"We're going to make cookies and watch movies and tell stories. And Faith's mom said she's going to put up a tent in the living room that we can sleep in. It will be like we're camping."

"That sounds very cool."

"Mommy said she used to camp when she was a little girl," Ashlyn told him, her smile fading a little. "She was going to take me, but she never did."

"I know she'd be happy that you're going indoor camping tonight, and one of these days you and I will go outdoor camping. I know some great places to go."

"Will we see bears?"

"Well, I kind of hope not," he said with a laugh. "But we can hike up to an amazing waterfall. You'll love it."

"Can Mia come with us when we go camping?"

His gut tightened. He'd like nothing more than for Mia to come with them, but he needed to be careful about making promises to Ashlyn that he couldn't keep. He wanted his daughter to trust him completely. But he didn't want to get into a heavy discussion now when she was itching to get out of the car, so he said, "We'll see if she's free. Let's go inside."

He walked Ashlyn into the party and watched her join the other kids with barely a backward glance in his direction.

"You going to be okay, Dad?" Kara asked him with a teasing smile, a knowing gleam in her eyes.

"It's just so strange. A couple of days ago, she could barely smile or speak to anyone. Now, it's like she's a new person. Once she was able to talk about what happened to her mom and cry it out on my shoulder, she got better."

"That's a good thing, Jeremy."

"I just want it to last, and I'm afraid that this night might be a bit much for her."

"I will make sure that she's fine, and if she's not, you will get a call. But honestly, Jeremy, I think it's going to be great. She's really good with the little kids. My two already love her to death, and Jeanette and Melody have decided she's their new best friend." She put a reassuring hand on his arm. "Go out and have some fun. I don't expect you've had much time to yourself the last month."

"No, I haven't."

"Are you and Mia going out somewhere tonight?"

Everyone had obviously decided he and Mia were a couple, which actually didn't sound bad to him. It had been a long day without her by his side; he was looking forward to their first real date. "I thought I'd take her to the Stonecreek Inn."

"That's romantic and expensive. Lucky girl."

"I'm the lucky one. She's an amazing woman. I've never met anyone like her."

"She is great," Kara agreed. "I like her a lot. She's friendly and unpretentious and fun. I wish she'd stay in Angel's Bay. I wish you'd stay, too."

"I don't know what I'm going to do."

"I know you have issues with your dad."

"I've resolved some of those, I think. Although, I thought he might come to the park last night for the movie, and he didn't. I don't know if he fell off the wagon again or just wasn't ready to meet Ashlyn and try to be a grandfather. But it doesn't matter. He's not going to be part of my decision."

"I'm glad. You can't let the negative people in your life control you."

"I agree. So is Colin helping you with this sleepover?"

"Absolutely. Are you kidding? I would not do this without him. He ran out to the store to get more eggs for our cookie baking bonanza."

"Great. I'll see you tomorrow morning then, if not before."

"Have fun, Jeremy. You deserve it."

He walked over to Ashlyn to tell her he was leaving. She gave him a nod and a quick hug and then went back to the game she was playing. *She would be fine*, he told himself again as he headed to his car. He needed to get on with his own fun.

As he drove away from Kara's house, he felt free, not just because he'd dropped Ashlyn off somewhere, but because his daughter was enjoying her life like a normal eight-year-old. He'd come to Angel's Bay to give her an environment where she'd feel safe, where she could heal, and amazingly that had happened.

How was he ever going to leave?

But that was a question for another time. Right now he had a date with a beautiful blonde.

⇀⇢⇠⇀

"Is it crazy that I feel nervous?" Mia asked Jeremy as

she got into his car just before seven. She'd put on a spaghetti-strapped sundress and wedge heels and actually taken time to curl her hair and put on makeup. She was feeling both pretty and not really herself. "It's not like we haven't had a meal together."

"Or had incredible sex," he reminded her.

"Or that," she said, flushing under his gaze. "But tonight feels different. It feels planned. Like we're making a choice."

"The only choice you have to make tonight is what to order off the menu. Stonecreek is known for its steaks, but we are by the ocean, so I'm sure the fish is good, too."

"It all sounds delicious. I only had a salad for lunch."

"What did you do all day—besides miss me?" he teased.

She laughed. "I didn't have time to miss you. I had a parade of people come through the yard. Christina Wykoff didn't find her painting and wanted to know what happened to it. Unfortunately, I couldn't give her an answer. She was not happy. Rita Phelps did locate her painting and took it out of the exhibition, which was fine with me, because it wasn't very good. Kent also came by, but he didn't locate his painting, either. He was more resigned to the fact that it was gone than Christina. She wanted to search the house."

"You didn't agree to that, did you?"

"No, that would be taking things way too far."

"I wonder what happened to the missing paintings," he mused.

"They could have been destroyed. We did throw a bunch of ripped canvases into the garbage. I suppose I should have looked more closely at them, but I just wanted to get the destruction out of my sight and out of my mind."

"Which was understandable. I still don't think anyone has a right to anything they left behind. You're being generous to try to help them, but you don't have to bend over backward for them."

"Hopefully, I won't have problems with any of the other artists. I also had a nice conversation with Didi Eckhart from the gallery. She liked the paintings and asked me to pick out the ones I like the best and bring them over this week. Then we'll figure out a date for the show. She also said she'd put the word out to see if we can find any of the other artists, just in case anyone else has a problem, which I hope they don't."

"You accomplished a lot."

"It did feel good to get something done." She paused. "Didi actually offered me a job."

He gave her a quick look. "Really? In the gallery?"

"She said she wants to turn her gallery into a more welcoming venue for local artists and her current curator is stuck in the old ways of her husband. She somehow thought I'd be perfect, even though we've only spoken for about thirty minutes."

"You make a good first impression," he said with a warm smile. "As well as a second and third and fourth…"

"Thank you, but I think she was basing her respect for me as much on her friendship with my aunt as anything else. Apparently, Carly helped her a lot when her husband died, and Didi felt like she found her feet again because of my aunt's inspiring words."

"Your aunt certainly did change a lot of lives."

"That was her legacy, right? It wasn't all the stuff she left behind; it was the people whose lives she touched."

"What about your mystery painting? Did you get any leads on that?"

"I heard from my friend in Paris. She confirmed my

suspicion that the painting was done by Henri de Toulouse-Lautrec. She said she thinks it was one of several paintings that he didn't deem good enough to sell or show. Apparently, after his death, there were numerous paintings found in his attic that no one had known about. Those paintings were later sold to a museum in Paris. Unfortunately, that museum was raided by the Nazis during World War II, and not all of the art was recovered. The pieces have ended up all over the world."

"So what's next?"

"I still need to hear from Kate. I want to know if the FBI has any leads on the painting's ownership after the war. I'll also need to get the painting appraised to see if it is in fact an original and not a copy, but I'll probably have to go back to San Francisco to do that. I want to be careful about how I handle this. Because the painting was found in my aunt's house, that could make her culpable of something."

He gave her a thoughtful look as he stopped at a light. "You don't think your aunt stole the painting, do you?"

"Of course not. But I don't know how to prove that. I need more information. Hopefully, Kate will get back to me soon, but I know she's on assignment in Japan, so who knows what she's up to."

"What is she doing in Japan?"

"I have no idea, but she sounded pretty excited about being there. She just finished her training, and I know she's eager to get into the action."

"She should be careful what she wishes for," he said, a serious note in his voice.

"Are you thinking about your own desire for adventure and how that turned out?" she asked.

He glanced over at her. "Your words did take me

back to the early days and also my first few assignments with Delta. We were considered the best of the best. We were the ones who would be sent into impossible situations to make miracles happen. It was a heady, powerful feeling."

"Is that what's so hard to give up now—that feeling of power?"

"It's more like the rush I got when I managed to do the impossible. Unfortunately, that didn't always happen. Not every mission was successful. And sometimes bureaucracy and politics played too big of a role, but that's the way the world goes." He turned into the parking lot behind the Stonecreek Inn. "We're here."

"It looks beautiful. Have you been here before?"

"Never, but I heard the food is great and the atmosphere is romantic."

She smiled at the look he gave her. "Looking for a little romance tonight, are you?"

"Definitely." He put his hand on her leg. "What about you?"

"We'll see how dinner goes," she said with a laugh.

They got out of the car and walked into the restaurant, which was tucked into a hillside. There were two decks: one on the front side of the restaurant overlooking the ocean and a side deck that looked over a picturesque creek and an ornamental bridge.

Their table was by the creek, and Mia liked the ripple of water over the rocks next to their table. It was very relaxing. They ordered wine, a vegetable appetizer and their entrées, then toasted each other with a drink and settled back in their seats.

She'd chosen the wild salmon with risotto and Jeremy had ordered a NY strip steak, both of which absolutely delicious. As they ate, they talked about nothing too serious: movies, books, baseball teams, fantasy football leagues and the legends of Angel's Bay— all the ordinary conversations that they'd somehow skipped in their very fast relationship.

Mia discovered that they shared a lot of the same views on the world, and on life. They also shared a similar sense of humor and had a crazy love of really bad movies involving robots and superhuman animals.

"I can't believe it," Jeremy said with a bemused shake of his head. "You actually liked *Rebel Robot III*. That is so not a girl's movie, especially a girly girl like you."

"I'm not that girly."

He laughed. "You're just the right amount of girly, Mia—soft, sexy, and we fit really well together."

"We were talking about *Rebel Robot*," she said, a little breathless from his seductive words. "I actually thought the second movie was the best."

"I liked the first one; the other two were pale imitations."

"There's going to be a fourth one next year."

"We'll have to go," he said.

It was an impulsive statement, she told herself. He wasn't making a promise, but his words still unsettled her a little, because she'd decided not to make plans beyond the summer with Jeremy. Not even movie plans. She couldn't look that far into the future, not because she was scared she would see them together having a relationship, but because she was afraid she wouldn't.

Her breath caught in her chest, and she reached for her water glass. She didn't want to admit she was falling in love with him, but she definitely felt like she'd lost her balance.

"You okay?" he asked, giving her a curious look.

"I think I got a crumb stuck in my throat," she said,

coughing a little and then sipping her water. "It's fine now."

"Good. I thought maybe it was my invitation to a movie next year that upset you."

He'd told her that what he loved most about their relationship was that they were honest with each other, but she didn't want to be honest now. Thankfully, she was saved from an answer by the ping of her phone. She pulled it out of her purse. "I'm sorry, do you mind if I read this?" she asked. "It's from Kate."

"Go ahead. I want to know what she has to say."

She read through the long text, her pulse beating a little faster with the new information. "Kate says the painting is on a list of stolen art from the museum in Paris that my friend told me about. Some of the art from that same museum was recently found in a palace in Bahrain." She looked at Jeremy. "Kate is worried that Aunt Carly was involved in either the theft or the knowledgeable acceptance of stolen art. But how could that be? I don't think Aunt Carly ever went to Bahrain. I don't even know where that is."

"Bahrain comprises a series of islands off the coast of Saudi Arabia," Jeremy said, his jaw tightening, his eyes darkening with shadows. "I was there a year ago."

"As part of a mission?"

"Yes."

"Can you tell me anything about it?"

"No. Sorry," he said in clipped tones. "I can't tell you about any of my jobs, Mia, not because I don't want to share with you, but because I can't. It would be a breach of national security."

"I understand. I shouldn't have asked. Anyway, I don't think my aunt ever went to Bahrain."

"She might not have had to go there to receive stolen

art. A lot of things go missing in that part of the world. There has been a tremendous amount of looting in the Middle East, and it's not always easy to tell the good guys from the bad guys."

"Kent said the same thing earlier. He told me that he'd never expected the enemy to wear so many faces, sometimes the face of a child."

"That was the worst," Jeremy agreed. "A kid walking toward us shouldn't have been threatening, but one day one of the kids we'd played soccer with showed up with explosives strapped around his chest."

Her stomach turned over. "That's awful."

"Which is another reason why I don't need to share my past with you, at least that part of my past. You don't need to know what I've seen. No one does."

His expression was harsh now, his eyes grim with painful memories.

"I wish you didn't have to carry those memories around, Jeremy."

"I don't carry them around; I locked them away a long time ago."

"But sometimes memories leak out. That's what happened to Kent, right? He came back to the safest place in the world and then found out he was more scared than he'd ever been. He told me that he painted his demons through the night—angry, hard brushstrokes, slashes of the brightest and darkest colors he could find. He said it was cathartic. And Kent had been with Jeremy in Delta—maybe in Bahrain.

Her stomach began to churn as she thought about the painting Kent had described. She hadn't put it together before, but his painting now sounded very much like the one she'd found covering the stolen painting.

"Oh, my God," she murmured.

"What?" Jeremy asked sharply, his gaze narrow. "What's wrong?"

"Kent's painting. He told me what it drew, and I just realized that it sounds like the one that was covering Toulouse-Lautrec's art."

Jeremy's jaw dropped. "What are you talking about?"

"Was Kent in Bahrain with you?"

Her question put anger in Jeremy's eyes. "Yes, but he didn't steal anything while he was there. He didn't smuggle out a painting and hide it in your aunt's house under his own artwork. That's ridiculous, Mia."

It didn't sound as ridiculous to her as it did to him, but then she didn't know Kent that well, and the man was like a brother to Jeremy. "I could be wrong," she said quickly.

"You are wrong. Kent is an honorable man. He has more integrity than anyone I know."

"It was just a theory," she said, realizing she probably should have thought a little more before sharing her suspicions with Jeremy.

"Maybe you should base your theories on facts, not wild imaginings. You're accusing a war hero of art theft."

"I wasn't exactly accusing—"

"Do you know what Kent went through when he was a hostage? He was tortured, Mia. They tried to break him, but he didn't break. He didn't give up secrets or people. He did what he was trained to do, and he helped bring down a terrorist cell. Does that sound like an art thief to you?"

She could see that she'd crossed a huge line. "I'm sorry, Jeremy. Let's talk about something else."

"No, we're going to finish this subject. If Kent stole that painting, why would he leave it at your aunt's house for a year?" Jeremy demanded. "Why would he cover it up and stick it in a closet? Why wouldn't he just sell it?"

"Maybe he felt guilty, had second thoughts after he got back."

"That's absurd."

"Well, I don't know."

"You don't know, because there's no way Kent is a thief. You just want to get your aunt off the hot seat. You want to blame someone else, when it's pretty clear to me that your aunt is the guilty party. It was in her bedroom closet, not even in the studio. She had to physically put it there. Maybe she didn't steal it, but I think she knew damn well what she had—that's why she hid it." He folded his arms across his chest as if he'd just closed the case.

She stared at him in shock, wondering how things had gone so bad so fast.

The waitress stopped by their table. "Who's in the mood for dessert?"

She shook her head, feeling like she might throw up if she ate anything now. Her stomach was churning with the heat of their argument. She and Jeremy had never really disagreed about anything, but this was big; this was personal and very intense.

"We'll just take the check," Jeremy told the waitress.

Her phone pinged again, and she glanced down at Kate's next message.

"What does it say now?" Jeremy asked.

"She wants me to turn the painting over to the FBI. She gave me the number of an agent to contact."

"Good, then you'll be out of it. And the real culprit will be caught."

She nodded, but she wasn't sure it was a good idea at all. She didn't want her aunt's name to be tarnished in any way, and who would defend Carly but her? Jeremy had accused her of throwing Kent under the bus to save her aunt, but wasn't he doing the same thing?

Jeremy paid the bill and then said, "Let's get out of here."

She was more than happy to leave.

They didn't speak all the way home.

So much for date night, she thought with a sigh, as he pulled into the driveway next to hers. There was nothing but tension and anger between them now. She'd been feeling so close to Jeremy, but now he was an icy stranger, and she knew she was getting her first look at the hard, ruthless side of his personality. But she also had to admit that his anger came out of loyalty to his friend, and that wasn't such a bad thing. It just wasn't great that she was the one who'd tested that loyalty.

Jeremy pretty much hated her now for accusing his friend of theft, and while she didn't know if she was right or wrong, she did believe she had some basis for the theory she'd put out. It might have been premature to talk about her suspicions, but she'd never imagined Jeremy would have such a strong reaction to her rambling thoughts.

When they got out of the car, she said, "I'm sorry things went downhill. I guess I shouldn't have read my sister's text."

"You shouldn't have accused Kent."

"And you shouldn't have accused my aunt," she retorted. Their fight had not been one-sided. Jeremy had given as good as he got. "I care about her and believe in her as much as you care and believe in Kent. But we're not going to agree, so let's just call it a night."

"Fine."

"Fine," she echoed. "I guess I'll see you around."

"Wait. You're not going to turn the painting over to the FBI, are you?" he asked. "You're going to keep looking into this yourself."

"I don't know what I'm going to do. I need time to think."

"Why don't you think about this? The aunt you admire so much had no real source of income. She rented the studio out for art. She traveled the world, but how did she pay for it? Did she inherit money? I know she didn't have a rich husband."

Mia stared back at him. "She used to teach art at the high school. And she gave art lessons, too. She did work."

"And those teaching jobs financed her worldwide adventures? She did all that on a teacher's salary?"

She hated that he was making her doubt her aunt, but he had raised a question she'd never considered. "I'm going to call it a night before we both say something we'll regret."

"I think it's too late to avoid that."

She didn't respond; she just turned and walked away, anger fueling her quick path into the house. She opened the door and let out a breath. She didn't bother to turn on a light; the darkness matched her mood. She felt angry and sad at the same time.

She didn't want a painting to come between her and Jeremy, but she couldn't take back her doubts about Kent, and he couldn't take back his doubts about her aunt.

Stalemate.

She walked down the hall and into the kitchen, shocked to see a figure standing by the kitchen table, the flashlight in his hand illuminating the painting on the table.

She flipped on the light. "Oh, my God," she said, meeting his gaze. "What the hell are you doing in here?"

Twenty

Jeremy threw his keys down on his kitchen table, opened the refrigerator door, stared at the contents, and then slammed the door shut.

Damn Mia and her stupid accusations.

And damn him for being such a fool.

He'd let a painting ruin what had been a wonderful night.

He'd just seen red when Mia had accused Kent of being a thief. She had no idea what Kent and the rest of them had gone through—the injuries they'd suffered, the horrors they'd seen—and they'd always put their duty first, beyond everything else. Kent wasn't a thief. He was a patriot, a soldier, and an incredible man. But Mia didn't know his world, and he couldn't explain it to her. But he also couldn't let her cast suspicion on his best friend.

He just needed to help her find the truth, he realized. Instead of being pissed off and attacking her, he should have just offered his assistance. The truth would not lead to Kent. Maybe it would lead to her aunt; he didn't know. But he did know that Mia wasn't going to give up until she figured it out.

Going out the side door, he walked down the

driveway and through the side gate. There was a light on in her kitchen. So he walked toward the sliding doors that led into the family room.

He'd planned on knocking but he was surprised to see the door open.

As he stepped into the darkened room, he heard a man's voice coming from the kitchen, and he froze at the familiar tone. He couldn't believe what he was hearing…

--->>><<<---

"I thought you were out with Jeremy tonight," Barton said.

"We got back early. What are you doing in here?" Mia asked.

"Taking back what's mine."

"The painting is yours?" she asked, shock in her voice. "You didn't stay in the studio. How could it be yours?"

"I stashed the picture when Kent was there. I covered it up with his really ugly painting. I didn't figure anyone would ever look behind that monstrosity."

"That was a year ago. Why did you leave it here all this time?"

"I was going to sell it like the others, but the trail was getting too hot. I had to stash it away for a while. Then it was mission after mission. I couldn't get back until now."

"You stole the painting from the palace in Bahrain, didn't you?"

"Well, aren't you a clever girl to have figured that out."

"How could you do that?" she asked.

"Don't act like it's such a horrendous thing that I did," Barton said, not a hint of apology in his voice. "The painting didn't belong to anyone there. It had been stolen two or three times by the time I took it."

"It was still wrong."

"You have no idea of what's right and what's wrong, what goes on in the other parts of the world. Jeremy, Kent, and I risked our lives every day for basically nothing. So I took a few things—so I made a little money. What's the big deal?"

"I can't let you take the painting."

"How do you think you're going to stop me? I don't want to hurt you, Mia, but I am taking this painting with me. I have a buyer, and he's ready to make a deal."

Jeremy had heard enough. "She's not going to stop you. I am," he said, walking into the room.

Barton jolted in shock, his gaze flashing with anger and guilt when he saw him.

"What the hell were you thinking, Barton?" he demanded to know. "You were looting during our missions?"

Barton's jaw tightened as he gave Jeremy a defiant gaze. "It was a few times, a few things. And you know that stuff was already hot."

"That doesn't matter."

"Of course it does." Barton stared back at him. "You're not going to turn me in, Jeremy."

Barton was the last person he wanted to turn in, but how could he let him walk away? It went against his conscience, his sense of right and wrong, everything he'd always stood for.

"I'm your best friend, Jeremy," Barton continued. "I've saved your life not once, not twice, but three fucking times. And you're going to try to put me in jail? I've been the biggest patriot the Army ever saw. So I took a painting from a terrorist. That's the crime that should end my life?"

"He doesn't have to turn you in. I will," Mia said, drawing Barton's attention back to her.

"You don't have any proof I took the painting, Mia," Barton said smoothly.

"You broke into my house."

"It doesn't look like I broke in. The sliding door was open, wasn't it, Jeremy? That's the way you came through."

"I locked that door," she said.

"Did you?" Barton challenged. "Maybe I just came by to check up on you, see how you were doing after the break-in. Maybe I was worried about you."

Jeremy couldn't believe the way Barton was talking to Mia without any regret or acknowledgement that he was in the wrong. He'd always had too high of an opinion of himself, but this was beyond ego.

"Why did you do it?" Jeremy asked, truly confused. "Did you really need the cash that bad? Or was it just a thrill for you?"

"It was both. I want to live better than I've been living. I've spent the last ten years in shitholes around the world, doing what most people aren't willing to do. I was owed."

"You chose that life; no one made you. You can't make this theft right, Barton. You can't spin it into something that's acceptable. You're no better than the person who took that painting in the first place. I'm calling Kent."

"Go ahead. I won't be here when he gets here, and you have no proof of anything. It will be my word against yours."

Barton gave him a challenging look, and he responded accordingly. He stepped forward and swung his fist into his best friend's face.

Barton's hand flew to his nose, as blood spewed out.

He looked at Jeremy in shock and then threw his own punch. Jeremy dodged the full force of Barton's fist as it grazed his jaw.

"Stop it," Mia said.

"Get out of here," he told her, as he tackled Barton once again. "This is between us."

"It's my painting, my house," she yelled.

He ignored her, his attention on Barton. They'd both been trained to fight. It would have been an even contest if he was at one hundred percent, but he wasn't.

Barton shoved him into the wall so hard a cuckoo clock came loose and bounced off Jeremy's injured shoulder. The pain stopped him in his tracks.

Barton got the edge again, landing a punch that made Jeremy's right eye feel like it had just exploded.

Blinded and enraged by pain, he swung his fist into Barton's gut, then used his feet to kick Barton off balance and on to his back.

Barton crashed into the stool by the island, taking it down with him.

Less than a second later, he was back on his feet, about to launch another attack when a spray of water hit them both in the face.

"I said, stop it!" Mia yelled, as she kept the hose from the sink on them. "You are not going to kill each other in my house."

Spluttering, he backed away from Barton.

Barton wiped the water from his face, giving Jeremy a wary look.

Mia turned off the water and stepped between them. "Now that I have your attention, here's what will happen next. You're both going to walk out of this house. I'm going to take the painting to the FBI and tell them I found it in the studio, and I have no idea how it got there."

"Mia," Jeremy protested. "Barton has to pay for what he did. You're not letting him off."

"He's going to pay." She looked at Barton. "You just lost the respect of the best friend you've ever had. I think that might mean more to you than a painting you lifted from a palace in Bahrain."

Barton stared at her, then his gaze swung to Jeremy. "I didn't do this to hurt you."

"Your motivation doesn't matter. Letting you off is too easy. And you don't care about my respect. If you did, you wouldn't have done this in the first place."

"You're wrong. I do care. This was never about you."

"But it was," he argued. "Don't you get it? What you did reflects back on the team. We fight with honor."

"This wasn't a fight. It was a damn painting. Don't you get that, Jeremy?"

"I don't," he said harshly. "I thought I knew you. I thought I could trust you with my life."

"You could and you can."

"Not anymore. And it's not just about the painting. You broke into Mia's house. You were the one who ripped up her studio, who slashed the paintings, who scared the hell out of her. How far were you willing to go to get this painting back?"

"I was never going to hurt her," Barton said sharply. "I knew you were out with her tonight. I figured the painting had to be in the house since the studio was cleaned out. I walked in, and here it was."

"Did Kent know what you did?" Jeremy asked, hoping that he still had one friend he could believe in.

"No. This was me, only me. The first buyer I had for this painting got cold feet. I had to stash it somewhere while I found another one. When I visited Kent at the studio, I couldn't think of a better place to hide a painting among dozens of others. I kept trying to get back to it, but it never worked out. After Mia's aunt died, I knew I better grab the painting before someone like Mia showed up to clean the house."

"So you didn't come back for your mother's birthday."

"I did, but I also wanted to get the painting. Unfortunately, it wasn't in the studio where I'd left it."

"Why did you have to destroy everything in there?" Mia asked.

"I had to make it look like kids had done it. You can't prove I did any of this, though. You can turn me in, but it won't stick."

"I wouldn't be so sure of that," Jeremy warned. "Someone else on the team might have seen you take that painting."

"No one on the team knew anything," Barton replied.

"But you had a buyer. We could find him or her," Mia put in. "Did someone in town help you—maybe Christina Wykoff?"

"Don't know who you're talking about," Barton said. "And good luck with trying to find my buyer. All you have is a stolen painting that you found in your aunt's house. You try to take me down, you and your aunt are going down with me. I don't think you want that."

"Well, you're not taking the painting," Mia said. "We're giving it back to its rightful owner."

"She's right," Jeremy said, standing between Barton and the painting.

"Fine. Whatever," Barton said. "I'm taking the job with Kinsey Security next week anyway. I'll have plenty of cash."

Jeremy did not want to let Barton walk out of the house and get away without being punished for what he'd done, but seeing the plea in Mia's eyes, he knew that he was going to do exactly that, because a stolen painting wasn't worth putting Mia and her aunt under a microscope.

"Good-bye, Jeremy. I don't expect we'll see each other again." Barton gave him a sad and mocking salute and then walked out the door.

"I can't believe I let him go," Jeremy muttered, as Mia handed him a towel.

"You're bleeding. I should take you to Urgent Care."

"I'm fine."

"What about your shoulder?"

"It hurts, but I'll survive." He paused. "I'm sorry, Mia."

"What are you apologizing for, Jeremy? You saved the painting. You saved my aunt's name from being dragged through the mud, and you saved me."

"Barton should pay."

"He will pay, Jeremy. Like I said, losing your respect is going to hurt him for a long time."

"I doubt that."

"I don't. He cares about you. You're a brother to him. I'm sure he never thought you'd find out. If we hadn't had that fight at the restaurant, we probably wouldn't have caught him in the act. He'd have taken the painting, and we would have never known it was him."

"I shouldn't have let you come into the house alone."

"You had no idea Barton was here."

"No, but I let my anger lead to a bad decision. I defended Kent to you, and while I was right about him, I was wrong about my other best friend. If you'd accused Barton, I wouldn't have believed that, either. I thought I knew Barton as well as I knew myself."

She gave him a soft, forgiving smile. "It's difficult to believe the worst about people we love. I didn't want to believe my aunt was a thief. We were both fighting to protect the people we care about."

"Well, she wasn't a thief. And neither was Kent. We were both right about those two." He paused. "I know you want this to go away, but the FBI may want to investigate the theft more than you do, Mia."

"If we return the painting, that might be the end of it. It's really hard to prove theft in cases like this, not just because we don't have proof that Barton took the painting from the palace, but also because the people in Bahrain probably stole it from someone else. No one is going to talk."

"You're probably right," he said. "So, what now?"

"Are you sure you don't want to see a doctor?"

He shook his head. "No. I'm okay. That might not be the case if you hadn't turned the water on us."

"I couldn't let you kill each other. I used to turn the hose on my brothers when they got out of control; I thought it might work."

"It did. Nice move. Although, I think I told you to run."

"I couldn't leave you on your own."

"You could have gone outside and called the police."

"If it had been someone besides Barton, I would have done that. But I just knew in my heart that Barton didn't want to hurt you or me." She paused. "I was shocked when you came through the door. I wasn't sure when I'd see you again after the way our dinner ended."

"I knew I'd made a mistake. Instead of getting angry, I should have offered to help you get to the truth. I should have trusted you not to do anything to anyone without proof. You wouldn't have hurt Kent unless you knew for sure he was guilty. I was coming over here to tell you that. When I saw the back door open, and I heard a man's voice, I was stunned. I couldn't believe Barton was in your house. I want to believe he wouldn't have hurt you, but I wasn't sure at that point. The man I knew seemed like a stranger."

"Thanks for the apology and for believing in me, because I wouldn't have hurt Kent. I might have asked uncomfortable questions, because sometimes my mouth gets ahead of my brain, but I just wanted to get to the truth. And it's my turn to apologize, too. I also know that you wouldn't have hurt my aunt's reputation unless you had irrefutable proof." She paused. "Now I'm going to get you some ice for your face."

"Wait," he said, grabbing her arm. "I need something else."

"What?"

"You." He drew her to him and pressed his mouth against her lips in a tender, poignant, loving kiss that put everything right with his world. "So we're good?" he asked her.

She nodded. "Really good. At least until the end of summer."

He shook his head. "No way. I'm not letting you go at the end of the summer. This is not a fling. This is a relationship."

Her eyes sparked at his words, but there was still wary caution in her gaze. "We've known each other a week, Jeremy."

"It feels like a lifetime. And I mean that in a good way. But I can't wait to get to know you even better." He took a moment, wanting to get the words exactly right. "I'm falling in love with you, Mia. Wait a second. I take that back."

"You do?" she questioned, her brows drawing together in a frown. "So fast?"

"I'm not falling for you; I've already fallen."

"Are you sure you don't have a concussion or something?"

He grinned. "I know what I'm saying. And I don't think I'm alone in the love department. Am I?"

She sighed and slowly shook her head. "No, I'm right there with you."

"That's a good thing, babe."

"There are still all those reasons we shouldn't get together: Ashlyn, your job, my job, the fact that I'm going back to San Francisco and you don't know where you're going. Should I go on?"

"We'll knock the obstacles down one by one. I'm not afraid of a challenge, and I don't think you are, either."

"Not of a challenge, no, but I am a little afraid of love," she admitted. "I want to get it right this time. This—you—feels too important; I don't want to screw it up."

"The only way you can screw this up is by not giving us a chance, Mia. I love you. Now you say it."

"You do like to give orders."

"And I expect them to be obeyed," he said lightly, needing her to say the words.

She offered him a warm, helpless smile. "I love you, too, Jeremy."

"Thank God. I think I just got my first Angel's Bay miracle."

"Or I did," she said. "We're really going to do this?"

"We really are, but there's one last thing. When I commit to someone, I go all in—forever. I want you to know that."

"Forever sounds perfect and exciting."

"I'll show you some excitement."

"Will you? Because you seem awfully interested in talking right now."

He laughed at her teasing smile. He didn't just love this woman; he liked her. Mia had quickly become his best friend, his lover, and one day he would make her his wife. He grabbed her hand and took her upstairs, so they could start the rest of their lives together.

Epilogue

*T*hree weeks later...

"I hope you're ready to meet the family," Mia told Jeremy as they pulled into the parking lot of St. Mary's Church in Santa Barbara, California. Her cousin Burke was about to marry the love of his life Maddie Heller, and Jeremy was about to meet her entire family.

He'd met her mom and dad a few days earlier. They'd stopped in Angel's Bay to check out the house before driving farther south to spend a few days in Santa Barbara prior to the wedding.

Mia had never felt so proud or so eager to introduce her parents to the man in her life. Sharon and Tim Callaway had liked Jeremy immediately and they'd loved Ashlyn even more.

Her mom had pulled her aside and told her that she'd never looked happier and that Angel's Bay had obviously worked its magic on her. She'd told her mom that it wasn't magic; it was Jeremy. Her mom had laughed and said, "Finally, one of my kids falls in love. Who would have thought my baby would be the first one?"

Of course her mom had then quizzed her about a

wedding, and she'd had to tell her to slow down. They were moving fast, but not that fast.

Jeremy turned off the car and said, "I think I can handle your family. Your mom and dad are okay; I expect the rest of the clan will be just as great."

"I think you'll like them," she said.

He turned in his seat to look at Ashlyn. "What about you, Ashlyn? Ready to say hello to Mia's brothers and sisters?"

Ashlyn beamed in her pretty new dress. "Do you think they'll like me?"

Mia smiled at the hint of vulnerability in her eyes. They'd gotten very close the last few weeks, but there were still times when Ashlyn worried that all the good stuff was going to vanish, that her life would change the way it had before. "They're going to love you, because I love you, and because you're wonderful."

"What about me?" Jeremy asked.

"They're going to love you, too."

"Because you love me."

"Because I love you," she echoed.

When they got out of the car, she said, "There's Mom." She waved to her mom and dad who'd just pulled into a spot a few feet away.

They walked over to the car to greet them.

Her mother wore a beautiful emerald green dress that set off her pretty green eyes, and her dad had on a dark suit. They were a striking couple, she thought, never having really considered her parents as a couple, but they were certainly a good example of the power of love and the strength of a marriage. They'd started their love story thirty-five years ago and were still going strong.

"Hello, Mia," her mom said, giving her a hug and then moving to Jeremy and to Ashlyn.

Her father followed suit. "How's everyone doing?" he asked.

"We're great," she replied. "Ashlyn is looking forward to her very first wedding."

"This is your first wedding?" Sharon asked. "That's so exciting. Do you want to come with me? I'm going to see the bride before she comes down the aisle."

Ashlyn gave a happy nod. Mia was beginning to realize that Ashlyn's true nature was outgoing and friendly. Now that she'd moved past her grief, she was blossoming like a flower opening up to the sun. Right now her mother was that sun, and why not? Sharon Callaway had raised six kids of her own. She knew how to deal with one small eight-year-old.

"We'll see you in the church," Sharon said, taking Ashlyn's hand. "Tim, are you coming?"

"Not to see the bride, but I do see my brother over there, so I'll catch up with you."

"All right."

"You know ever since you told your mother the two of you were together, she's started thinking of Ashlyn as her granddaughter," her father said with a twinkle in his eyes. "So do I, to tell the truth. Maybe we'll be at your wedding one of these days."

"Dad," she protested. "Don't push."

"Just saying." He grinned and took off to meet her Uncle Jack.

She turned to Jeremy as her father left. "That was pointed."

"I want to marry you, Mia. I hope you know that. I haven't formally asked, because I didn't want to rush you into anything."

"I know. I didn't want you to ask yet. I wanted us to figure some things out first before we planned a wedding.

Now that I've decided to take the job at the Eckhart Gallery, and you've decided to give being a police officer in Angel's Bay a try, I'm feeling more ready to move forward."

"Really? Should I get down on my knees right now?"

"No," she said with a laugh, grabbing his hand to stop him from making that move. "Today is Burke and Maddie's day. We'll have our own day."

"It's going to be soon. And I think we should talk to your parents about buying your aunt's house."

"Do you really want to do that?"

"I do. It's a great house, and you can keep the studio going in whatever way you want. It's perfect."

"It's not perfect, but it's perfect for us. If I've learned anything in the past several weeks it's that I don't need perfect; I just need what's right for me, and that's you. We're going to have a great life together, Jeremy. You, me, Ashlyn, and hopefully a few more kids—if you're up for it."

"As many as you want. I think I'm getting better at this dad thing."

He'd barely finished speaking when she heard a feminine squeal. She turned to see her two sisters walking across the parking lot.

Annie and Kate arrived with breathless greetings and hugs.

When that was done, they both gave Jeremy a speculative glance.

"So you're the man who's stolen my sister's heart," Kate said.

"That would be me."

"I'm Kate."

"And I'm Annie."

"It's nice to meet both of you," Jeremy said. "I've

heard a lot about you."

"All good, I'm sure," Annie said with a grin.

"You do know if you don't treat Mia right, you'll have to deal with us," Kate told him.

"I do know that," he said solemnly.

"Or them," Annie said, tipping her head to three men getting out of another car. "Our brothers have been known to beat the crap out of a few of our dates."

"I can take care of myself," Jeremy said.

"You don't have to worry," Mia said with a laugh. "You're a war hero. My brothers are going to love you."

"We should go inside," Annie said. "It's almost three o'clock."

On their way into the church, Mia introduced Jeremy to her brothers and her cousins Emma and Shayla as well as Nicole and Ryan, and their brand new baby. By the time they found a seat, the church was filled with Callaways and friends.

"You weren't kidding about your big family," Jeremy said, as she slid closer to him to make room for more people in the pew.

"We're quite a crowd when we're all together." She looked around the church, and her heart swelled with love. "When I was little, I used to feel like I was insignificant in this big group of people. I wasn't the loudest or the tallest or the most athletic or the best at anything, but now I realize that I was always surrounded by unconditional love and acceptance. That's something I want to pass on to our kids."

"You will," he said, taking her hand.

"And I'm really thrilled for Burke and Maddie. Burke lost his first fiancée in a tragic accident. I didn't know if he would ever find love again, but then Maddie came along, and she turned his world upside down."

"I know that feeling," Jeremy said. "That first day, when I helped you off the roof, and I looked into your amazing blue eyes, I knew I was in big trouble. I told myself to stay away from you, but that didn't work out too well."

"And I told myself not to sleep with you, because I knew better than to jump into bed with a man who could easily break my heart, but that plan didn't work out too well, either."

His fingers tightened around hers. "I'm going to make you happy, Mia—every day of the rest of our lives."

"I know. I promise to do the same."

The music began to play and as the crowd rose for the bride's entrance, she leaned over and kissed Jeremy's mouth. "I love you."

"I love you, too."

—◆◆◆—

Kate looked over at her twin sister making out with her hunky boyfriend and felt a twinge of jealousy. She was super happy for Mia, of course, but her own heart was a little empty.

The last year had been a whirlwind of activity: getting accepted into the FBI, training at Quantico, and now handling actual assignments. Her career was going great, but she had to admit the love in this church was making her want more than a career.

As Maddie made her way down the aisle, Kate's gaze moved to her cousin Burke. He'd always been handsome and strong, the kind of man who could handle any challenge, but today he looked softer, his gaze almost needy as it focused on the woman making her way to his side.

That was the problem with love; it made a person vulnerable and sometimes weak.

It was a complication that would not serve her well in her job.

Not that she was in love with anyone, but she couldn't help thinking she might want to be one day.

Burke took Maddie's hand and they walked up to the altar while the crowd sat down.

She glanced at Mia.

Her sister gave her a happy nod. She definitely didn't have to worry about Mia anymore.

Her phone vibrated and she glanced down at the text coming in.

She'd wanted something to get her heart pumping, and now she had it—her next assignment. She had no idea where it would take her, but she was ready to go.

"Everything okay?" Mia whispered.

She looked into her twin's eyes and nodded. "Yes, but I have to leave right after the ceremony."

"To go where?"

"I'm not sure yet, but I know it will be exciting."

Mia smiled. "You love your job, don't you?"

"I do. I think I might even be good at it."

"I know you will be. Just make sure you come back for my wedding."

"What?" Kate said a little too loudly, drawing the attention of her brother Ian, who gave them an irritated look. "What?" she asked more softly. "You're engaged?"

"Not officially, but we will be, and you'll be my maid of honor, of course."

"When?"

"I don't know yet, but promise you'll make it back, no matter where you are, no matter what you're doing."

"I wouldn't miss your wedding for the world."

"Good. You know something, Kate?"

"What's that?"

"Love is the greatest adventure of them all," Mia said.

"You might be right, but I'm going to try some other adventures first."

For her, love would have to wait...but maybe not too long.

THE END

The next book in the Callaway Series:

TENDER IS THE NIGHT

will be released in March 2016

——➤➤◄◄——

Keep on reading for an excerpt from

Barbara's #1 NYT Bestselling Novel

SUMMER SECRETS

Excerpt - SUMMER SECRETS

Prologue

Ship's log, Moon Dancer, July 10
Wind: 40 knots, gusting to 65 knots
Sea Conditions: rough, choppy, wild
Weather Forecast: rain, thunder, lightning

Kate McKenna's fingers tightened around the pen in her hand as the Moon Dancer surfed up one wave and down the next. The ship's log told nothing of their real journey, revealed none of the hardships, the secrets, the heartbreak, the danger they now faced. She wanted to write it down, but she couldn't. Her father's instructions were explicit: Nothing but the facts.

She couldn't write that she was worried, but she was.

The weather was turning, the barometer dropping. A big storm was coming. If they changed course, they would lose valuable time, and her father would not consider that option. They were currently in second place—second place and heading straight into the fury of the sea. She could hear the winds beginning to howl. She feared there would be hell to pay this night. Everyone's nerves were on edge. Arguments could be heard in every corner of the boat. She wanted to make it all go away. She wanted to take her sisters and go home, but home was at the other end of the ocean.

"Kate, get up here!" someone yelled.

She ran up on deck, shocked to the core by the intensity of the storm. The spray blew so hard it almost took the skin off her face. She had to move, had to help her father reef down the sails to the storm jib. But all she could do was stare at the oncoming wave. It must be forty feet high and growing. Any second it would crash over their boat. How on earth would they survive?

And, if they didn't, would anyone ever know the true story of their race around the world?

Chapter One

Eight years later...

"The wind blew and the waves crashed as the mighty dragon sank into the sea to hide in the dark depths of the ocean until the next sailor came too close to the baby dragons. The End."

Kate McKenna smiled at the enraptured looks on the faces before her. Ranging in age from three to ten, the children sat on thick, plump cushions on the floor in a corner of her store, Fantasia. They came three times a week to hear her read stories or tell tales. At first they were chatty and restless, but once the story took hold, they were hers completely. Although it wasn't the most profitable part of her bookstore business, it was by far the most enjoyable.

"Tell us another one," the little girl sitting next to her pleaded.

"One more," the other children chorused.

Kate was tempted to give in, but the clock on the wall read five minutes to six, and she was eager to close on time this Friday night. It had been a long, busy week, and she had inventory to unpack before the weekend tourist crowds descended. "That's all for today," she said, getting to her feet. Although the children protested, the group gradually drifted from the store, a few mothers making purchases on their way out the door.

"Great story," Theresa Delantoni said. "Did you make that up as you went along, or did you read it somewhere?"

"A little of both," Kate told her assistant. "My dad used to tell us stories about dragons that lived under the sea. One time we were sailing just outside the Caribbean, and the sea suddenly seemed to catch fire. Dragons, I thought, just like my father said. It turned out to be phosphorus algae. But my sisters and I preferred the fire-breathing dragon story."

"A romantic at heart."

"It's a weakness, I admit."

"Speaking of romance..." Theresa's cheeks dimpled into an excited smile, "it's my anniversary, and I have to leave now. I promised I wouldn't be late, because our baby sitter can only give us two hours." Theresa took her purse out of the drawer behind the counter. "I hate to leave you with all those boxes to unpack."

"But you will." Kate followed her to the door. "Don't think twice. You deserve a night off with that darling husband of yours."

Theresa blushed. "Thanks. After eight years of marriage and two babies who need a lot of attention, sometimes I forget how lucky I am."

"You are lucky."

"And you are great with kids. You should think about having some of your own."

"It's easy to be great for an hour."

"Brrr," Theresa said as they walked out of the store together. She stopped to zip up her sweater. "The wind is picking up."

"Out of the southwest," Kate said automatically, her experienced nautical eye already gauging the knots to be between twelve and fifteen. "There's a storm coming. It should be here by six o'clock. Take an umbrella with you."

"You're better than the weather report," Theresa said with a laugh. "Don't stay too late, now. People will start to suspect you don't have a life."

Kate made a face at her friend. "I have a fine life." Theresa was halfway to her car and didn't bother to reply. "I have a great life," Kate repeated. After all, she lived in Castleton, one of the most beautiful spots in the world, a large island off the coast of Washington State, one of the several hundred islands that made up the archipelago known as the San Juans.

Her bookstore at the northern end of Pacific Avenue had an incredible view of the deep blue waters of Puget Sound. It was one of the interesting, quaint shops that ran down a two-mile cobblestone strip to Rose Harbor, a busy marina that filled every July with boats in town for the annual Castleton Invitational Sailboat Races.

Castleton was known for its rugged beauty, its fir and evergreen-covered hillsides and more than one hundred miles of driftwood-strewn beaches. Most of the island traffic came via the Washington State Ferry, although boaters were plentiful, and small private planes could land at the Castleton Airport.

The unpredictable southwesterly winds created swirling, dangerous currents along many of the beaches and had driven a few boats to ground on their way to shelter in the harbor. But the winds didn't stop the boats from coming or the sailors from congregating. Tales of sails and storms could be overheard in every restaurant, café, and business in town. There were more boat slips in the marina than there were parking spaces downtown. The lives of Castleton's residents weren't just by the sea, they were about the sea.

Kate loved her view of the waterfront—loved the one from her house in the hills even better—but more than anything she appreciated the fact that the view didn't change every day. Maybe some would call that boring, but she found it comforting.

The wind lifted the hair off the back of her neck, changing that feeling of comfort to one of uneasiness. Wind in her life had meant change. Her father, Duncan McKenna, a sailing man from the top of his head to the tips of his toes, always relished the wind's arrival. Kate could remember many a time when he had jumped to his feet at the first hint of a breeze. A smile would spread across his weather-beaten cheeks as he'd stand on the deck of their boat, pumping his fist triumphantly in the air, his eyes focused on the distant horizon. The wind's up, Katie girl, he'd say. It's time to go.

And they'd go—wherever the wind took them. They'd sail with it, into it, against it. They'd lash out in anger when it blew too hard, then cry in frustration when it vanished completely. Her life had been formed, shaped and controlled by the wind. She'd thought of it as a friend; she'd thought of it as a monster. Well, no more.

She had a home now, an address, a mailbox, a garden. She might live by the water, but she didn't live on it. The wind meant nothing more to her than an extra sweater and a bowl of soup for dinner. It didn't mean that her life was about to change. Why couldn't she believe that?

Because of the boats.

They'd been sailing into the harbor for the past week, every day a few more, each one bigger, brighter and better than the last. There was an energy in the air, a sense of excitement, purpose, adventure. In just a few days the race would begin, and next Saturday the biggest and brightest would race around the island in the Castleton Invitational. Two days later, the boats would be off again, racing to San Francisco and then on to Hawaii for the Pacific Cup. The sailors would battle the elements and one another. In the end, only one would be victorious.

Kate didn't appreciate the direction of her thoughts. She didn't want to think about the boats or the damn race. Ten days. It would all be over in ten days, she reminded herself as she walked back into the store and shut the door firmly behind her. She could handle the pleasure cruisers, the fishermen, the tourists interested in whale watching; what she couldn't handle were the racers, the fanatical sailors who lived to battle the ocean, to conquer new seas. She knew those men and women too well. Once, she'd been one of them.

The door to her store opened, accompanied by a melodious jangle from the wind chimes that hung outside. A man entered, dressed in khaki pants and a navy blue polo shirt. He had the look of a man on business. There was energy in his movements, a gleam in his deep blue eyes, and an impression of power and purpose in his stance. As he ran an impatient hand through his dark brown hair, Kate felt her pulse quicken. Strangers came into her store all the time asking for books, directions, information about the island, but none of those strangers had given her heart such a jump start. Maybe Theresa was right. She definitely needed to get out more.

"Hello." His voice had a bit of a drawl to it. The South? Texas? She wasn't sure where he'd come from, but she had a feeling it had been a long journey.

"Hello," she said. "Can I help you?"

"I certainly hope so."

"I'm betting you need directions, not a book."

He gave her a curious smile. "Now, why would you bet that?"

"You don't look like an armchair adventurer."

"You can tell that just by looking?"

She shrugged. "What can I say? I'm good."

"Not that good. I don't need directions."

"Oh. A book about sailing, then?"

"Wrong again."

Kate studied him thoughtfully. He hadn't stood still since he walked into the store, shifting his feet, tapping his fingers on the counter. He looked like a man who couldn't stop running even when he was tired. Hardly one to settle into a recliner with a good book.

However, she couldn't refute the fact that he had come into the bookstore of his own free will, so he must have had a reason.

"I know." She snapped her fingers. "Gift book. You need a book for Aunt Sally or Cousin Mary, or maybe the girlfriend whose birthday you forgot."

He laughed. "No Aunt Sally. No Cousin Mary. And, regretfully, no girlfriend."

Kate had to bite back the incredulous *really* that threatened to push past her lips. She settled for "Interesting. So what do you want?"

"I'm looking for someone."

"Aren't we all?"

"You're very quick."

He was quick, too, and it had been awhile since she'd flirted with a man. Not that she was flirting; she was just being friendly. "So, who are you looking for?'

He hesitated, and it was the small pause that made Kate tense. That and the way his gaze settled on her face.

It had been eight years since someone had come looking for her. It wasn't likely this man was here for that reason, though. What were the odds? A million to one.

"A woman," he said slowly.

Kate licked her lips, trying not to turn away from the long, deep look he was giving her.

"I think I've found her," he added.

So much for odds.

"It's you, isn't it? Kate McKenna?" He smiled with satisfaction. "The oldest sister in the fearsome foursome that raced around the world in a sailboat. I recognize you from the photographs."

"Who wants to know?"

"Tyler Jamison." He stuck out his hand.

Kate gave his hand a brief shake. "What do you want?"

"A story."

"You're a reporter?" She had to admit she was surprised. She'd once been able to spot a reporter from a block away. She'd gotten complacent. That would have to change right now. "I can't imagine why you'd be looking for me. That race was a long time ago."

"Eight years. That would make you twenty-eight, right?"

Kate walked over to the door and turned the sign to *Closed*. If only she'd done it five minutes earlier, she would have missed this man. Not that he wouldn't have come back in the morning. He had a look of stubborn persistence about him. She suspected that he was a man who usually got what he wanted.

"I'd like to do a follow-up story on what's become of one of the most interesting sailing crews in ocean-racing history," Tyler continued. "It would tie in nicely with the upcoming sailboat races."

"I don't race anymore, but I'm sure I can find you some interesting racers to talk to. Take Morgan Hunt, for instance. He raced in the Sydney to Hobart last year and could tell you tales that would curl your toes."

"I'll keep that in mind. But I'd like to start with you and your sisters. Your father, too."

Duncan McKenna would love the publicity, adore being in the spotlight, but Lord only knew what he'd say once his tongue got going, especially if his tongue had been loosened by a few pints of beer, which would no doubt be the case.

"My father loves to talk about the past," Kate said, "but just like those fishermen whose stories of catches grow bigger by the year, so do my father's stories about that race. You can't believe a thing he says."

"What about you? You'd tell me the real story, wouldn't you?"

"Sure." She gave him what she hoped was a casual shrug. "Let's see. We sailed forever, it seemed. Some days were windy; some were hot. The wind ran fast, then slow. One week turned into the next with more of the same. The food was terrible. The seas were treacherous. The stars were always fantastic. That's about it."

"Short and succinct. Surely you can do better than that, Miss McKenna. A woman who appreciates books should be able to tell a better story."

"I sell books; I don't write them. Besides, there were a dozen news stories about the race in the weeks that followed our return. Everything that needed to be said was said. If you're interested, I'm sure you could find them on the Internet or in the library." She paused. "Do you write for a sailing magazine?"

"I'm a freelancer. I go where the story takes me."

Kate frowned. This was great. Just great. Another

man who went with the wind. Why did they always stir up trouble in her life? "Well, there's no story here. We're all very boring. I run this bookstore, not exactly a hotbed of commerce, as you can see." She swept her hand around the room, forcing him to look at the cozy chairs by the window, the neatly stacked shelves of mysteries, fiction, fantasy, romance, children's books and, of course, the ever-popular books on seafaring.

Although she was trying to downplay the bookstore, she couldn't stop the sense of pride that ran through her as she looked around the room that she had decorated, remembering the care she'd taken with the children's corner now brightened by posters and stuffed animals. She'd turned the bookstore into a home away from home, a place of delicious escape. It hadn't been easy to build a business from nothing. But somehow she'd done it.

"It's nice," Tyler said. "From sailboat racer to bookstore owner. Sounds like an interesting journey. Tell me more."

She'd walked right into that one. "It's not interesting at all. Trust me."

"You're avoiding my questions. Why?"

"I'm not avoiding anything," she said with a laugh that even to her own ears sounded nervous. "It's like this—I was barely out of my awkward teenage years during that trip. I'm an adult now. I don't particularly want to rehash that time in my life. It was no big deal."

"It was a huge deal. Most people who win ocean races are seasoned sailors, sponsored by big corporations, sailing million-dollar boats. But the McKenna family beat them all. I can't understand why you don't want to talk about it. It must have been the biggest and best thing that ever happened to you."

"We had fifteen minutes of fame a long time ago.

And our race was different. It wasn't filled with racing syndicates but with amateur sailors who had a passion for sailing and a longing for adventure. The racing world has changed. No one cares what happened to us."

"I do."

"Why?" Something about him didn't ring true. He seemed too confident, too purposeful to be after a fluff story. "Why do you care?"

"I like to write about adventurers, ordinary people who accomplish extraordinary things. And I'm fascinated by the thought of three girls and their father alone on the ocean, battling not only the other racers but the wind, the icebergs, fifty-foot waves. I've read some accounts of the trip, especially the harrowing details of the terrible storm during the second-to-last leg of the race. I can't imagine what you must have gone through."

There was a passion in his voice that bespoke a genuine interest, but why now? Why after all these years? Why this man—who had appeared out of nowhere and didn't seem to work for anyone? Why him?

"You look familiar," she said, studying the sharply drawn lines of his face. "Where have I seen you before?"

"I just have one of those faces. An average, everyday Joe." He paused. "So, what do you say? Will you talk to me? Or do I need to track down your sisters, Ashley and Caroline?"

Kate couldn't let him talk to Ashley or Caroline. She couldn't let this go any further. She had to get rid of him. But how?

"You're stalling," Tyler said. "I can see the wheels turning in your head."

"Don't be silly. I'm just busy. I have boxes to unpack before tomorrow, so I'm afraid we'll have to do this some other time."

The phone behind the counter rang, and she reached for it immediately, grateful for the interruption. "Fantasia," she said cheerfully. Her heart sank as she heard a familiar voice on the other end of the line. Will Jenkins ran the Oyster Bar on the waterfront, her father's favorite hangout. "How bad is he?" The answer put her heart into another nosedive. "I'll be right there. Yes, I know. Thanks, Will."

"Trouble?" Tyler inquired as she hung up the phone.

"No." She opened the drawer and pulled out her purse and keys. "I have to go. And so do you."

"You look upset."

"I'm fine." She opened the door, the breeze once again sending goose bumps down her arms. There was change in the air. She could feel it all around her.

"You don't look fine. Is someone hurt?" Tyler waited while she locked the door behind him. "Can I help?"

Kate told herself not to be taken in by the concern in his eyes. He was a reporter. He just wanted a story. "No one can help. You should go home. Back to wherever you came from."

"Thanks, but I think I'll stay a while. With all these sailors in town, I'm sure someone around here will talk to me."

"Suit yourself."

Kate hurried to her car, which she kept parked in back of her store. Tyler Jamison was a problem she hadn't anticipated, but right now she had a more pressing matter to deal with. She turned on the ignition and let out the brake. Her small Volkswagen Jetta shook with another gust of wind. Her father always said if you can't own the wind, you have to ride it out. She had a feeling this was going to be one wild ride.

———⋙⋘———

"Get me another beer," Duncan McKenna demanded as he put his fist down on top of the bar. He'd meant to slam it down hard, make the glasses jump, but he was too tired. "There was a time when a man could get a beer around here, Will."

The bartender finished drying off a glass at the other end of the bar. "You've had your limit, Duncan. You'll get no more from me tonight. You need to go home and sleep it off."

Sleep it off? He couldn't sleep. Hadn't for years. Oh, he dropped off now and then once the liquor took hold of his mind and gave him a blessed few hours of peace. But that didn't happen often, especially lately...

"Dammit, Will, I need a drink. I need one bad." He could hear the desperation in his voice, but he couldn't stop it. The need had been building in him all day, growing fiercer with each boat that sailed into the harbor, each dream of a journey, of a race to be sailed and to be won. That had been his world. God, how he missed it, missed the pitch of the waves, the power of the wind, the thrill of the race. Missed the pounding of his heart, the spine-tingling, palm sweating moments when all would be won or all would be lost. What a rush his life had been.

"I need a drink," he repeated.

Will walked down the length of the bar and gave him a hard look. "It won't do you no good, Duncan. I called Kate, and she's on her way."

"Why the hell did you call her?"

"Because you need a ride. You've been in here all day."

"I can get myself home." Duncan tried to stand up, but the room spun around, so he sat back down and held on to the edge of the bar for dear life.

"Sure you can," Will said dryly. "Just sit there. Don't try to leave."

"I'll do what I want," Duncan snapped. "I've been around the world upside down and backward. I won the goddamn Winston Around-the-World Challenge. No one thought we could do it. But we did, me and my girls." He paused and let out a weary sigh. "We were the best, Will. The very best. My girls got heart, just like their old man. They don't quit. I don't quit. McKennas don't quit."

"Yeah, yeah, I know."

And he did know because he'd heard it all before. Will was only a few years younger than Duncan, but he'd been tending bar for more than twenty years. Duncan couldn't understand how a man could be happy staying in one place for so long. Twenty years ago, Will had had hair on his head, a flat stomach, and girls lining up three-deep to flirt with him. Now he was bald, soft in the middle, and married to a librarian. Hell of a life he'd made for himself.

Will walked away to serve another customer at the end of the bar. Duncan turned his head and saw a woman sitting at a nearby table. As she moved, her hair caught the light, and he lost his breath at the glorious, fiery shade of red. Eleanor, he thought impossibly. His beloved Nora had hair the same color, and deep blue eyes that a man could drown in. He'd gone overboard the first time he'd seen her standing on the docks in a summer dress that showed off her long legs. His gut twisted in pain at the memory. Eleven years she'd been gone, but he still missed her. His heart felt as heavy as a stone. He wanted a drink. He wanted oblivion. He wanted—so many things.

"Dad?"

He tried to focus, but he couldn't see clearly. It's the

alcohol, he told himself, but when he wiped the back of his hand across his eyes, it came away wet.

"Are you all right?" Kate asked with concern on her face.

Kate had the look of Nora in her eyes, but her hair was blond, her skin a golden brown and free of the beautiful freckles that had kissed Nora's nose. Kate's face was stronger, too, her jaw as stubborn as his own. There were other differences as well. Nora's love had never wavered. But Kate's...

"The boats are coming, Katie girl. There's a wind brewing. You know what that means? You know where we should be?"

"Not today," Kate replied.

"You never want to sail anymore. I don't know why." He shook his head, trying to concentrate, but his head felt thick, his brain slow. "What happened to us, Katie?"

"Let's go home."

Home? Where was home? He'd had to sell the Moon Dancer. It had almost broken his heart, selling his beloved boat. Now he lived in a small old sailboat. He'd wanted to call the boat Nora, but he couldn't quite bring himself to paint his wife's name on the side. Nora wouldn't have been proud of this boat or of him. Kate wasn't proud of him, either.

"I'm sorry, Katie. You know how sorry I am?"

"You're always sorry when you drink." Kate put out her hand to him. "Let's go home."

"I can't go now. I'm telling Will here about our big race."

"He's heard it before. I'm sorry, Will," Kate said.

"It's no problem," Will replied.

"What are you apologizing for?" Duncan demanded. "I ain't done nothing. And I'm your father. You don't apologize for me." He got to his feet, wanting to remind her that he was bigger and stronger and older than her, but the sudden motion caused him to sway unsteadily. Before he knew it, Kate had a hand on his arm. He wanted to shrug her away. In fact, he would do just that as soon as he caught his breath, got his bearings.

"Need some help?" a man asked.

Before Duncan could answer, Kate said, "What are you doing here?"

"I was thirsty."

"Can't blame a man for being thirsty, Katie girl," Duncan said, feeling more weary by the second. "I gotta sit down."

The man grabbed Duncan's other arm as he started to slip out of Kate's grasp.

"Your car?" he asked.

"I don't want to go home," Duncan complained. "I want another drink."

"The alcohol is going to kill you, Dad," Kate told him as she and the man managed to walk him out of the bar and into the parking lot.

"Better the alcohol than the loneliness," Duncan murmured. Kate pushed him into the front seat of her car. His eyes closed and he drifted away. He was finally able to sleep.

Kate saw her father slump sideways in his seat. For a moment she felt a surge of panic that he wasn't just sleeping, that something was happening to him, that he was sick or—no, she couldn't think the word, much less say it. Her father was strong as an ox. He wasn't even that old, barely sixty. He was just drunk. A terrible, lousy drunk. A terrible, lousy father for that matter. Why was she worried about losing him when it was so apparent that she'd lost him a long time ago?

"You'll need help getting him out of the car," Tyler said, interrupting her thoughts.

She'd almost forgotten he was standing there. "You've gotten yourself quite a headline, haven't you? 'Victorious sailor turns into worthless drunk.'"

"Is that how you think of your father?"

"No, but it's probably what you'll say."

"How do you know what I'll say?"

"I've been interviewed before, had my words twisted."

"Is that where your resistance comes from?" he asked with a thoughtful expression on his face. "I'm not interested in embarrassing you, Miss McKenna. I just want an interesting story. Fame, success, adventure— those are things that change people's lives forever. Most people never experience even one of those, much less all three, the way you did."

Kate didn't know what to say. She needed time to think, to figure out the best way to handle this man Maybe if she told him just enough, he would go away. But what would be enough? Would he start digging? And if he did, what would he find?

"I need to take care of my father," she said. "Maybe tomorrow, if you want to stop by the bookstore, we can talk."

"Why the change of heart?" He sent her a skeptical look.

"You don't look like someone who gives up."

"That's true." Tyler tipped his head toward the car. "Will your father be all right? I could follow you home, help you get him into the house."

"No, thank you."

"Where is home, anyway? I don't think you said."

"I don't think I did." Kate got into her car and shut the

door. "I don't know what to do about that man," she muttered, glancing over at her father. Duncan's response was a very unhelpful snort. She'd have to take care of Tyler Jamison herself.

Tyler stared down the road long after Kate's taillights had disappeared. What had seemed so simple had suddenly taken on new and disturbing dimensions. The first was Kate herself. She wasn't what he'd expected. For some reason, he'd thought tomboy, tough girl, overachiever, but she hadn't looked all that tough in black pants and a clingy T-shirt that matched her light blue eyes. Her blond hair had fallen loosely around her shoulders, and she'd moved with a feminine grace, spoken with a soft voice. She had a great smile, too, he thought, the kind that invited you to come in and stay awhile, the same way her friendly little bookstore invited customers to stop in and browse. Not that she'd been all that friendly when she'd discovered he was a reporter. Despite her casual manner, he'd sensed a wall going up between them with every question that he asked.

Tyler reached into his pocket and pulled out a folded piece of paper. It was a magazine cover from eight years ago. Three blond, sunburned girls stood on the deck of a sailboat, holding an enormous silver trophy in their hands, their proud, beaming father in the background. The McKennas had conquered the world's toughest oceans. But were there secrets behind those smiles? Was there another story of their trip, one that hadn't been printed? Tyler suspected the answer to both questions was yes.

In fact, if one looked closely at the picture, only Duncan looked really happy. The girls appeared shell-shocked. It was the only word he could think of to describe their expressions. Maybe he was reading more than was there. He'd spent most of his life living by the facts and only the facts, but this story was different. This story was personal.

Kate McKenna hadn't wanted to talk to him. As she said, it was an old story, so why the resistance? She was hiding something. A drunken father—not the biggest secret in the world. There had to be something more. Tyler had a hunch he knew what that something was.

He folded the magazine cover, slipped it into his pocket and took out his cell phone. He punched in a familiar number, then waited.

"Jamison residence." Shelly Thompson, Mark's private nurse, answered the phone in her no-nonsense voice.

"Shelly. It's Tyler. How's Mark doing today?"

"Not good. He tried to stand, but his legs couldn't support his weight. He's very depressed."

Tyler let out a sigh filled with frustration, helplessness and anger, emotions that swamped him every time he thought about his younger brother who had once been such an accomplished athlete. "Can I talk to him?"

"He's asleep. Do you want me to wake him?"

"No. But when he gets up, tell him I found the McKenna sisters." Tyler ended the call, slipping the phone back into his pocket. The McKenna sisters might be good at keeping secrets, but he was even better at uncovering them.

END OF EXCERPT

About The Author

Barbara Freethy is a #1 New York Times Bestselling Author of 45 novels ranging from contemporary romance to romantic suspense and women's fiction. Traditionally published for many years, Barbara opened her own publishing company in 2011 and has since sold over 5 million books! Twenty of her titles have appeared on the New York Times and USA Today Bestseller Lists.

Known for her emotional and compelling stories of love, family, mystery and romance, Barbara enjoys writing about ordinary people caught up in extraordinary adventures. Barbara's books have won numerous awards. She is a six-time finalist for the RITA for best contemporary romance from Romance Writers of America and a two-time winner for DANIEL'S GIFT and THE WAY BACK HOME.

Barbara has lived all over the state of California and currently resides in Northern California where she draws much of her inspiration from the beautiful bay area.

For a complete listing of books, as well as excerpts and contests, and to connect with Barbara:

Visit Barbara's Website:
www.barbarafreethy.com

Join Barbara on Facebook:
www.facebook.com/barbarafreethybooks

Follow Barbara on Twitter:
www.twitter.com/barbarafreethy